Rob Parker is a married father of three, who lives in a village near Manchester, UK. The author of the Ben Bracken books *A Wanted Man, Morte Point, The Penny Black* and *Till Morning is Nigh,* and the standalone post-Brexit country-noir *Crook's Hollow*, he enjoys a rural life on an old pig farm (now minus pigs), writing horrible things between school runs.

He writes full time, as well as organising and attending various author events across the UK - while boxing regularly for charity. Passionate about inspiring a love of the written word in young people, Robert spends a lot of time in schools across the North West, encouraging literacy, story-telling, creative-writing and how good old fashioned hard work tends to help good things happen.

Ben Bracken Book One

A
Wanted
Man

Rob Parker

LUME BOOKS

LUME BOOKS

First published in 2017 by Lume Books
85-87 Borough High Street,
London, SE1 1NH

ISBN 978-1-83901-184-9

www.lumebooks.co.uk

For my girls: Becky, Ava and Sylvia.

Prologue

I don't want to wake up yet. Don't make me. The horror and pain of what put me to sleep is too raw.

But the smell – acrid, mouldy, coppery – is too weird to ignore. If I'm alive – and so much of me wishes I wasn't – I'll have more battles to fight. The pain is coming back too, in my leg, head, arms, chest – damn near everywhere.

My arm. It feels numb. Something strange. I have to see what's going on here. I crack my eyes open.

It's dark. The floor is metal, blotched with puddles of fetid water. The bullet hole is still just above my left knee, my shirt ripped and clinging to my bloody torso in strips, but my left arm is tied behind my back. That's new.

I reach for the binding when a voice booms suddenly in the metal cave, which I can see better all the time as my eyes adjust.

'Behave yourself!' The sound bounces tinny off every surface.

I know who it is, brooding in the darkness, flanked by other men in the murk. The Turn-Up. Terry 'The Turn-Up' Masters. I can just about make out his smug-bastard leer.

Something lands on the floor in front of me. It tinkles and glints in the aquamarine light from a far doorway. A kitchen knife.

'Only one of you is leaving,' Masters announces in his thick cockney drawl, all apples, pears, and ponies. An immediate shuffling starts from somewhere to my left, a scrambling of shoes. Another man is here with me. I see him now, his own left arm tied behind his back. I root around in my larynx to find my voice.

'I knew you were a piece of shit, but this…' I croak.

Masters' comeback is immediate.

'You've disrespected me with your self-proclaimed balls of steel all day. I just don't get it – I don't get it at all. I've been in my little bubble, you've been in yours, happily going along until you decided to make a problem.'

There's no point arguing with him. Not when everything seems so finite and hopeless. Not when he has proven to be exactly what I thought he was. I speak. 'Are we going somewhere with this? It's been a long-arse day.'

'He's a fucking waste, but I want you to make him go that extra yard to prove he has some kind of point,' Masters says, his eyes fixed on me, and I look to the other man. With horror, I recognise him as Masters' own son, Markland. I watch him slide out and reach for the knife, grasping it with a shaking hand. 'How much do you want to survive? It's a question I extend to both of you. Sing for your suppers.'

'Dad…' Markland whispers like a man who knows that the nepotism that got him so far in life has finally run dry. To me, he's no real threat, but a knife is a knife, and deserves respect, even if he is holding it like he's going to paint my caricature with it rather than drive it into me with purpose.

I rise to my feet, pain pulsing through my leg above and below the wound, mere movement scattering jagged sparkles before my eyes, as Markland lunges at me with the blade, his own eyes bulging with fear. It stinks of piss-poor commitment, and I sidestep it easily. I'm not happy with this. Not happy at all. It's Masters I want, not his mewling spawn.

If I can get the knife, just for a second, I might be able to throw it at Masters.

I watch Markland's right shoulder, waiting for it to betray his next strike. It tenses, and the knife is moving again. I block the thrust easily with my own right arm, twisting into it, and in the same motion swing for his face. I miss, and he bobs away. There might be a move or two to Markland after all.

I want this over. I want the threat neutralised. I want Masters.

I head straight in, driving at Markland chest to chest – a primal move that shocks Markland enough to allow me to lunge for the knife, gripping his hand in mine. We tussle, locked in an embrace of survival, then lose our balance. Markland trips forward, forcing me down too, and I roll, my knee flaring in agony. Markland lands hard with a wet gasp, and that's all I need to know: something bad has happened. Sure enough, the knife is buried in his sternum. His face belies no pain, but I know that look a mile off. The knife has punctured Markland's heart. It's not the gasping wheeze of someone whose lung has been punctured, nor the agonised writhing that follows an intestinal piercing. It's the cold result of a fatal tear to the heart. The end for Markland is very near, and he stares at me with eyes fixed in an ever-loosening glaze of panic.

I didn't mean it. I didn't want to kill him.

I swing round to where Masters Senior had stood before, but the room is empty. No – it can't be. I check everywhere, but the shadows are empty.

Pursuit. Freedom. Go.

I reach down to Markland and place my good knee on his chest, pressing down to let me pull the knife out with one sharp upward tug. The result is horrible: the knife is slick with bright-red blood, which geysers out of him. Markland stares at the ceiling, breathing shallowly, blood splashing up onto his face in crude crimson flickers.

Using the knife to free myself, I have use of both arms again. I'm going to catch up with Masters, and put this knife to good use. I can't see an exit, but I'm ready to hunt it out. Then suddenly the quiet of the chamber is shattered once again by a voice, this time one I don't recognise, shouting only one word:

'Freeze!'

Moments later, when I finally can see where I am, I can't quite believe what's happening. The police march me along dank corridors, up two flights of stairs, and out onto the deck of a ship – a rust-bucket freighter moored beneath a halogen cascade from a white scaffolded structure, which I realise in amazement is the London Eye. I'm on the Thames.

My escort is met by tactical support units, and I am abruptly cuffed – left bewildered, saddened, and surprised. I look around at the vessel I have been dragged from, found standing over a dead man's body and holding the knife that ended him, and I know two things. One, I was done like a kipper. Set up. Two, I'm the same as that ship: a piece of once great use and worth, shoved aside and abandoned by those who had promised to care for it, now only fit for dirty work and left to decay. And as I'm led away to the waiting van and a very uncertain future, I know that I only have myself to blame.

1

My two years in prison ended just how they started – with a stabbing. As soon as Craggs drove the makeshift dagger into Quince's belly and the recreation room filled with prison staff waving batons, I was moving. I knew they would arrive quickly, and I knew that the door would swing shut just slowly enough for me to slip through. The place erupted in noise and violence, but I didn't look back. I haven't done since.

Now, I am running. I can feel my mind bathing in the electric warmth of adrenaline. People are looking at me from a bus waiting at the traffic lights and I try to rein in my stride just a touch. If only they knew what I knew, they might understand why I can't adopt a more leisurely pace. I need to keep moving.

Hello, Manchester, it's me, Ben Bracken. I am back. It's nice to see you, my adopted home town. I'm just sorry it's under circumstances like these.

I'm arrowing right into the heart of the city, right into the bustling centre, with the sole intention of hiding in the urban congestion. I'm familiar with the city, its quirks, crevices and people, and I know just what to do when I get in there.

The suit I wear, a gigantic, ill-fitting grey coverall of stinking, sweat-soaked canvas, was the chief warden's only moments earlier. As is the shirt, which will soon be dripping with both our sweat, at this rate. I took both from him as I left the prison – I couldn't very well come out in my prison issues – and left him there on the steps of the prison in his underpants. He is such a nasty, vile *shit* of a man. He absolutely deserves it.

He shouldn't be bothering me for a while, which is thanks in full to the contents of the only item I carry, hanging off my shoulder: a tattered green duffel bag. I can scarcely believe what is inside, but as insurance policies go, this one is ironclad. And I know that as long as it is safe, I am safe with it.

I cross the road and head north towards the Printworks, an entertainment oasis from where I can easily head to my destination, the Northern Quarter. But first, I need to make a call. And the Printworks has a bank of payphones.

It is mid-afternoon, just about 3:45, I think. Thursday. Cold, late October. The city has that quiet afternoon throb about it. The long-lunchers have all gone back to work by now, hiding boozy excesses on their breath with too much gum, and the early leavers haven't quite summoned the courage to sneak for the door just yet.

It feels so good to walk on these streets again, for so many reasons. It is a surrogate home now, and after all the travelling it's still one of the only places on earth where I feel comfortable. I was sent overseas as a soldier, one of Her Majesty's loyal hounds, setting right the wrongs others had perpetrated against human rights and democracy. A ten-year career mainly stationed in Iraq and Afghanistan saw me reach captain. I was the pride and joy of my family, the 'Toast of Rawmarsh' they used to call me back in my home village in Yorkshire. Such memories become more vague all the time. Then I had to make a very difficult choice, which was my undoing. I was cast out, ripped of my purpose, medals and duty, viewed as scum by my peers, dishonourably discharged and sent home in disgrace – and hated by the society I gave everything to protect.

That same society changed a lot in the decade I was away fighting for it, and now I barely recognise it. It now strikes me as an ideal dining out on its rich history. Yet somehow my sense of duty remains. I can't help it. I don't believe in My Great Britain anymore, nor even trust it to do the right thing for the people on her shores… But it's like we were married, Britain and I, long since divorced – yet I'm still inexplicably devoted to my bitch of an ex.

The Printworks is just ahead. I cross the street again, bobbing between the cars, and head in via a side entrance. The Printworks, once the largest printing house in Europe, is now a cavernous converted warehouse, filled

11

with bars, restaurants, cinemas, and a bank of cash machines and payphones. I head straight to the nearest phone and check the pockets of the suit. Two twenty-pence pieces and a ten. Perfect. Thanks, guv'nor. Picking your pocket felt damn good. I know I could call the number reverse charge anyway, but that doesn't stop me from enjoying getting one over on Chief Warden Harry Tawtridge just one last time.

I dial the number I've committed to memory for this very moment. Three rings, then the call is answered not with words, but with silence. I know he is there, though. Bob 'Freckles' Froeschle got out three weeks before me, although *his* exit carried Her Majesty's consent. This moment was rehearsed, and I feel a buzz at putting our prep into practice.

'The package will be there from midnight tonight, and I'll cover it with you as agreed,' I say. 'Thank you. I am grateful.'

I hang up. Job done. The insurance policy is almost there. The last strand of the escape plan executed to perfection. I am pleasantly surprised. I'm used to responding to instructions ordinarily with violence. Not this time: I'd used my brains and hadn't laid a finger on anybody myself. I'm inwardly pleased, which is a damn sight better than the bitterness and anger I was stuck with before.

I know I shouldn't but I find myself popping another coin. I dial again from recollection, having called Kayla's house countless times when I was on leave. Before prison, before everything changed.

A voice answers, but it is not Kayla, it is a young boy. 'Hello?' he says, not a care in the world.

'Joshua?' I say.

'Yeah, who's that?' he replies, playing along. I can feel myself ready to bottle it. So much for being ruthless and decisive.

'Tell your mum it was Uncle B. Tell her, Uncle B sends love to you all, that includes you, Joshua. And tell her I'm going to do my best.'

'Umm, ok.'

What the hell am I doing?

'Bye, pal,' I say, before hanging up. I wish I had more in me to say, but I don't know how to say it.

I owe that family so much, more than they will know, but I also know that hearing from me will hurt. It was a selfish gesture to call, damn it all. But they need to know I'm thinking of them. Of him – of Stephen, the man I killed. Joshua's father and Kayla's husband. Because if I forget about them, none of what I broke out to achieve will mean anything.

I leave the booth and crack on with something I'm far more comfortable with.

I see a bar opposite, Waxy O'Connors. An Irish bar. I would bloody love a pint, perhaps a cold pint of Guinness. I haven't touched a drop of alcohol in twenty months now – the length of my stay in Strangeways. I could easily pop in for one, and head into the Northern Quarter after, but my remaining thirty pence probably wouldn't get me much in there save for a bag of pork scratchings, and I'm almost gagging in this filthy suit anyway.

I use the front exit of the Printworks, passing the Big Issue sellers, and head left, up towards the Northern Quarter. Within a couple of moments, I'm running again, inhaling the cold, grey air that only Manchester ever really seems capable of providing. It's like an elixir and I gulp it down.

Between a pair of streets I see the entrance to an alleyway that I recognise. Above the mostly garish shop fronts, the second floors of the buildings are still all set perfectly in the 1940s. It gives the Northern Quarter away immediately: Manchester's little piece of Manhattan. Movie crews come in to shoot period-set New York films here because it's cheaper, and it's a nice little corner you can always head to for a warm welcome, a cold beer, and a good atmosphere.

Damn. The beer popping into my head again. I wasn't expecting to only be out of the nick for twenty minutes and already be thinking about having a beer. But it signified freedom to me when I was inside, and I certainly have that freedom now. I'll get my chance. Besides, I'm nearly there. Church Street.

The street is very quiet, and a scrappy alley cat slinks along the pavement, pausing to look at me with that look all cats give humans: how've you managed to get this far with just one life compared to my nine? It leaves me to it and I walk up to the glass doors of an apartment complex nestled between two businesses. I call up to the fifth-floor flat I have been to only once before.

A female voice answers. 'Hello?'

'It's an old friend. Last time I saw you, you were in your nightclothes,' I say, keeping an eye on the street.

The intercom is quiet for a moment, presumably while a decision is being made. I hope she recognises either my voice or the occasion I was alluding to. She should do.

'Please come straight up,' she says.

The door buzzes open, and I enter and head for the lift. I am not expecting anyone to be looking for me, at least not quite yet, but I don't want to stay here long. I'm convinced I'll be ok, and my previous captors will leave me to it, because it is simple: if they reveal I've escaped, I break out my insurance plan. The authorities would come crashing down on that prison like a ton of bricks, and the disgraceful, corrupt management of that facility would be dragged into the light. So I would imagine that for all intents and purposes, Ben Bracken is holed up in his cell, patiently living out the remaining fifteen years of his sentence.

Fifteen years – that should be enough time to get more than a few things done.

It's heartening to know that nobody will be looking for me, but still, taking care keeps you alive. Care means I should keep this visit fairly brief. Especially while I still carry the damn insurance policy under my arm.

The flat's at the end of the corridor, and the door is ajar. I knock and push it open a touch.

'Hello?' I call out.

The door is slowly pulled open, to reveal a beautiful woman staring at me, her eyes filling a little, her hand creeping up to cover her mouth. She has shoulder-length brown hair, eyes wide as side plates and browner than melted chocolate, and I instantly recall the last time I saw her. Bruised, frightened, and in a very bad way. Her name is Freya, and last time I saw her, I saved her life.

'I stink. I really smell bad,' I say, holding my hands up, but she is on me before I can say anything else.

'Ben,' she whispers, throwing her arms around me. I'd been nervous about what welcome I might receive, but that has been quickly put to bed.

'I'm sorry for dropping in out of the blue,' I say, hugging her back. I'm genuinely glad to see her. We both went through a lot that day, and we haven't seen each other since I sent her scampering down an emergency staircase in her nightie.

'What the hell are you wearing?' she asks, wrinkling her nose and smiling.

'You don't like it? It's always a bit hit and miss when you buy suits off the rail.'

She lets me go, and we enter the apartment. It is as nice as I remember – warm wood floorboards under an open living space, bare brick walls, and vast floor-to-ceiling windows, which overlook the low rooftops unique to this end of town. If I ever were to settle down anywhere, it would be in a place like this.

'Tell me to get stuffed, or whatever you like, but I wondered if I could trouble you for a change of clothes, fifteen minutes internet access and, if you are feeling especially generous, a shower?'

Freya smiles and dabs at the corner of her eyes with the sleeve of her dark jumper.

'Of course,' she replies.

I love seeing her like this – doing well, and safe. Then, I notice a glitter on her hand that makes me catch my breath.

'The wedding ring... You and Trev?'

'Yes,' she says, looking at the ring. 'After what happened, we... didn't see any reason to wait anymore.'

I find myself beaming. Everything I did, and the reasons I had for doing it, has been justified. I feel new strength – new steel in my resolve. I feel reinvigorated.

'We wanted to invite you,' she says softly.

'Don't be daft – I can be tough to pin down.' I smile. 'I'm thrilled for you both. Were you ok after what happened?'

She sighs, looking pensive, but she retains the slight fundament of a smile.

'Yeah. It took some time, but we both got there.'

'That's great, Freya. I mean that.' I need to get down to it. I'd love to reminisce but with any luck there'll be less pressing times. 'Freya, I've just got out of prison – kind of. I don't believe that anyone is after me, but I don't want to put you in a difficult position – and I already have, just by being here. I need to keep moving but I need help, and yourself and Trev are my best bet. I'm afraid I'm not supposed to be out of prison. But I am. And I don't want it to come back to bite you.'

Freya takes a step towards me and puts a hand on my shoulder. That warmth again.

Trev is a lucky man, but it was nearly so different. Two years ago, he got home late from his IT job to find the apartment ransacked and Freya missing. A nasty piece of work called Keith Sinfield was running a child sex ring from a flat in the biggest high-rise at the other end of the city, and by accident his laptop, from which he conducted the whole operation, ended up in Trev's possession. Sinfield kidnapped Freya to force the return of the laptop.

Trev called me. Truth be told, when the phone rang I was being sick into a bin at a crummy budget hotel on the other side of town, on the bottom end of a self-pity bender, but I helped get her back. It was a messy one.

'After what you did for us, we will do anything we can to help.' She turned me and gave me a little push. 'Hit the shower, and I'll get some of Trev's clothes together. He'll be home soon after five, so if you can wait that long, please do, he'd love to see you. Bathroom's second door back there. We owe you our lives, Ben.'

I have spent what feels like a lifetime undertaking grim tasks and never getting a word of gratitude in return. Receiving it now renders me awkward, overwhelmed and grateful.

Freya leaves me to it, and I head for incredible luxury: a real, private shower, in freedom. Such a simple thing, but a signifier of so much. It feels like a new dawn, a symbol: to wash away my previous life, all its mistakes and sadness, and start afresh.

2

After my shower, I crack the bathroom door open to find a pair of dark jeans and a black t-shirt, which will do just grand. I pull back on my old grits (you can't have everything) and then the jeans, which I am surprised to find are skinny. I have never worn skinny jeans before. It feels like I am wearing a denim wetsuit below the waist, something I'm not entirely comfortable with. The t-shirt fits a gem, and the smell of non-industrial-strength detergent is most welcome. It feels just great to be wearing civvies again.

I pad out into the hall in my bare feet. The warm, polished wood flooring feels like a luxurious massage to my concrete-battered toes. I savour the steps to the living space. Freya is there, at the kitchen end of the room, pouring coffee from a steaming cafetière into ceramic mugs. The smell of fresh-brewed coffee fills my senses and I find myself grinning from ear to ear: the luxuries appear to be endless. I notice three mugs as opposed to two.

'There he is…' a voice softly exclaims, and I turn to see Trev. Trevor Houghton, my old school friend and later, university compadre. 'I made my excuses as soon as Freya texted me. It's good to see you, pal.'

'I'm an expert at dropping out of the blue to piss you two off,' I counter, our old rapport back with one exchange. I am smiling as I move to meet him, delighted to see him well. I have not seen him either since that terrible day, and now it feels like that matter can truly be put to bed.

'Hi Trev,' I say, and he envelops me in a monster bear hug that would have crushed me like a bag of old pistachio shells if I hadn't offered a little stout resistance.

'Thank you,' he says, with as much honesty I have ever heard in his voice.

We were close pals at university, drinking buddies and football team-mates, before I left it all to pursue what I felt was my destiny in the armed forces. And now to hear that truth in sentiment that only true friends show each other… it makes everything I did worthwhile. He lets me go, as Freya moves into the room carrying a tray of steaming mugs. I am ushered to a sofa, which I let swallow me. Perching on matching armchairs, Trev and Freya sit opposite.

'Needless to say,' Trev begins, 'it is so good to see you.'

'I said you would,' I reply. It's true – I had. And I do like to keep a promise, even though this was one I wasn't sure I could keep.

'We couldn't keep track of the trial,' he says. 'The media barely covered it. But I'd imagined you'd end up back in our neck of the woods.'

'I took the plea. Not much for the papers to sensationalise when it's all agreed beforehand.'

'And now Freya tells me you just got out of prison.'

'After a fashion. I've taken a leave of absence, you could say.'

Trev looks at Freya. 'We don't care,' she says. 'We don't care what you did or why.'

'Thank you,' I respond. I mean it, too. I have spent the last couple of years being judged from pillar to post when, largely, the right thing is the only thing I've ever tried to do.

'Freya says you are not being pursued. Do I even ask how you can break out of prison and that be possible?' Trev asks, struggling to keep a grin off his face.

'My lips are sealed. The more I tell you, the more trouble you'd be in if I somehow come unstuck. I'm not expecting that at all but I didn't come here to drag you into anything bad. I still want to be careful, for you two just as much as me.'

'I can respect that,' says Trev. I raise my mug to him before sipping noisily. My word, it is good. A rich, exotic, caffeine buzz damn near smashes me bolt upright.

'What is your plan?' asks Freya.

'When I knocked on the door, I asked for some clothes and fifteen minutes with an internet connection, which, I assume, given your IT-related employment, you have.' I nod at Trev, who last I was aware worked at PC Planet repairing computers.

'By all means,' Trev says.

'Thanks. Don't worry, I won't be doing anything traceable here. I used fake social media accounts to get things arranged when I was inside, using a kind of ham-fisted code. It was crude, but it got the job done.'

'No problem at all. I kind of have my own sort of paranoia-inspired firewall in place here anyway. In my line of work, you read a lot about what a simple Google search can open you up to. Can't be too careful.'

'Even better.'

'Your mum and dad know you're out?'

'No way. Haven't seen them since the trial. Don't think they'd approve somehow.'

A little silence falls, as if we wonder what the next thing to say might be. I am enjoying their company greatly, and this little taste of a normal life they've afforded me. But we all know I'm a fugitive. And I have places to go and people to see.

'You can't stay? Just for the night?' Freya says.

Trev turns his gaze back to me. 'It's the least we can do.'

I wish like hell I could just say yes, and enjoy an evening of good conversation, maybe with a decent bottle of wine going around. But my duty has always got the better of me, its engine a sense of purpose that is now much greater than before.

'No. Thank you. Seeing you both has been…' I don't finish, but I hope they get it. 'I'll come back when things settle down and we'll have a few beers and put the world to rights. But for now, I'm sorry, I can't stop.'

I'm not very sociable, nor am I great with feelings. I suppose that's thanks to a soldier's life and the fundamental lack of trust the end of that life filled me with.

But I trust Trev and Freya. I do care for them. And I find it genuinely painful not to stay with them a little while longer.

'Just the internet, please.'

3

We exchange goodbyes, promising that, drama permitting, we will keep in contact. I am the secretly proud recipient of two warm hugs.

I step out onto the street into the steadily creeping twilight. Cars are trying to slowly funnel out onto the ring road and then out into the spiderweb roadways of Greater Manchester and beyond. The air is increasing in icy bite, enough so to make me zip the old leather bomber jacket Trev leant me. I should probably have shaved back up at Trev and Freya's. The battered duffel bag under my shoulder doesn't exactly do much to dispel my vagrant image, either.

My appearance was always pristine thanks to my calling, and it's only now, being mindful of scrutiny, that I notice it: scruffy, with a half-beard and hair longer than usual. Through force of habit more than anything else, I'm still attached to my old no-nonsense military cut. I can't get used to the fashion of being unshaven, but I suppose, for the time being, I'll just go with it. I really don't want any giveaways to my military background, however minute.

I cross the street and walk back down the gloomy alleys as a light drizzle falls. A kebab shop on the corner spills steam out into the haze, and it smells like heaven. I don't have a penny on me, so I couldn't go and get something if I tried. But that is the next port of call, after all. Cash. And a meeting with my old mate Jack Brooker.

I emerge through the backstreets into the cold grey expanse of Piccadilly Gardens, dodge a couple of trams, and drop onto Princess Street. At the far end, its apex almost lost in low, blue cloud cover, stands Beetham Tower, presiding over everything below it like an omnipresent benefactor. A flat, a few floors down from the top, was where I rescued Freya from. Some men had to die, and their boss Keith Sinfield ended up going through one of the plate glass windows, out into the dawn air. I never saw what became of him, but I assume a drop of forty-six stories will give you more than a couple of lumps and bruises.

Hitting Oxford Road, I turn left and after a few moments I see The Temple, moreover I see its blinking sign over its descending entrance stairwell. I take the stairs down. I had used Twitter to set the meeting up, as we agreed before my trial. The only tweet the two accounts will ever exchange. Totally anonymous. Totally untraceable.

I enter the bar, and half expect people to look at me in horror – the escaped convict – but of course, nobody does. The Temple Of Convenience, as it is properly known, is a tiny shoebox that used to be a Victorian public toilet and I'm relieved to see it is quiet with only a couple of customers. The solitary barman looks bored and tired, buried in a creased paperback. I don't have any money (yet) and therefore can't buy that first beer of freedom. I take a seat at a table facing the door and enjoy the dimly lit drinking hole. It is definitely good to be in a place like this again. Tiny, authentic and real.

So much of my training and subsequent career was based on punctuality, and that has given me a good judge of timing. Jack is late. I tell myself to relax, to just let things be for the moment. I can't control everything, so why worry about it?

It's the fear, albeit slight, that I will be recognised. I know that it won't happen. I know that the last thing the chief warden will do, when he eventually douses the riots I started, is report that I'm gone. No. Ben Bracken will be in his cell, patiently seeing out the next fifteen years. Because if that doesn't happen, Chief Warden Tawtridge will regret it, thanks to my insurance. Simple as that.

A couple enter the bar, laughing, not a care in this world. I envy them, in so many ways, but pity them in others. They haven't seen the cruelties in life, the bluntness and trauma of a frontline existence. Look at them: effortless and trendy, slaves to nothing more than the latest corporate advertising protocol. But who am I to judge? After all, I am sitting here in a rather cool-looking leather jacket and a half-beard. I fit right in. Good. I'm supposed to be blending in.

'Hi, mate, it's been some time,' says a voice, and I turn.

Surprise hits me immediately. This is not the Jack I remember.

He sags into the seat opposite me. It's been two years since I last saw him but *Christ* he looks older. A lot older. He looks aged to hell and back, pale, weathered and ill. His piercing blue eyes are bloodshot and the lids droop, but still look like they could burn a valley on Neptune – that intense. His chin is fluffed with patchy unconvincing stubble, although his dark shaven skull remains the same. He used to be a handsome, youthful lad, young-looking even for his early twenties, with a mischievous permagrin. The change is staggering.

'Jack, how are you pal…' I begin, but feel compelled to address his appearance. 'What the hell happened to you?'

'Yeah, I've… got your money here,' he mutters, placing a blue and red bank card on the table. 'I haven't touched any more than was agreed.'

I am worried about him. He has genuinely helped me, without fuss, and again I remember how different he was when I first met him, which was right here in The Temple of Convenience.

He has held my cash for me, right through my prison stay. A hundred and eighty grand, all that was left of my army wages. It was in return for a favour the night we met. I was on a self-pity spiral after my army discharge, and had taken to drinking my way around the city. I was by the bar just at the back there when Jack appeared, just twenty at the time, shaken but trying to hold fast. Turned out he'd spilt a pint on someone he shouldn't have in another pub and he'd ended up here lying low. I have never, *ever* liked a bully, so I went back up the steps where a couple of Burberry-clad thugs were waiting for him and I sorted it. Easy when you know how.

Jack was very grateful, and said if he could ever do anything for me all I had to do was ask. I told him to forget it and we met up for a pint quite regularly after that. He was a student at Manchester University where I'd been, and we swapped university war stories. He was a business under-graduate, not sure where he really wanted to end up in life but game to give it a go and equip himself with the best tools at his disposal. I told him how I'd only lasted eighteen months of an English Literature degree and how that somehow rose-tinted my view of our country, so much so that when my dorm TV screens were full of images of a dusty war in Iraq in 2002, deep seeds of patriotism were planted that eventually led to me leaving my degree and joining the forces.

His company kept me from dwelling too hard on my own troubles, and I was grateful for that. He knew I had my darker secrets but he never asked. For the most part we just had a laugh.

Then I went up Beetham Tower and threw that bastard Sinfield out of the window.

I found myself on the run, away from Manchester, setting in motion a chain of events that would lead to more mayhem and my eventual arrest. I needed to get my money somewhere safe should I need to get my hands on it, and I immediately called Jack. Student bank accounts don't go through the same tax and accounting rigmarole as others, and my cash would be safe. He really came through for me, and I feel strong pangs of empathy as I look at him now.

'Thanks mate, but… Forgive me, you look like dog shit.'

'I'm fine,' he says quickly. 'I'm glad you're out. I won't ask anything else, but I certainly wasn't expecting you for a while yet.' He glances at his phone as he talks.

'What's happened?' I ask.

Jack doesn't answer. He rises. His eyes are red, his hair all over the show, and the overwhelming impression is one of near-overpowering anxiety. I want to ask more, but man-code comes into play. Some men say, 'I don't want to talk about it,' when all they really want to do is spill their guts. The way Jack is speaking – the curtailed yet polite words, the curtness – suggests that he really doesn't want to talk. I've been around so many brooding soldiers that I know it's best to pay him that respect.

'Jack, thanks for everything you have done for me. I won't forget it. If there's anything I can do for you ever…'

'No, we are square,' Jack replies, and starts backing towards the door. 'Four five zero nine,' he adds, before turning and heading out of the bar. The wind whistles through the door and up to the table, chilling me as

I watch Jack exit, heading back to whatever has him so fiercely in its grip. This wasn't the reunion I was expecting.

I suddenly don't feel like a beer anymore, and I pick up the card. *Four five zero nine.* There's still a couple of hours before the high street stores close. Best get started.

*

I think I have all the immediate essentials, so I lay them out on the bed in my hotel room. It was easy to get a cheap last-minute deal on a room at the Premier Inn on the edge of town. I checked in as Jack Brooker, the name on the bank card I used to pay with, which is what I'll have to do until I can set up a fake bank account somewhere backed up by a fake identity. But it will do for now.

I also handed over my duffel bag at reception, saying a friend would pick it up later. Hopefully, sometime during the night, my 'friend' Freckles will indeed come as planned and whisk the bag away to our prearranged secured location: a lockbox at Nationwide Building Society, where I'm hoping it will gather dust for a good few years.

The room is clean and spacious. The bed is a double – a real bed, something else I'm looking forward to. And the Wi-Fi is free.

On one side of the bed sits a thirteen-inch MacBook Pro, a Samsung Galaxy smartphone loaded with a pay-as-you-go sim, a Swiss army knife, some basic clothes from Primark – combat jeans, a flannel shirt, three dark t-shirts, and the least ridiculous underwear I could find – a pair of hardwearing dark brown Timberland boots, a toilet bag preloaded with toiletries, a mini first-aid kit, a waterproof backpack to stuff it all in, a pair of Steiner Nighthunter low-light binoculars, a compass, pen and paper, and the finishing touch: an Italian BMT foot-long Subway with chipotle sauce.

I stretch out on the empty half of the bed, flicking on the TV, ready to wolf down the sub. I think about Jack: what's happening there? Maybe the fact that I had to save him from those two thugs a couple of years back suggests he has a habit of getting himself into trouble, and maybe he has gone and done it again.

I pick up the smartphone, enter the passcode I have assigned for security and load up the preinstalled Twitter app. I type in the login details, and the planet's most poorly populated Twitter account comes to life, with only two deliberately generic names. I select Direct Message, and type.

@MUFC4Ever1995 to @MUFCFan2654
21:46 on Thursday 27th October
07893 629087 if you ever need anything.

I grab that sub, ready for some food that actually tastes of something. Then I'm going to pack and get ready for bed. I'm off first thing in the morning, back to the Big Smoke, back to settle old scores and correct the mistakes I've made. Back on the hunt for the one that got away, the smug, wily, powerful old bastard, Terry 'The Turn-Up' Masters. The man who got me locked up, blew out my knee, and stuck me in a one-armed knife fight with his son. The man I need to sort out before I can do anything else.

4

That was the best night's sleep of my whole life. A fitful first fifteen minutes gave way to a bottomless, floaty vacuum. I dreamed a bit, I think, but given that it can get a bit dark in my head at times, I don't bother trying to recall it.

Breakfast isn't bad: a full English with all the trimmings, although the coffee is frankly crap compared to Trev and Freya's brew over on Church Street last night. I had sauntered down to the hotel restaurant just like any other guest, a touch of purpose in my stride to suggest I was just another guy who wants to get shit done on a Saturday. The clock over the cereal table reads 7:37 a.m. The room is mostly empty, with just a couple of early risers peppered about at the window tables. Blokes with their own backstories, just like me. They go through the motions of eating their breakfasts with a dull precision suggesting an oft-repeated routine.

As I watch the two other diners, I notice that they are hooked to their smartphones, barely able to peel their eyes away from them.

I certainly haven't got used to the all-consuming smartphone fetish yet – in the Afghan dust there wasn't much use for Angry Birds. I smile, acknowledging my own hypocrisy. I buckled and bought one last night, on the salesman's promise I could use Twitter from it.

Thinking of such things, I remember my Twitter appeal to Jack Brooker. I take out my own device. If you can't beat them...

The first thing that hits me when I see the screen, is a missed call from a mobile number. It can only be Jack, as he's the only person who has this number. There's a little funny looping symbol in the top left of the interface, which I haven't seen before. It looks like a cassette tape... and the penny drops. Answerphone. After a few seconds of fumbling, I manage to access the message.

It opens with an automated female voice: '*Message left today at 4:53 a.m.*'

Then follows a full five seconds of silence, although as I listen, I know: it definitely *isn't* silence. There is a scratching, and as my ears strain across the soundscape, I begin to hear breathing. Ragged breathing. Then a deeper rumble, a popping Dopplered hiss – a car passing. Then another. A voice speaks.

It is Jack.

'*I've called you... because I don't know what else to do, nor who to trust. I thought I could do this on my own, but I can't.*'

Silence again. I pull a pen from my jeans pocket and make ordered notes on a napkin. '*It's my dad. When I saw you last night, he had been missing for two days. I've been going mad trying to find him. I've tried every way I know, but I got nowhere.*'

That explains his state last night. I'm guessing he hasn't slept since he found out his father was missing.

'*...And about an hour ago, the police found him. Shot dead, in a disused warehouse out beyond the runways at Manchester Airport.*'

Jack's voice cracks, emotion beginning to pour out.

'*Someone shot him. My dad. You seem to know how to handle yourself... Please help me find who did this. I don't trust the police, they are fucking time-wasters, it took them long enough to find him, and they can't tell me a bloody thing.*'

Jack's request is totally unexpected, and twirls my brain. I'd like to help the lad, but getting involved in a potentially messy situation in the city whose primary prison I have just wandered out of? Not what I had in mind. Plus, I've got my own agenda – one I'm dead set on.

'*Please. Call me.*'

The line goes dead, and robot lady comes back on, asking whether I want to delete the message or save it. I delete it, and pocket my hasty notes.

I drink coffee and try to bring order to what I've heard. Jack's father goes missing but turns up dead in a warehouse at Manchester Airport. Shot. Who has access to firearms here in the UK? Farmers, the police, and organised crime. I can't picture an angry pig farmer losing his shit and heading to

Manchester Airport to clip someone. Nor can I especially imagine a police officer doing the same thing, although stranger things have happened. And that leaves the last one. Organised crime.

I was heading down south to tackle organised crime, but the whole point was that it was away from here, with a very specific target. The Turn-Up.

I most definitely don't want to get involved in something up here.

But… I feel a nagging. That familiar tug of duty. I carry it everywhere with me even now, bound by it, cajoled by my gratitude to Jack. I even feel protective of Manchester, odd as that may sound. I found myself in this city. I don't want bad things happening on this city's streets.

No. I'm letting my heart rule my head. This city is like any other, with its darker corners. But Jack… Damn it.

My problem is compounded by my brittle, unique moral compass. My idea of good and bad is very black and white, with great streaks of grey smeared straight across the borders between the two – the zone in which I have been known to take matters into my own hands. Those grey areas demand I owe Jack some assistance, even if it is outside of my self-imposed remit.

Thumbing open the smartphone Twitter app, I send him one word via private message: *WHERE?*

Out in the lobby, I check the time. My train to London leaves at the exact same time tomorrow. Let's give Jack twenty-four hours and see what I can turn up. I approach the prim, alert receptionist.

'Can I extend my stay for an extra night?' I ask.

'That shouldn't be a problem, sir,' comes the smiling reply, as her fingers flick over the keyboard.

'The package I left last night. Did my friend collect it ok?'

'Yes, she came just after midnight,' she replies, not looking up.

She? Who the fuck is *she*? Freckles knew the drill, knew the arrangements. He was supposed to pick it up himself. Him and nobody else. What is he playing at? A bead of panic threatens to surface, and I hold it tight. Freckles may have had to change plans, and such is our agreement of 'no foreseeable contact' that he had to go ahead without me. Ok. I try to seek reassurance in the possibility.

I hastily cancel my room request. I'll find somewhere else to stay, while things are up in the air. The question stands, however, burning bright: who the fuck has my insurance policy, and where in Christ's name is it?

*

I take the stairs two at a time, eager to get my stuff and get moving, and within a matter of moments I am swiping my room door open with the keycard.

My room is dark. I'm pretty sure I'd left the curtains open, but maybe the housekeeper has been in. I make for the window to open the drapes, but something makes me pause. My instincts feel snagged, frayed, unravelling further with every step. I stand still, and listen.

Something is amiss. My senses subconsciously pull focus, a feeling I know all too well. Years of training have rendered me a highly perceptive sensory panel, and enable me to decipher tiny disturbances in my midst – the slight temperature increase as another body shares the space, the faintest audio signature of hushed breath. I am not alone.

But my visitor doesn't know I have any inkling of his or her presence – if I carry on as normal, I might be afforded a couple more moments to locate him.

I whistle a little (surprised to find my 'go to' whistling tune is *Somewhere Over The Rainbow*), and drop my pocket change noisily onto the dresser. I take off my jacket as my eyes scan the room.

The bed appears untouched. It's a solid bedstead, so nobody could be secreted underneath. The bathroom could hide anybody, but it's the curtains I'm interested in. They cover the entire window, right down to the floor, and there's easily space to conceal a person. There is no bulge, but as my eyes sweep the floor, I see the giveaway.

A hint of shadow in the far right-hand bottom corner, where a person leaning against the window is blocking the less-than-blazing morning sunlight from reaching the floor. I reach for the TV remote, and flick it on. Diversion. As soon as the TV crackles to life, I run for the window.

Feeling my footsteps, the visitor flinches and moves forward, creating an outline in the purple curtain – an outline of someone about six feet tall, solid-appearing, with a strange jutting bulge midway up his body, pointing

29

out into the room. As I run, the bulge spits fire in a hushed, harsh *flick*, creating a hole in the curtain. A silenced pistol.

I have dealt with the assailant before I even know I have: I duck low, then rise as I meet the bulging figure, firing my right arm up to my opponent's upper torso. When my arm meets his shoulder, I grip it and rip my target to the floor in a basic, but effective, judo throw.

The curtain rips from its rail, raining sunlight and little white curtain runners down on us both, as my opponent's head hits the floor. I reach for his legs, mindful of where the gun might be in this tumbling mass of fabric, arms, and legs, and manage to grab both his ankles. He starts to buck, as he recovers slightly from the head impact, but I kick low and hard into the curtain. I hit something meaty, and waste no time in interlocking his legs in an upside-down cross-legged yoga pose. I then insert my right hand between the two crossed calves, grabbing the lower of the two and pulling upwards with a yank.

A sharp scream lets me know I've got it: a modified Indian death lock, as the weight of the hanging body exerts immense pressure on the crude coat hanger shape I have made out of his legs. I lift higher, to intensify the scream – an extremely vicious volume button – as the strain against the bones intensifies. As I lift, suspending my visitor in space, still swaddled in curtain, I kick again, just to get the message home that I'm in charge now.

'Put the gun down or I lift again,' I say. I lift slightly to show him just how nasty it could get, and the man cries out. 'I lift higher, and your tibias snap just below the knees. And your ligaments, well… they'll strip from your knee joints as they try to hold your fucking legs together.'

'Shit! Ok!' the man screams, the gun flopping out and thudding on the carpet.

'I'm only interested in the truth. For every second I think I'm not getting it, I lift. The higher I get, the closer your legs get to snapping. If you're having trouble with that I'll make sure you get the idea pretty quickly.' I lower his head to the floor, allowing some of his weight to rest while keeping the strain on. It must hurt like hell. It's a rum move I picked up outside of the traditional training avenues, and it never fails. When the hold is in place, gravity does the rest, and the rest is *horrible*.

The man breathes heavily, undoubtedly feeling some relief. I'd like to get a look at him, see if it's anybody I would recognise, but I don't want him to see me just yet. 'How many's with you?' I ask sternly. 'Outside or in?'

'One man, in the car park,' he splutters.

'You've come here to take me out, correct?'

The man is silent for a second, so I lift him up a touch to remind him the urgency of my question. It has an immediate effect.

'Yes… Yes! But I'm only following instruction. I don't know you. *Fuck*,' he wails.

'Because, of course, that makes all the difference doesn't it…' I say, lifting higher again. I feel the joints straining against each other.

'No, no, of course, *Jesus*…'

'You're a fucking dogsbody, aren't you?'

'What? I don't… Shit…'

'Who sent you here, dogsbody? If it's orders you are following, who issued them?'

He inhales and exhales raggedly, spluttering and gasping as the blood floods his inverted cranium. His vision will be blurred by now, and his senses completely disorientated. He doesn't answer, so I drag him higher, and he screams. I nearly have him entirely off the ground now, and he will surely be in real pain. I need answers, and he really doesn't want to give me the name of his employer. I change tack.

'What's my name?' I hiss.

'What?'

'My *name*… What is it?'

I lift higher again, his head now completely off the floor, eliciting a strangled yelp.

'Fuck you, I'm not gonna give you the satisfaction—'

I yank higher one last time.

'*What is my name?*'

'Jack Brooker!' he screams.

I drop him to the floor. He's talked, and now I need to shut him up. I grab the gun and smash the pistol butt down hard on his head – or rather, its shape beneath the fabric. The impact is fierce, the resulting silence immediate.

I pull the curtain back to find a battered and bruised face. He's about mid-thirties, perhaps, similar to me. And he looks of mixed descent, perhaps English and Chinese.

The grim truth is that someone wants Jack Brooker dead. And that same party has enough reach and power to know when the name 'Jack Brooker' books into a hotel, or makes a credit card purchase. Shit – it would have been good to get that name too before I had to put him out.

I need to get out of here. Whoever's got that kind of reach will have eyes and ears in all sorts of places. I grab my belongings, shovelling them into the rucksack in ten seconds flat. I take the gun too, even though I feel uneasy about it. Me and guns haven't often ended well.

It feels strange to the touch, a little lighter than I remember. That added weight of bad intentions is gone. I check it over: a Glock 17, somewhat modified for the silencer. The Glock 17 is one of the most popular pistols in worldwide law enforcement, but this… this is something a little different. Despite my unease… I like it. I stick it in my waistband, and I'm out the door.

I need to get to Jack. I also need a new place to stay, and a new identity, quicker than ever. I can't go around town pretending to be Jack Brooker when there's quite obviously a hit out on that very name. I might as well wander around with a sandwich board advertising myself as the man himself.

Two questions loom like fat, dark storm clouds: What on earth is he involved with? And what's he done to make people want him dead?

5

The taxi slows to a stop in a charming neighbourhood about fifteen minutes' drive west of Manchester, in Worsley. The properties, shrouded in balding trees, are handsome, with the ornate appointment yet modest size of above-average wealth – and the sun even threatens to shine. According to the taxi clock, it is 8:50 a.m.

I pay the driver with cash I'd got from a petrol station cash machine, and hop out. I took the maximum the machine would let me, £250, in the hope that I won't have to use that marked cash card for a while. On the way over I'd also called Freckles, and left a message that would get full marks for being right to the point: '*Where is my insurance policy?*' I left my new number with him and urged him to get back to me.

There are autumn leaves all over the street, and this picture-book scene of successful England is pretty appealing. It immediately piques my interest in Jack a little more. The guy who helped out a murderer (that being me, even though he might not know that) with what can only really be classed as money laundering (he *definitely* knew about that) lives here in this quiet, comfortable set-up. I walk to the house in the corner, to the address he specified on our Twitter exchange.

The house itself is a white-stone beauty, with two pillars either side of the door, manicured gardens, and two stories of living space. The door is a solid slab of mahogany, and, as I use the heavy black iron door knocker, I hear the echo of polished floors on the other side.

I wait, then try again, harder. Still no answer.

I crane my neck up to look at the windows. All the curtains are open.

I glance back at the street. Empty. Is this odd? I wouldn't know. I haven't been in a fairly opulent neighbourhood in a while. Doing my best not to look like a burglar, I walk around the side of the house.

I follow the fence to a small back garden. It is well kept, canopied by oak trees, and much smaller than I expected; but the property backs onto an expansive, beautiful golf course. Stunning view. And then I notice Jack, sitting on the decking that leads up to the back of the house and its porch doors.

He's wearing a hoody and sweatpants, holding a glass of orange juice, and staring out over the golf course. There's a half-full, trademark-blue bottle of Bombay Sapphire gin by his side, no doubt in there with the OJ. I head over.

'I'm sorry, mate,' I say.

Jack turns to me, his face ruptured by fear and sorrow. His eyes scream for help, but his gritted teeth seethe vengeance. It's a complex, dangerous look, which I have seen many times in the haze of Middle-Eastern deserts. It is a look that, when left to brood and build, usually leads to dangerous places.

'I can give you twenty-four hours,' I say, hoping that that will serve to calm him a little and offer hope, even though I've no idea what we are up against.

Jack swigs a heavy slug from the tumbler. The orange juice looks pale, and I can almost smell the gin from where I stand. This isn't a good sign. Much more of this and he'll need the majority of those twenty-four hours to sleep it off. I point to the tumbler.

'Jack, mate, I need you to go easy on that,' I say.

Jack looks at me with a flash of indignation, but cools it quickly. He drops the glass to his lap.

'You're a man who's, done things, clearly... What did your training tell you to do when your world is ripped out from under you?' he asks.

It seems a genuine request.

'I'm not one for lying. It never gets easier. You never get your head around it. You never comprehend it. But time helps you learn to live with it. And that's all you can ever hope for.'

Tears begin to well messily in Jack's eyes, and spill uncontrollably.

'I just want to fucking kill everybody...' he seethes.

'Just take it easy. I'm here for twenty-four hours, ok? Now, if you listen to me, and let me do things my way, we can get a fair amount done in that time. But we need to act fast and you need to be honest with me.'

'I will. But you must promise me something.'

I was expecting this. A request straight out of the male pride playbook.

'I know what you are going to say. You want me to agree that if we find who did it, you can be the one to put them away. Correct?'

He looks at me with that burning gaze, trying to make his case.

'At times like these everyone always wants that,' I say. 'It's not a smart move, and it's not something I'll promise.'

'Promise me,' he says. I see that vehemence in him again. I think of the scene in the hotel room earlier. There's nothing to be gained from telling him some people want him dead too. Not yet, at least.

'No. You want my help, then stop wasting time. We need to get started. Now.'

Jack releases the mental coil a little, enough to glance out at the golf course.

'In a minute,' he says.

He gestures out to the golf course. I follow his finger to a woman with a startling peroxide bob coming our way. I glance back at Jack.

'Just go with it,' he says. 'She lives in the estate on the other side of the golf course. At the very least it'll explain a few things.'

As she gets closer, I can see that she's about Jack's age, early to mid-twenties, and wears a dark winter jacket, jeans, and red wellies. She is soft and pretty, although her features are augmented by the streaming mascara tracking her cheeks like rivulets of ink.

She notices me, and I simply nod to her and smile. She hops the fence into the garden and walks straight up to Jack, who still hasn't risen. She too looks shattered by grief.

'Jack, I'm so, so sorry,' she says, bending to pull him close. Jack doesn't return the gesture enthusiastically, he just opens his arms to accept her embrace. Because he remains seated, she has to bend down awkwardly to him.

'What can I do?' she whispers.

'Zoe, you can start by telling me if there's anything I should know,' Jack says softly.

Zoe lets go and glances over at me. She looks unsure of me, and vulnerable. I smile again, to try to reassure her. I don't want to scare her off if she has any light to shed.

35

'I can give you guys some time, if you like?' I say, knowing full well I intend to go nowhere.

'No, it's fine. Zoe, this is…' Jack opens his palm to me, allowing me to fill in the blanks. A smart move, which I am grateful for, allowing me to construct the lie on which to base my future. I haven't thought of a false name yet, but I am blessed with one of the most popular names in the UK.

'Ben,' I say.

'Ben is an old friend of mine. He is completely trustworthy, and he is experienced in affairs like ours,' Jack says.

Interesting. What *affairs* are these?

'Hi,' says Zoe, offering her hand. It's cold but she seems most genuine; I can't tell if she's an astute judge of character or simply naive.

She turns back to Jack. 'I really want to ask how you're doing, but I would imagine that would be a bit… counterproductive,' she says.

'On the money, as always. Want to take a guess at Saturday's Lotto numbers while you're on form?' Jack replies.

Zing. Not what I was expecting. There is clearly an interesting dynamic at play between these two.

'Funeral is at three, a week yesterday. The best we could do. Everything's taken care of. Grandad thought you'd like to be free of the hassle.'

'Six foot tall to six feet deep in six days flat. Is that about the sum of it?' Jack looks at her sharply. Zoe sighs and seems to try to brush it off. I'm staying out of this, but the questions I have for Jack are mounting.

'It's at Altrincham Crematorium, Jack. Grandad said that was your dad's – Royston's – wishes,' says Zoe.

Jack arches his eyebrows. 'Hey, what do I know, right?'

Zoe stares at him, her brow wilting. She looks exhausted, hurting, committed but sad. Silence surrounds us for a moment, punctuated only by a distant *swipe-splack* of a tee shot somewhere on the golf course.

Then quite suddenly, Jack combusts.

He stands so quickly, his chair flips backwards onto the decking, his glass of gin and juice smashing on the wood. His words come out like machine-gun fire. Zoe takes a step back.

36

'I will tear this fucking city to shreds! I promise you. Why my dad? Why Royston Brooker? Why him? He was no junkie, no snitch, and you know it. He always did the right thing by me, by you, by those fuckers he called family!'

Zoe stands firm, and doesn't break eye contact, and my eyes are flitting back and forth between the two like I'm watching a tennis match that has devolved to non-physical warfare.

'It seems your dear grandad has taken care of everything in death, but where the fuck was he in life? It's no good making hasty funeral arrangements, if he could have done something about this. He is with you for that sole reason, isn't he? Under the wing, in house, that's what it was about, wasn't it? Under that golden fucking umbrella? Well, in case you hadn't noticed, it turns out that golden umbrella means exactly fuck all!'

Jack turns away, breathing heavily. Zoe still says nothing but watches him with strength; she's not that shaken. I am impressed by her and her obvious backbone. My eyes drift to the golf course, where two nattily clad golfers stand staring at the scene on the decking.

'Stop eyeballing and mind your business!' I bellow. They shuffle along, dragging their golf trollies with added urgency.

Jack turns back to Zoe, crunching glass under his feet.

'No one can tell me anything! The police have been over, they don't seem to know their arse from a hole in the ground, all they seem to be doing is insisting on me seeing a grief counsellor.'

He takes a step towards her.

'Zoe, I know you are aware of more. I don't know how much more, but I promise it'll be more than me. If there's anything you know – about what happened, or about anyone involved, you have to tell me. If your grandad is the man that everyone seems to think he is, he must know something. You *have* to tell me. Or I will go into that city and I won't be held responsible for what'll happen there.'

Wow. This is definitely not the Jack I left behind a couple of years back. Much has clearly happened in the intervening years, and the boy clearly has become a man of resolution and character. I'm reminded of recruits after their first tour – they go away timid, nervous yet ready, and return bold, sure, and weathered.

'I can't pretend I know what you are feeling,' Zoe says, 'but I can tell you that we are all right behind you. I know that goes without saying, but I thought it is something you could do with hearing.'

'Whoop-di-fuckin'-doo,' Jack fizzes sarcastically. 'I'll make it very simple: Can they or can't they tell me who did it?'

'Jack… you know Grandad is devastated over this, too. You know Royston felt like blood to him. You must see that this has cut him deeply, and he is doing everything he can to sort it. I can promise you that. He is just as broken as you are.'

That seems to placate Jack a little – and I'm suddenly very interested in this grandad character. Seems like sticking around wasn't such a bad plan after all.

'You have my mobile number, don't you?' says Zoe ruefully. 'I can see there's not much I can do here.'

Jack looks down, and speaks quietly, as if a little ashamed of his outburst.

'I have it,' he says.

She motions to go, sticking her hands in her pockets. Then she turns to me.

'Keep an eye on him, please, Ben. It was nice meeting you,' she says.

'Likewise, Zoe,' I say. 'I'll keep him in line.'

I don't really know whether I intend to keep to that, but I feel Zoe has an important role to play here, and I want to keep her sweet.

She turns to Jack. 'Just… lie low. And look after yourself,' she says. Her eyes plead with him, and his veneer breaks down a bit more.

'I will. Thanks. For coming down. I know we haven't spoken in a while…'

'Forget it. Behind the scenes, things are underway. I'll keep you in the loop. And if I don't see you beforehand, I'll see you Thursday.'

And with that Zoe leaves, walking back across the lush fairways from whence she came, a peroxide, winterised will-o'-the-wisp.

I turn to Jack. 'You have a car here I can drive?' I ask.

Jack doesn't answer. He seems lost in watching Zoe go. My senses are tingling at the prospect of dark forces at work, a mysterious force at play in the shadows, and I want to get a damn good look at it.

6

We drive silently to the McDonald's on the East Lancashire Road, the A580 that leads straight into the heart of the city. We had taken what I assume to be Jack's late father's Lexus GS450, a snazzy, sporty luxury saloon that goes like shit off a hot shovel. After twenty months away, I enjoy the feel of being back behind the wheel.

The sole purpose here is to sober Jack up with a stodgy carb-fest. I order on his behalf: black coffee, a breakfast wrap meal, two extra hash browns, and a bowl of rather gloopy ready-porridge. I take a bottle of water for myself.

We head upstairs, which is dead. Jack's demeanour is quiet, reserved. He knows he's got to talk. He also looks like he is processing the conversation he had with the enigmatic Zoe – that earnest, delicate, attractive young woman who seems to be not-too-secretly hard as nails on the inside. The prospect is also pretty real that Jack may be about to reveal things that suggest he is not who I pegged him for.

We sit down, and I put the tray in front of him.

'Eat up,' I tell him. He looks at me, cockeyed.

'I bet it was a bundle of fun sharing a prison cell with you,' he says.

'You'd have to ask him… although my last cellmate ended up killing someone.' A true story for another time.

'Sounds about right,' he says with a petulant snap.

'You eat. Then you tell me everything. If you want my help, it's no time for secrecy, right?'

Again the cockeyed look, then we sit while he eats. He eats lazily, and at times like the very thought of another morsel might make him spew. But he gets there.

I sip water and wait. My mind drifts to basic strategy but I know that's still too early. Before long, Jack is mopping up ketchup with the last scrap of hash brown.

'I'll tell you everything I know. But don't judge, ok? This is a situation I was born into, and I wish I wasn't. I wish things were different, now more than ever. The events of the last few days have completely proven I was right all along.'

He looks broken, resigned, and even apologetic.

'If this is difficult, Jack, I can ask the questions,' I suggest.

'No, it's fine,' he replies. 'I'll start from the very bottom but there is a lot to include. If I get muddled, or there's something I fail to explain properly, just pull me up on it.'

'Fire away.'

'Everything changed when I was twenty-two. I go into Dad's office – back at the house – looking for an ink cartridge for uni stuff. I think he might have one stashed away on his shelves. I accidentally knock a framed picture off the shelf and it smashes on the floor. It's not a picture inside, but a certificate. A certificate for an award recognising '*Exceptional Enterprise By A Small Business*' in favour of Quaycrest Mortgage Brokers. It was Dad's business. Well, he was a sole trader, but traded under that business name. He acted as an intermediary between homebuyers and mortgage lenders, negotiating favourable rates in exchange for commission. He had done it as long as I could remember.

'I reach down to pick it up, but I notice the embossed hologram has flaked right off. It's a fake. A forged certificate. Out of its frame, the smart certificate looks like just a printed piece of A4, nothing special about it at all.

'So I do a little digging into Quaycrest, like on Dad's website and stuff and everything looks fine, there's a bunch of testimonials and the like, and a commission pricing structure set out but… nothing rings quite true. I'd never looked at Dad's business before, in any detail. When I finished school he didn't offer me a job with him on the assumption I wasn't interested. He was right – I wasn't at all.

'I check through Dad's filing system at his records and letters, and there's surprisingly little of it. I mean, basically there's nothing, except for commission receipts from clients. No correspondence with banks and no actual correspondence with clients. It quickly becomes obvious that Quaycrest is a hollow entity, all backed up by receipts but with absolutely no substance once you look below the surface.'

'Money laundering,' I say.

'Right. But what for? So I challenge him on it. And it catches him cold. He ignores my question and goes straight out of the house, speeding off into the night. I sit there, in the wreckage of this lie, as I realise that my life has also been one big lie. And I try to process it. I have – I had – a great relationship with my dad, and didn't want to believe that he had either lied to me or was anything different than who I thought he was.'

He's so obviously upset, I let him have the Freudian introspection. I keep tabs on the facts.

'Later, Dad comes back. He sits me down in the kitchen, then he pulls the fridge from the wall – literally just pulls it out. And behind it is a safe. I have no idea what is going on at this point. He opens this safe and inside is a collection of items. Three or four mobile phones, about ten five-by-five-inch Perspex cubes containing these little fish, a small stack of passports and ID cards, a picture of Mum, and a pistol – a real pistol. And underneath that, on a bigger shelf, is a load of stacked cash.

'And then he looks me straight in the eye and tells me about my birth.'

I'm hooked again.

'Now you've noticed that I've never mentioned my mum, haven't you? I mean my dad just gets killed, I should be with my mum, right? Well, grab the tissues, because she's dead, too. I had always been told she died giving birth to me, which is true. But the version from my upbringing missed some pretty important details.'

He pauses a moment. I can almost see him pooling strength behind his eyes. He continues.

'My mum gave birth to me in the bath, with three bullets in her. One in the shoulder, two in the chest. My mum, in bloom, had been with Dad when they were victim to a carjacking. Dad had taken a wrong turn somewhere near Longsight, and he was pulled out of the car at the lights.

41

A struggle followed, Mum and Dad managed to get away in the car, but shots were fired, all of them ending up in Mum's body.'

Jack's eyelashes quiver, but his speech remains strong.

'Remember us talking about Zoe's grandad? His name is Felix Davison. Dad drove in a panic to Felix's house, at which point Mum's trauma had triggered a disastrous chain reaction in her body. She was helped into the bath, and I was born, delivered by Felix himself. Mum died straight after, right there in the bath. Apparently, she held me for a moment, smiled, and slipped away.'

Jack drinks, and I let the image he has just given me sit in my head. His poor mother, desperately using her last remaining strength to give life to her son as she loses her own. *Jesus*.

'The night of my birth... Dad was looking for alcohol – he thought he could treat her wounds – and could only find brandy, and when he came back up the stairs, he and Felix swapped what they were holding – the baby and the brandy. Dad held his baby son for the first time, while Felix had a stiff drink after delivering a baby in his bathtub, both of them trying to process the loss of my mother, and work out how they would make sure those that killed her would get what they deserved.'

'Go on.'

'After I pressed him on it, Dad told me that the carjackers weren't just lowlifes looking for a quick boost. They were the PGM, the Plymouth Grove Massive. Well, what the PGM didn't know, was who they had fucked with.'

Jack swallows, his eyes suddenly distant.

'Within three days of my mum's death,' he says, his voice little more than a whisper, 'the Plymouth Grove Massive was gone. Nobody has ever heard of them again, and imagination has filled in the rest. An urban legend was born. A sort of tale of warning, power, and retribution. Of what your actions will cost you. *The Baby And The Brandy*. You mess with certain people, you will live to regret it.'

'I'm picturing some organised crime connection here?' I wasn't expecting this kind of story.

'Exactly. A neat little organised crime group called the berg, run by Felix Davison, Zoe's dear grandad. They hid everything from me, absolutely everything, because, as Dad said when he fessed up, he wanted me to make my own choices. He wasn't blood to Felix, he wasn't born into that life, but he thought I might not get those choices if I was born straight into the fold. He kept me separate, so I could be free to do what I wanted when the time was right. And when I found out what was what, they asked if I wanted in.'

'What did you say?'

'I said *no*. I said I didn't want to be involved. Dad respected that. Felix did too, as did the rest of the berg. And everything seemed to be fine. Until three days ago when Dad went missing.'

'That is quite the story,' I say, leaning back in my chair.

'It's just the start, really. But it's a start nonetheless. There's more, but you have the crux of it there.'

'What is your gut telling you about your father's death?'

Jack ponders this for a moment, and gazes out of the window at the drizzle and the steady stream of traffic crawling into Manchester's belly.

'There are a hundred and sixty organised crime gangs in Greater Manchester. Can you believe that? And, from what I've learned and heard, the berg are right at the top. Whether I want to believe it or not, Dad was a power player in a powerful group. A group that people look at with envy. Who knows how many people want to bring the berg down a peg or two?'

'And you think Felix might have an idea about Royston?'

'If anyone wanted to know about a high-profile organised crime hit in this city, Felix would be my first port of call.'

'Then it should be ours, too.'

I stand, ready to get moving. Jack runs a hand across his shaven head, and sighs.

'The story of *The Baby And The Brandy* is a legend. It's part of North-West crime folklore. Nobody knows I was the baby in the story, or what became of the baby, and they think it's a simple little fable about not messing with the wrong people, something that, in killing my father, some people seem to have forgotten.'

He stands up and looks at me, eye to eye.

'But I'm going to show them. I'll remind them. And by the time this is through, I'll make sure they know damn well who I am. That legend is going to get a surprise ending.'

43

I survey Jack with sadness, and feel for his situation. I have made some appalling choices in my life, choices that reaped terrible consequences. But Jack never chose any of his. His father did, and it resulted in the death of both of Jack's parents. And now he is left alone, with more questions than answers and a grief that is pushing him towards harm's way.

But now... he is not completely alone. My mind is swimming with the detail I have heard, the injustice and intricacies of Jack's predicament, not least of all – the way that organised crime has claimed another innocent victim. Not Royston Brooker, but Jack himself... and I know I will fight his corner until the bitter end.

7

We leave McDonald's and re-enter Manchester's ashen, urban embrace. I drive, Jack only having ended his bender an hour or so ago.

Before we go, I try Freckles again, this time with a direct call to the number I reached him on yesterday, but I am met with nothing. My concern grows, although I know I need to focus on the task at hand. I'm ready to get started, but in the strange position of being unsure of what to do first. Jack clearly sent a message with Zoe, if she cares to deliver it. He wants a name, and he wants to spill blood on receipt of it.

'Do you think your plea to Zoe will get you a name?' I ask. 'Will Felix give you one? I mean, do you think he even *has* one?'

Jack thinks this over, as fat raindrops speckle the windshield.

'Because,' I say, 'if he doesn't know anything and we wait for something, we are just wasting time, when I could go out there and have a little poke around myself.'

Straight after getting kicked out of the army, I came back here, and my spiral took me closer to the underground than I'm prepared to admit. I could make a few waves in the hope that somebody knows something, however tiny.

But if Manchester really is bent unto the will of the berg, then Felix really should know *something*. Or at least give us an idea of which doors to knock on, which rocks to turn over. I can't sit and wait. Inaction has never been my forte.

'Look, if you are not sure your conversation with Zoe will get a name, you need to force Felix's hand. Illustrate to him how urgent this is.'

'We wouldn't get near him. The berg are super tight and super protected, and with one of their own getting killed, they'll have the shutters down. No chance.'

'How would you contact him? If the relationship between your dad and Felix was so tight, I'd have thought the least he would do is call you!'

'Well… we are not exactly on speaking terms. I… recently told him not to contact me again.'

'Dare I ask why you did that? I mean, I know you want nothing to do with these people…'

This seems to poke at a fresh sore.

'Let's go,' he says. 'Take a left on the way out.'

Progress. Better. I ignite the engine and we hit the road again. 'He… tried to recruit me. For real. A few months ago.'

I angle the car into the flow of traffic. 'How do you mean, recruit?'

Jack looks as if he is wrestling with something, but I'm unsure what. 'Take the next left again.'

I do, while Jack continues.

'There was a case of cash – berg cash – that went missing up in Edinburgh. One of the berg, a little charmer called Leonard Freund, took something *of value* up to Scotland, although I've no idea what it was. In exchange, Leonard was given a case containing £1.25 million, but it went missing. Felix got a tip-off – or I should say, his son Michael did – that the money was on the move, headed down to London, in a silver BMW. Directly between London and Edinburgh sits Manchester, which this BMW had to pass through to get where it was going. The berg were completely stuck, they couldn't intercept him, and I stepped in. I didn't mean to, but they were in trouble.'

'You helped them?' I ask, my eyes fixed on the road.

Jack sighs.

'I saw the BMW, and I forced it off the road. I… I didn't like the fact that this guy had stolen from my dad, and I wanted to stop him. I forced him down into a ditch by the M62. It got a bit out of hand. The car was fucked, that beautiful Beemer all twisted up like tinfoil, and the guy inside was scrambled egg. But the case was intact on the passenger seat.'

'You impressed them…' I say, leading him, trying to hide my surprise.

'They intimated as much,' he replied. 'First they replaced my car with this one. I hate it.'

'I love it.'

'Then they asked me outright. I got the full spiel, the whole explanation as to who they really are and why they do it, but with all the grim details spared. It felt like the Hollywood version, with the harshness glossed over, but after I'd seen that guy crushed to a pulp in that ditch on the M62… There's no glamour there, only ugliness. A life lurching from one grim fandango to the next. I didn't want it and told them so.'

'But your hands are already dirty, aren't they?'

Jack looks down into his lap, wearing regret like a lead cloak.

'Yes. In trying to help Dad, I… made compromises I can't take back. So you see, I *do* know what it's like to kill. I've shown I have what it takes.'

The revelations keep coming. With the scale of money involved and the activities discussed, we are talking about some serious organised crime players here. Old adages about being in the right place at the right time seem appropriate. I mustn't forget the last time I tackled organised crime, with that snake Terry Masters, I bit off more than I could chew.

But I'm stronger now, there's less of an angry haze inside. I feel more assured, and ready.

Out of nowhere, the berg are firmly on my radar. That can be my secret, for the time being. Find Royston Brooker's killers, and bring them to whatever justice we can manage. Then I'll turn my attentions to the berg.

I look at the man Jack has become. It's with a shred of sadness that I feel him now over on my side – joining me in the murk of lawlessness. We are both killers, but we only ever wanted to do the right thing. Those are the hands we were dealt, and we both chose to play them – and for that we only have ourselves to blame.

8

Only five minutes of stop-start travel has passed before Jack directs me off the main carriageway, and down by a principal intersection next to Old Trafford, the vast, cavernous home of Manchester United. I watch the high red neon lettering blink in the drizzle as the car wheels down around the stadium towards the water of Salford Quays.

My phone beeps in my pocket, as a text comes through. It can only be Freckles, so I sneak a peek.

The text is light on detail but heavy on implication. *HAD TO CHANGE PLAN. TAWTRIDGE KNOWS ABOUT ME.*

I drop my phone into the little coin bin next to the gear stick, and breathe out hard. I'm glad Freckles had the foresight to adapt to any problem, but being on the outside of a situation that so involves me leaves me edgy. I have no reason to question Freckles' loyalty, but I'm not happy about this. I want to know where my insurance plan is, because as sure as the Mancunian rain, I'm fucked without it.

How the hell did Tawtridge get to Freckles?

'You all right?' Jack asks.

'Yeah, just the usual bullshit,' I murmur.

We follow the road around, parallel to the water. The Quays are essentially a trade stop-off along the Manchester Ship Canal, which now shows off Media City, the northern home of the BBC, and the Lowry Centre, a commerce and theatre flagship. All of this is bolstered by a heady volume of commercial and residential real estate, offering luxurious waterside living just outside Manchester city centre.

I haven't been back here since I left the city for the armed forces, and the changes are wholesale. It is barely recognisable from the quirky shipping district I remember, and now there is more than a hint that this is a place to see and be seen in.

'There's a right ahead, just take it and park up,' Jack instructs. I do just so, and we both hop out of the car in a small car park that overlooks the entirety of the Quays. It's a good sight, and I feel a hint of pride at my adopted city's accomplishment.

'I take it you know where we are?' Jack asks, with a dark undertone to his voice.

'Yes. Salford Quays,' I reply, resting against the railing to take in the view, the gentle surface of the canal about fifteen feet beneath my feet.

'That's the Manchester Ship Canal, runs right out along the Mersey to the main ports in Liverpool. Pretty handy in an import/export sense, wouldn't you say?'

I nod once.

'Another big bonus,' continues Jack, as he turns and points to the sky over Old Trafford, where a plane is banking right to change course, 'you're just a hop, skip and a jump from Manchester Airport.'

I can certainly see the appeal of this particular part of Manchester, if covert international business and quick getaways are your sort of thing.

'So, Felix has a warehouse down there by the Lowry, and a residence up there just by the main waterside properties. It's that one with the tall windows, just away from all the others.'

Jack points, and I follow his finger from a medium-sized blue warehouse – nothing more than a big corrugated iron box with a jetty – to a beautiful-looking piece of property that could only be described as palatial. Floor-to-ceiling windows from the floor of the property to the ceiling of the second floor – a wooden-clad waterside retreat of the highest order.

'It's perfect,' I say. 'You can see everything from there.'

'That's right,' Jack says. 'Including us.' And with that, Jack waves at Felix's house. He follows it up by standing for a couple of seconds with outstretched arms, his features imploring recognition. 'Like you say – we get his attention,' he says.

49

I'm growing increasingly wary. If this group, the berg, really are apex predators in Manchester's grimy criminal ecosystem, prodding a wounded animal when they have just lost one of their own is perhaps not the best thing to do. But Jack seems to think he's untouchable as far as Felix is concerned. I hope he is right.

Playing with fire like this, it suddenly seems clear how underprepared we are, and an old adage springs to mind, one that stuck with me from day one of training at Sandhurst: Fail to prepare, prepare to fail.

The prospect of action, at this point, is cloaked in fog, not laid out in the ordered, staccato time frame I'd prefer. If this is the way for Jack to get the information we need, then that's fine. But there are a shitload of variables to this one. And waving at a crime lord's house does not sit atop the pile as the shrewdest thing to do. It makes me feel more than a little like a sitting duck.

I sit on the bonnet of the Lexus, and wait. Jack sits next to me. Our eyes are fixed on the house across the water, our ears are filled with the soft hush of breeze and the shriek of gulls.

'Jack?' I say, but I speak again before he can reply. 'Don't get carried away. Front and centre, you want a name. If Felix has one, take it. Then let's plan the next move accordingly. I am no good to you if you bugger off on your own, flying off the handle. If you get a name, we get our heads together, and we build something with a beginning, middle, and end, with entrances, exits, and contingencies. If we need to act with urgency, then we'll take that as it comes. Do you understand?'

'Ok,' Jack replies.

'You sure this is the right way to go? Goading them like this?'

'I'm not goading them, I'm making them address me. They'll be here in a couple of minutes, I reckon.'

'I'm not happy about that, either.'

'You have to let me do this. I know these people. I need answers from them.'

I can't argue with that but something else is bothering me. I spit it out.

'I don't quite get it. These days you seem to be able to handle yourself, and given the chance, you'll end things your way. I don't know why you need my help.'

Jack doesn't shift his gaze at all from those perfect windows. He takes a minute to think about it, before answering.

'I don't want any mistakes. The way you took care of those men a couple of years back, you didn't fuck about, you just did it. You didn't think twice – that is something I need. And I need the people who did this to be dealt with.'

'But you've realised there can be a big difference between the ways it gets done,' I interrupt. 'You know that there is a certain detachment to pulling a trigger, a certain distance to running someone off the road in a car. And you imagine it will be a lot different if you have to pull someone close and slide a knife between their ribs, move it back and forth a couple of times to really hit something important. You need me to make sure, if that's what's got to happen to get what you need, that's what's going to get done. And I'm the best way to make sure it will happen.'

I turn to the view again, leaving Jack to his silence. I survey what lies before me, both the view and the wider picture.

Regardless of who killed Royston Booker, and what might happen to them, curtailing the berg's criminal activities is something I definitely want to factor in. If I can use the berg, with Jack's help, to bring justice to Royston's killer, I might be able to use what I have learned to bring the berg to account at a later date. Perhaps get some evidence of criminal activity I can drop at the police's doorstep, something that would see them arrested, and result in their operations being shut down.

My ulterior motive is taking shape. Jack doesn't know about my reasons for escaping prison, my new plans and purposes. He must think I'm just happy to be out and doing him a favour. Well, I will do that – to an extent. And then it's my turn.

A soft rattling *swoosh* heralds the arrival of another car, which pulls up next to us. Two men jump out. One wears a dark jumper, jeans, and work boots, looks about forty-five, salt-and-pepper hair in a strange mid-nineties centre parting. The other is in full Nike sportswear, athletic but with bulk, like a wide receiver. Lots of muscle. He looks like he could chase down a Mack truck and stick it in a headlock.

Salt-and-Pepper speaks. 'Hey, Jack, do you have a minute?'

He doesn't even glance at me. Zero acknowledgement that I am there at all.

'You know I do, Michael,' replies Jack. 'What do you think I'm doing here?'

Sportswear says nothing, merely opens the rear passenger door, then rests his arm against it.

'So… shall we?' says Michael, running a hand through his carefully styled hair. Neither of them pay me any attention at all, as if I'm nothing more than Jack's imaginary friend.

I can do nothing but let this situation play out, as much as being a bystander makes my gut twitch. This all feels wrong, letting Jack go with them, but the intel could well be worth the risk.

'Absolutely,' says Jack, walking towards the car. He turns back to me. 'Would you mind the car for me?'

I merely nod back, while keeping an eye on the other men. Neither of them meets my gaze. They seem cool, experienced, regimented almost. Well oiled. Well versed.

They pull out into the roadway, then accelerate gradually. As they go, I can just make out Sportswear glancing in his wing mirror at me, but I can't be sure. I turn back to the waterside and let the cool breeze float across me. It smells icy – icy and dark. Like the rivers I visited on holidays in my youth. Gulls shriek through the low whistle, but I don't see them. My eyes are centred on the house opposite. Felix Davison's house.

It's as grand and beautiful a home as I could ever hope for, and I know that, thanks to my actions and choices, I will never live in such luxury. But there's no point in moaning about it. The only thing I'm interested in is forward momentum and progress – both of which can be achieved in that beauteous glass lair across the sloshing murk of the Manchester Ship Canal.

9

My foot gleefully reunited with that Lexus gas pedal, I weave my way back to the city centre, looking for a new base. I'm staying. Tricking myself that I'm heading to London right now would be pointless – Jack's plight is too intriguing. Besides, Masters will still be there, down in London, unwittingly awaiting my return.

I don't think I can leave yet anyway, even if I wanted to. There's the disconcerting question of my insurance policy, and where it's got to, and that's a question whose answer ties me to Manchester as much as anything else. I can't leave the city until that situation is sorted; I'd end up forever on the run, choked by uncertainty. All I can do at the moment is trust that in whatever way he has crafted it, Freckles has the situation well in hand.

I need somewhere quiet and unfussy. I know of an old haunt that could do with some work, but will be fine for the immediate future. I'm not proud, I'm not picky, and the Campanile on the edge of town doesn't ask for ID. It's only a couple of minutes away.

My mind floats off and around to Jack, and where he went with those blokes. They had to be related to the berg, and his father. He recognised them, and there was an obvious rapport between them – even if they were effectively demanding him go with them.

But I have to leave it be; I've got work of my own to attend to. Digging.

I remember, as I pull into the hotel car park, that there is something else I need to source on the internet, besides the searches on the berg I had planned – something which I think will prove a lot more difficult. I need to find someone who can fake me an identity. Someone trustworthy, reputable, and experienced. Someone who will forget me as soon as they create the new me.

I know that, to do that, I'll have to brush shoulders with the very social bacteria that I'm trying to scrub away. But it's a necessary evil. A Nietzschean quote from my studies all those years ago comes to mind: '*When you gaze long into the abyss, the abyss also gazes into you.*' To get close to the evils of this world, those very same evils will impact upon me. It's a price I'm going to have to pay, and I must think of the greater good. I must make no compromises. Compromises eke the cracks of failure.

I park up and head for the entrance. Within minutes, having paid in cash and signed the register as a Mr Sean Miller, a name plucked from thin air, I am ensconced in a booth in the empty hotel bar, laptop open, logging into the complimentary Wi-Fi. I place my phone on the table next to it, ready to eye updates. The clock on the front reads 10:30 a.m.

Once in the network, I start with Google, and in the search box I type '*the berg manchester*'. Within a second, the search results blink up and I'm faced with pages dominated by an ad agency in Manchester called berg Advertising, and ex-Manchester United defender Henning berg. Page two of the results is about the same. Page three, same again. By page seven, I'm losing hope, but there is one result that catches my eye. It's a newspaper report, from the *Manchester Evening News* website, and the date of the result is eight years old. I bring up the article. The headline, followed by the brief article, reads:

'POLICE OFFICER WAKES FROM COMA

A Greater Manchester Police officer, beaten and left for dead in Salford, has recovered consciousness after an 11-day coma. Officer Jeremiah Salix, 27, was found in the Ordsall area, unconscious with multiple injuries. He was placed in a medically induced coma, and operated upon by surgeons at St Mary's Royal Infirmary. He has been in intensive care ever since.

Last night, Officer Salix woke for the first time since he sustained his injuries. Staff Nurse Mary Robertson describes the moment he came around. "It started with blinking. He soon became lucid and asked for his girlfriend. We are so happy to see him come back, as we were very concerned."

The investigation into what happened to Officer Salix continues, but rumours that it was connected to an organised crime gang known as the berg are unconfirmed.'

Bingo.

The berg seem as elusive and rare as a UFO sighting, now nearly a decade since they featured in the media and popular culture.

I reroute my thought process to the names I do know, and what I can learn through their carelessness.

One of the men who picked up Jack was called Michael. I know his surname to be Davison, so I type in '*michael davison manchester*'. All I find is a solitary Facebook photo tag, which I click through. The owner of the photo is Leonard Freund – a name I remember from Jack's stories earlier.

On opening the picture, I make a positive ID straight away. The picture itself is a standard nightclub snap: bright flash, pitch-black background, all the glamour and excitement of the moment itself stripped away, leaving the bare facts. Just two men at a table next to a mostly empty club dance floor. A bottle of champagne on the table. And that's it. Neither looks too pissed, neither looks too happy, or too bothered. They look bored to tears. I notice the pupils. Saucers. Drugs? Possibly.

One of the men is clearly Michael Davison, the man from before: that hair could belong to nobody else. His name appears at the bottom of the image, along with Freund's. Hovering the cursor over the names I see that Freund's is clickable, and Davison's is not. Davison has no Facebook profile. I click on Freund's and it quickly becomes obvious that this man is a social media obsessive and a consummate narcissist.

For starters, his profile picture looks like a homemade modelling shot. Black and white, high contrast, and shades. An oddly out-of-date pencil moustache completes the look. I scroll down. There are meals as photo updates – just pictures of plates of food. And cars, a few nice sports models. There's a fancy watch called a Breitling. A few clichés of a stereotypical high life: jacuzzis, first-class air travel, gadgets.

Is this what makes this Freund tick, or what he thinks people want to see? He's like a ten-year-old with a Facebook profile, living out his fantasies – only none of these are Photoshopped.

I check the time – I thought Freckles would have got back to me by now with more news. I hate it, but I'm absolutely at his mercy. It makes my guts squirm, this lack of control.

My phone buzzes on the table, and I jump. I half think that Freckles must have felt my unease telepathically and finally called to put me out of my misery, but caller ID lets me know it is Jack.

'Yes?' I answer.

'I've got it,' Jack says hurriedly. He sounds a little out of breath.

'You got…?'

'A name. They gave me a name.'

Jack's meeting clearly went well, and he won't want to sit still for long. 'Do you recognise it?'

'Kind of. Anyway, I know where we are going.'

'You want to get started right away, I take it?'

'No. We'll wait till tonight.'

'Can you give me any info?'

'The Floating Far East. That's where we are headed.'

I have no idea what that is, or where it might be found. 'Anything else?'

'Not now. Meet me at eight thirty, at the ice rink in Spinningfields.'

'I'll be there.'

The line goes dead, and my mind transforms instantly. My senses tighten and my mind clears. I am back on the frontline, battening down of the hatches, ready to do what needs to be done. The calm, the pause, the reflection… then the unavoidable descent into harm's way.

10

I walk along the standstill jam of the M602 on the city outskirts, which funnels the motorway traffic right into the city centre. I'd spent the early afternoon researching The Floating Far East and its surroundings, and on finding myself restless, headed out. I'm free now, I've got time until meeting Jack later. Let's go and find Freckles and find out what the hell is going on.

The city looks compact and imposing from here, and I take in its peaks and troughs. When you look at a city this way, from this distance, you only see the bits that reach for the heavens, you don't see that which crawls and festers around its ankles. But that's Britain for you. Always reaching, always pressing on. It was that indomitable spirit I fell in love with, twinned with a history that stands proud alongside any. Nostalgia seems to put an arm around my shoulders.

I drop through a quieter road that cuts between a few apartment blocks, the street lined with hastily parked cars sitting at jaunty angles, and I feel a wave of déjà vu. I went to a party in one of these apartments, high up on one of the upper floors. I think I kissed a girl there. That must have been a decade ago. It's a sobering thought.

I exit the loop road, cross the dual carriageway, and pass past an NCP car park, whose customers bottleneck through its solitary exit. The afternoon is beginning to cast longer, lower shadows, the October glow of the city blinking more to life with every passing minute. The road flattens out, with nothing but an unfinished concrete shell on my right, haunting a long-abandoned building site. Must have run out of money on that one.

A couple more minutes, and I'm surrounded by high blocks of flats again on either side, and I see the one I'm looking for. I've never been here before, but I'm following an educated guess. I know Freckles lives in a residential complex on this street, City Road East, called City Walk Apartments. Before we got to know each other properly, we had idly chatted about where we lived in the city we were both so familiar with. I had no fixed abode, but he let his slip. And there it is ahead.

The door is locked, a keypad offering me the chance to ring up to be buzzed in, but I don't know the flat number, and wouldn't bet on him letting me up in any case. I loiter.

Twenty minutes pass as the early twilight settles around me like a violet blanket speckled with neon and halogen. A young couple is walking down the street, arm in arm, deep in what looks like a fragile conversation. They are not rowing, but they are not on the best of terms, with her leaning into him with an urgent expression, large Bambi eyes testing the limit of their sockets, and him staring fixedly at the ground as if he's following a breadcrumb trail out of the encounter.

I take my phone out, feign making a call, and hold it to my ear.

'Yeah, mate, just arrived,' I say to nothing and nobody. The couple are disentangling and opening the front door. 'Yeah, nah, you don't have to buzz me in, door's open.'

The couple enter the building, and the guy holds it open for me. What a gent. 'Yeah, I'm on my way up now,' I say, then mouth *thanks* to the helpful man.

I go straight to the post boxes on the left-hand side and pause to get my bearings. I'm standing in a tall, open-air space that must function as a kind of communal garden for the residents. There are a couple of dotted benches and tired brown-green ferns, struggling where the sun fails to reach them. It smells close, muddy, and the air is humid, even in October. I glance upwards to the sky, and see the windows of all the apartments above, most of which are open.

And that's how I'll find him. I take out my phone and call. The phone dials, and then suddenly up high over my head, I hear it – the plaintive ringing of a house phone. I step into the garden to get a better fix on it, holding the phone at my side, hoping now that Freckles doesn't pick up.

I follow the noise across the windows for a bit. Maybe up one more, and… yes: there. That's the one. Three floors up, six windows from the right-hand side. It looks dark up there. I hope he's in.

Through a pair of glass double doors I am quickly offered lifts and stairs. I take the lift to the third floor, and count the doors along to the spot that should be my target. The white gloss wooden door has '33' painted on it below a small peephole.

I knock loudly. Freckles will know it's me, so soon after my call, and he won't be able to ignore me. Plus I'll kick this door in if I have to. My freedom is at stake here.

There is a shuffle beyond the door, a pause. Then:

'You shouldn't be here.'

'If you'd have stuck to the plan, I wouldn't,' I reply. I hear him unlock the door, and he pulls it open. No light seeps out, as if he's been sitting in the dark, but the glow from the hallway lets me see Freckles – and it's a sight that jars me.

It's Freckles all right: medium height, pudgy build, longish hair raked back from his face. It's the first time I've seen him in civilian clothes, but that's not the shocker. The shocker is the quilting of deep, fresh, purple bruising covering his entire jaw, left earlobe to right earlobe, the scrapes across his forehead, the nose bashed cruelly off-centre, and the blackened, sunken eyes.

'*Jesus*, Freckles,' I say.

He says nothing, just looks at me with those eyes that are wet with remorse and accusation – and pain. I don't need a body language expert to tell me what he's suggesting. *This is your fault, pal.*

'Tell me what happened,' I say, crossing the threshold. We walk down the hall, cream-carpeted and lined with shoes both male and female, yet still dark. Freckles walks with a limp, and holds his upper body with care – as if his ribs are a kid's school project made of papier-mâché and eggshells. He stops and turns back to me. The hallway is close and the atmosphere is closer.

'You said y-you'd call me…' Freckles stutters in a fluttering, fraught voice. It must hurt like shit to talk with a jaw that mangled. 'You said you'd call me when you got out, that you'd have something for me to hold onto.

59

Ten K, no questions asked, you said. You needed it putting in a deposit box. You never told me what it was, or when it would be coming. You're not supposed to be out, are you?'

My lack of response speaks volumes.

'Shit, Ben, what did you take from them? Fuck's sake, Ben! Tawtridge tracked me down in a flash, just a couple of hours after you called me. Sent two of the wardens down to meet me after work.' He gestures helplessly, and grimaces with the effort. 'You can see how well that went. Tried to intercept what you were giving me,' he says, running a hand through his hair.

'Where is it now?' I ask.

'Christ…'

'I'm sorry for what has happened, Freckles. I really am. But I can't change that now. Where is the bag?'

'My wife has it. I told her what to do.'

'Where is she now?'

'Fucked if I know. I told her to go to ground until things settled down.'

I let this information sink in for a moment. All is not lost – yet. But I never intended to cause trouble for people. This was just supposed to be a way of getting my insurance policy to a safe place while I got a march on.

Freckles was only doing a couple of years for benefit fraud, which actually seemed a bit harsh. He had knee issues, had to stop working. He got signed on, then after eighteen months or so, a surgeon tried something new and got it sorted. But he couldn't find a job, and the benefit money came in handy to paper over the financial cracks. The irony of it was that if he'd just quit the disability benefit and applied for Jobseekers Allowance, he'd have been getting money just fine. The court didn't see it that way, and made an example of him. Down he went.

'I'm sorry, Freckles. I mean it. I'll make it fifteen K for the trouble,' I say.

'This is really bad for me, you know. Stace is proper onside, she's savvy, knows what she's doing… But I'm just getting my life back together, and this happens. I finally get a job, and I get the shit beat out of me outside work. Employers usually see that kind of thing as bad for business. And now Stace is out there somewhere with a bag of God knows what, hiding out for God knows how long.'

'Who came after you?'

'It was two of the kangas on our block, Adams and Polanksi.'

Kanga, kangaroo, rhyming slang for *screw*, nickname for prison officers. Two of Tawtridge's team. He hasn't given up on me yet.

'What did you tell them?'

'Told them I didn't have it, which was the truth. They thought I was lying, that I had it stashed somewhere. Hence this.' He gestures to himself.

'You didn't tell them where it was going to be?'

'No, I didn't,' Freckles sighs.

I put an arm on his shoulder. 'You did good, mate. Really good. I'll sort this out, then I'll let you know when your wife can come home. I'll get right onto it. I won't forget what you've done for me. I owe you a massive favour.'

'Too right you do.'

I turn for the door, but Freckles catches me.

'What is in the bag?'

'I won't tell you specifics, but it's an insurance policy. And Tawtridge knows that as long as I have it, or it's safe somewhere, I'm untouchable.'

That won't last forever. I need to find a way of getting Tawtridge off my back, for good.

'When you hear from your wife, let me know. I'll get the bag off her so you can put this behind you.'

Freckles thinks about that for a moment. 'You're a complicated guy, Ben.'

I leave. It's funny: I always thought of myself as quite simple. I check my watch. 4:30. I can make one more stop before I meet Jack, and it's one that has been tormenting me ever since I contemplated breaking out, and even now I'm not sure I'm ready for it. But I have a window, and I believe in taking the opportunities life deals out – royal flushes, bum hands, and all.

11

I take the M60 out of Manchester and head for the Peak District. I realise I don't have that much time for this one, given that I can't be late for Jack, but my curiosity just won't give me a break any longer. I've been out of prison one day, and I can feel something unexpected: the strange pull of home. I'm curious to see how things are now. What has changed, if anything, in my absence.

As I drive, I think back to poor old Freckles' bad luck. Tawtridge must have heard my request, or one of his screws did. In rec room one day, when we were cleaning, I asked Freckles if he'd hold on to something for me when I got out, and I'd iron out the details later. That was the only part of the conversation that was ever held in an open setting, and Tawtridge, the resourceful bastard, must have got wind of that little bit of info and filed it away in case he ever needed it. And now he did.

I leave the motorway networks as the daylight fades and trundle through the bleak stone township of Glossop, as wild hills begin to sprout out either side of the settlement. I know where I am going, and follow the 'V' in the horizon where two hills meet and a road carves through: Snake Pass. Suddenly, the buildings and pavements disappear, and I'm out in the open, rolling through a picture-book patchwork of varying landscapes: undulating rugged grasslands, steep canyon drop-offs, vast forests of tall firs, and a softly lapping reservoir. You could be lost out here, but still feel in touch with the gods. It's *Lord of the Rings* country, Tolkien's inspiration. It's Britain at its most beautiful, most powerful, most respectful.

The bricks and mortar I grew up inside might stoke memories, but it'll be the people inside the house – my parents – who'll make this visit succeed or fail.

My parents. They never visited me in prison, and I know my fall from grace really hurt them, but I can't help wondering if they are ok. They are my parents, after all, so supportive and proud when I was progressing through the ranks, and so awash with loving relief whenever I was home. I miss them terribly – it's the one weak spot my backbone won't extend to, and I wish it wasn't the case.

I won't reveal myself to them. I won't knock. At least I don't think I will.

Snake Pass spits me out on the outskirts of Sheffield, the Steel City. I take the ring road round, circling the city from the outside, before dropping off the bottom of the city and back into the flow of traffic out. Sheffield is a good, decent city, and being the biggest one close to home, one that I guess you could say I did most of my growing up in. I came in here to chase girls, watch football, listen to live music, enjoy independence, but I'd always get the train home.

Home to Rawmarsh.

It's not long before I am there again. Haugh Road, right in the middle. Everything looks the same, right down to the chewing gum on the pavements. There's the old off-licence, the pub I used to drink in. There's the phone box I'd call my mates from, out the front of the house I called home for thirty years.

My heart feels a hot stab at seeing it, worse than I expected. Home.

It's a terraced house that could do with some work. The lawn is a bit longer than Dad used to have it, by quite a bit, actually, and the PVC window frames we had put in on a government grant to promote greener living a few years ago are a bit mucky. The door is still painted red, with a brass knocker.

What are you doing here, Ben? Are you going to invite yourself in for a cuppa? Or stand out here like a stalker?

I hadn't really thought that far ahead. But somehow, I needed to see it. I needed to see something concrete, to remind me where I came from… Christ, this fucking *neediness*… I don't like it.

I feel abandoned by them, for sure, but they had their reasons. They were so proud, and suddenly all that pride was gone.

And now, with my visit this evening? I suppose I just need to know that, even though everything else is chaos, things back here at home remain the same. We wouldn't even need to talk, just…

In fact, despite the curtains being open, it doesn't look like they are home.

Wait. I can see in through the front window, despite the dwindling light. Something's different: On the left-hand side, Grandma's mirror is missing, the one passed down to Mum when she died. It had a gold frame – well, gold edging on top of tin – and it was Mum's pride and joy. And the curtains that are open… there *are* no curtains. Looking closer I can see the tie-back hooks stand visible and empty.

I walk up the path, leaving prints in the long grass, and peer inside, and more and more of my past looms up in front of me the closer I get. But this nostalgia, and the stir of anticipation that has arisen despite my efforts to subdue it, is quickly replaced by something cold, something bitter.

The room is empty.

I can see through to the kitchen along the old carpet that runs right through the downstairs, which in the emptiness now looks more threadbare. There's nothing.

They've gone. My parents have left here.

I stand simply staring into the hollow space, and feel as if I'm gazing into the very emptiness that has been abruptly carved inside of me. My feeling of loneliness is complete.

I have no way to contact them. They are gone, and from the look of things, gone for good. And considering that they never sent me a forwarding address while I was in prison, they clearly don't want me to know where they are.

All I wanted was to see that they were ok, but as far as I can tell, they didn't even want me to have that. They have disowned me. I should have guessed from their passive stares in the public gallery at my trial, fixing on any point but their own son's searching gaze. I can't help but stand and dwell.

I quickly decide that I've had enough. I walk away because there's nothing for me here anymore, not for the first time. Rawmarsh is no longer my home. I feel I could cry, but I won't. No chance – those bastards, they won't get that from me.

I walk down the path to the scuffed, mucky pavement. The gum on the concrete beneath my shoes, some of it is undoubtedly mine. My DNA lies at my feet, inseparable from my town, my past. That DNA is now the only evidence I was ever here. Thirty years of love, life, family – all reduced to a dirty bit of gum on an old pavement.

This will steel me. Toughen me. It has to. Because this would, could, should break a lesser man.

12

I get to Spinningfields early, in the cooling, prickly evening air. There must have been twilight rain while I was on my ill-fated jaunt to Yorkshire, because the atmosphere retains a post-downpour clarity. If Manchester wasn't so alive, I'm sure I'd hear a pin drop.

After dumping the car, I make the short walk along the backstreets from my hotel, keeping a fix on the upper floors of Manchester Civil Justice Centre, a huge, preposterously balanced filing cabinet of a building that stands in the centre of Spinningfields.

There's a space in me. A dirty great hole with red, raw edges. I feel excavated since my trip to Rawmarsh, and have had plenty of time to stew on the ninety-minute ride home, but now I've shoved it all roughly to the back of my mind so that I can focus on the task at hand. There's just no use wallowing.

It's not long before I get where I am going, having passed the old, disused Granada Studios, home of TV greats such as *Coronation Street*. This city has transformed, the tired, older generation making way for a brave new one, eager youth taking ever-bolder steps to modernity. Business has flocked to Manchester, and I remember reading, as I step into the smartness of the pedestrianised Spinningfields site, that within these smart tower blocks sit sixty-four of the *Sunday Times*' list of the top one hundred companies.

The site is a square of five blocks, cut off from cars apart from service vehicles and adorned with plush bars and restaurants alternating with big-business premises. In another lifetime, I might have enjoyed getting a nice easy nine-to-five, and might even have had friends I could meet for a drink after work, before going home to my family. I watch the groups of bright young things cavort in their loosened ties and pretty dresses, as they mill about from bar to bar.

The firearm pressing against the outside of my right hip pulls me back to the present. I'm not one of those people. I never will be.

With the pistol in my waistband I feel a little like a Wild West gunslinger. Coming into possession of it is a great piece of luck. Usually, if you want a firearm in this country, there aren't a great many avenues to hand that don't have the same effect as strapping a neon sign to your head announcing that you have very bad things in mind.

The only other things on me, are my Swiss army knife, wallet, and phone, the latter two wrapped in sandwich bags I borrowed from the hotel kitchen to keep them safe and dry.

The ice rink is ahead, framed in twinkling halogen. In this quarter, Manchester is clearly thriving, but there are darker corners out there, and the man leaning against the ice rink railings on the left-hand side looks like he has his head, heart, and soul firmly preoccupied with one.

I approach Jack, who looks about ready to detonate, with a taught, fused posture and determined expression.

'Tell me about today,' I say, pleasantries abandoned.

'Felix is a mess, it seems all the guys are,' Jack replies, unblinking.

'By guys, you mean the berg?'

'Yeah, Michael and Samson. They were the ones who picked me up.'

'So how did the conversation go?'

'Felix was in tears, he didn't want to give me anything. Just a broken old man. I told him if he didn't give me a name I would hold him responsible for whatever is to come next.'

'And that did the trick?'

'It did.'

I wait a few beats. 'And…?'

'Sparkles Chu.'

'Sounds like a Korean pop prince. Who is he?'

'He runs the restaurant I told you about, as well as a criminal organisation specialising in cocaine, a touch of meth, and arms.'

'Sounds lovely.'

'The Floating Far East appears to be their centre of operations. And that's where we are going tonight.'

I remember my homework, a map of Manchester springing into my head, but on a zoom from the heavens right down to a riverside street six hundred yards from where we stand.

'I know it. Any special intel you have on it, that you can't get from the internet?' I ask.

'Not really. Just that it's a restaurant out front and there's a room at the back that seems to be a meeting room. Michael told me.'

'So far, so clichéd. How do they know this? What's their source?'

'They used to do a little business together, although nothing too major. Michael has been there a couple of times representing Felix and the berg's interests, and has seen Sparkles there holding court.'

'But how do they know that this guy Sparkles was the trigger man?'

'According to Michael, they had recently tried to up the ante with Sparkles and his friends, collaborate on some higher-profile business. This time it was Dad that made the approach, after Michael had opted out on the basis that he was unsure whether to work with them again. Dad thought it was a good idea. He went there, had a conversation, but it didn't go as planned. He came back with a death threat.'

Icy hatred seems to sweep over Jack.

'They didn't like the manner of his proposal,' I suggest.

Jack spits out: 'I suppose not.'

'But that doesn't irrefutably tie Sparkles to the hit. How is Felix sure?'

'He's not. But he's the only name he has. He said Dad didn't go around collecting grudges. On the contrary, he had a fair way of business that made friends rather than enemies. And Sparkles and the River seem to be the only party big enough to attempt it.'

'The River?'

'I just picked it up from them. Whenever they referred to the party that operates out of that floating restaurant, they referred to it as *the River*. A pet name, I guess.'

'Are this group of Eastern origin? And by Eastern, I mean China?'

68

'I would imagine so, yes. Although I've never laid eyes on them.'

'This morning, just before I came to see you, a man tried to kill me in my hotel room.'

Jack's eyebrows head for his hairline, his eyes going widescreen.

'More specifically, it was a man of, I believe, part-Chinese origin. And he wasn't trying to kill Ben Bracken, he was trying to kill Jack Brooker.'

Jack scowls. 'And you only mention this now?'

'Figured you had enough on your plate, without thinking you are a marked man.'

'They were trying to tie off loose ends. Those fucking bastards. Kill the father, kill the son who's looking for answers.'

'All I'm saying is, it seems realistic to assume that a powerful group with a Far East connection does indeed want you taken out. Which is why you might be right.'

I don't like giving Jack news like this, but it backs up his story and will strengthen his conviction, and that is what we need to take with us to that restaurant. I take charge.

'Ok, if you want this… I'm in charge, we do this whose way?'

'Your way.'

'I've mapped the place out, entries, exits, all accounted for. You follow my lead, and I'll explain on the way. You have your dad's piece?'

Jack nods grimly.

'Good. That feeling you have, that spite, that outrage – let it spill up to here.'

I hold my hand up to my Adam's apple, as an old battlefield speech comes back to me on an occasion when I was about to help some boys become men.

'Let it boil below there, but never past here. You let it get past here, you'll start to fuck up. Your body needs to be ready to execute at all costs, but it needs to execute what a cool head tells it to. Keep it bottled, but don't lose it. It's your secret weapon. Let's get going.'

With that, I start walking. I know exactly the narrow paths I want to take to get to the restaurant, which route will take us there the quietest. No point rattling the hornet's nest when you're about to stick your hand in it.

13

We walk and I give the orders. I make them as clear and concise as I can.

As we wind through the backstreets from Spinningfields towards the high banks of the River Irwell, the lights of the city centre dimming on our backs, I feel that welcome readiness sweep me. For the first time since Jack contacted me, I feel in control and prepared, and the uncertainties of Freckles and my parents are shelved.

I have taken us through the alleys and passageways in case there are any restaurant employees on the streets close to the riverbank, where the restaurant is permanently moored. I don't want to flirt with recognition. If the restaurant indeed is a secret business-within-a-business, then a street-side presence will probably have a fair idea who Jack is, never mind myself, 'that bloke who fucked up cousin Whatnot's legs'.

The riverbank is now ahead, the water twenty feet below us, rippling moonlight back up at us.

'There it is,' Jack says, pointing off to our right. Sure enough, two hundred yards away, floats our destination. A huge Chinese junk, fit for inclusion in any exotic armada, adorned with festive lights from the tip of the bow all the way to the highest point of the mast and right along the angled red sails. It is quite the sight. The main cabin of the vessel seems multilayered, and deep. Portholes stippling the hull spill a warm light out onto the river. It's the kind of place you'd go to impress your better half.

There is a man under a little covered shelter next to a broad gangplank which serves as the restaurant entrance. He is facing away from us as we approach.

'You all set?' I ask Jack.

'Yes,' he whispers.

'The gun – you're comfortable with it?'

'Yeah, I think so.'

'You give me some bullshit about playing lots of Xbox, I'm turning around…'

'I have held this gun before, yes. I know how it works.'

'Heavier than you think, isn't it? Your conviction – keep tapped into it. You'll get the hang of the rest.'

Jack doesn't answer, and I think I may have ended up patronising him. Good – he'll be desperate to prove me wrong.

Now, a hundred yards away, I motion Jack towards the bankside railing.

'Hop it,' I order.

Jack looks at me in confusion, but doesn't question. When he is on the other side of the railing, his back to the river on the ledge, I check the doorman. Still facing down the river towards the brighter lights of the main road, from where a couple is approaching, arm in arm. Best get to it before they see us.

I hop over also, steady myself, and look down below me. There it is. I had noticed it on Google Street View, using the road on the other side of the river as a virtual vantage point. A very narrow ledge, more an outcropping of brick about seven feet below us. I don't know whether it is there for a purpose, perhaps to measure the water level, or merely a nineteenth-century cosmetic addition, but it looks strong enough to support us. I lower myself slowly, using my arms for leverage. I grip the concrete ledge, keep my stomach tight to the wall, and drag my toes along the brick until they bump the ledge. I take the weight, then whisper to Jack: 'Slowly.' He ably copies me.

Glancing down I see the ledge is about six inches wide, with my heels sticking out into space. It will be just fine. I look at Jack, who is distinctly reluctant to look down.

'It's ok. Follow me,' I say.

He nods, and I turn to my left, my nose brushing the moss-flecked wall and filling up with a musty, earthen aroma. I fix my eyes on the hulking vessel, and start edging along the ledge. I can hear Jack shuffling along behind me, and we make steady progress, one step at a time, one hand over the other.

It doesn't take long before we are directly below the gangplank. The air carries that woody, peat-infused odour only a running river can impart as it washes over something fixed and solid. The boat has clearly been here for some time. I check on Jack, who is just a yard or two behind me. Good lad.

The gangplank is made up of a series of sturdy wooden beams joined together, almost like a thick horizontal ladder, complete with gaps between the beams in which to insert fingers and gain purchase. I listen hard; the last thing we want is our fingers getting crushed by the feet of patrons coming on board.

I wait for Jack to reach me. 'One at a time,' I whisper. He nods.

It is quiet above. The water moves swiftly and silently beneath us. I poke my fingers through the slats, get a grip, and swing out into the murk. The edge of the wood is slippery, and for a second, I think I'm going to lose my hold. I squeeze hard, and, like a big kid on scaled-up monkey bars, I slowly swing my way the ten feet to the boat.

There is a thick rope surrounding the hull of the vessel, bowed intermittently, which will function as a step. I loop my left leg around it, straddle the thick coil, and sit in the slack. I gesture for Jack to follow, and he reaches up to the makeshift bridge with some hesitation. I crane my neck up to peek over at the doorman, who is looking at the sky, seemingly bored to tears.

Jack makes steady progress, so I start the final stretch of the journey: navigating this thick rope around the front of the hull to the other side of the vessel, where I know the porthole to the gents' toilet is located. Incredibly, some bloke took a selfie in the toilets, uploaded it to the web (because of course everyone wants to see a picture of you just after you've performed a basic bodily function), and Facebook's location services did the rest. Voilà, a picture of the restaurant toilets, complete with porthole entry point.

I shift my weight over the drop, grip the rope with hands, calves, and ankles, and slowly start a gradual journey along the rope to the bow, taking care at the points where the rope bows up to its fixings. I check on Jack, relieved to see he is not far behind.

I round the bow, which is a bit more tricky, and involves letting go with my legs and hanging in space while I swing my body around the point to the other side. Safely on the other side, while giving my arms a momentary rest, I wait for Jack, and when I see him, offer a hand to lighten the load.

I pull him around the corner, and we are right by the porthole. Jack gets comfortable on the rope, and pauses to rest. I bring my index finger to my lips in a silent *shush*.

Peeking up to the muck-covered glass, I look in, the soft bathroom light splashing my face. Urinals on the far wall, sinks and mirrors to the left, toilet stalls to the right. At the farthest right urinal, a man stands, legs well apart, rocking slightly, apparently having an epic piss. I take the Swiss army knife from my jacket pocket, and use the flathead screwdriver to remove the screws around the bottom of the porthole window frame. I leave the top fixing intact, so that, when we are inside, the window will slide back into place, covering our tracks.

The man at the urinal is animatedly finishing off, and if more than a shake is classed as playing with it, he's damn well conducting a symphony in there. *Come on.*

As soon as he's gone, I twist the plate of glass upwards, and the warm air from the bathroom gushes out, along with the stench of stale urine. I hoist myself through, feet first. When I'm in, Jack pokes his feet through almost as quickly. I replace the glass with care.

Deep breath time. This is enemy turf. Bringing the fight into their territory will throw them but if they have done the things we believe they have, they certainly won't think twice about using deadly force here and now. I gesture for Jack to stand behind me, as I edge around the open doorway of the gents.

A corridor. Dim lights, wood floors, art prints on the walls. Glimpses of modernity encased in ancient dust jackets. Nobody in sight, but I can hear chatter, and music. The restaurant floor must be just around the corner at the end of the short corridor. We move casually in case anyone should see us, and the murmur of voices increases in both depth and volume. At the end of the corridor there are very conveniently placed potted lilies, which mask me a little. It's enough to give me a good look at the place.

The first thing I notice is the barrels. The ceiling is obscured by huge, hanging, horizontally racked barrels, presumably used as containers when the ship was an active trade vessel, although they appear to have been converted. There are plastic pipes branching between them, and each barrel appears to have a tap system at one end. There is a metal unit attached at the head of each system also, presumably providing scientific readings of the contents. Temperature, pressure and such. A suspended distillery.

I'm actually rather impressed by that. Below the hanging moonshine factory sits the restaurant, and it's a beauty. Never mind bringing a date here – this is where I'd propose to her. It's spacious, with dark wooden surfaces, authentic Chinese ornaments and art, lush potted plants of varying species, all illuminated by soft tea lights on the tables and glowing lanterns overhead. You could lose yourself easily in here, an active imagination transporting the diner to another time altogether. Rows of intimate round tables, in varying sizes, with booths on the far left and the entrance door on the far right. On the back wall, immediately opposite, is a well-stocked bar. The place is a fantasy floating upon the spoiled, polluted debris of an inner-city northern river, and they have done a great job with it.

The restaurant is about half full, which is entirely as expected. Chinese traditions often dictate a much later dining time, so this place will be bedlam no earlier than midnight. The barman opposite is a stocky Chinese man with a shaven head, and, like the captain of this vessel, he watches out over the restaurant. I turn to Jack.

'Let's go for a drink,' I say, and step out from beyond the corner. Jack follows me, and we begin an unhurried stride across the centre of the restaurant. Nobody pays us any attention at all.

As we walk, I take in the bar, the front door, and the large windows over the booths on the left. Our best exit is that front door, as the gangplank seems to be the only dry route off here. We pass under the barrels too, and I glance up. A clear liquid is visible through the plastic pipework, and an idea strikes me. A sliver, a scratched instinct.

At the bar, I give the stocky man my full attention.

I gauge quickly that this man, although strong and intimidating, doesn't recognise us. I make a show of ordering. 'What are you on, mate?' I say animatedly to Jack, perching on a barstool.

'Lager,' says Jack.

'Hi, mate,' I say to the barman. 'It's a lager for this gentleman, and for me... I'm sorry but is that *baijiu* up there in the barrels?'

He looks genuinely startled and I can tell I've caught him off guard good and proper. I took some of my training abroad, and picked up the odd thing. I have a solid hunch that in those barrels is indeed *baijiu* – a very strong traditional Chinese liquor, about 110% proof. It is a drink that is increasing in popularity worldwide as China's international power and influence expands, and if all these barrels contain such a temptation, hanging above us is a liquid fortune.

'Yes. Yes, it is,' he responds in an authentic Manchester twang wrapped around a deep baritone.

'Could I try some?'

'Of course,' the man replies, keeping his eyes on me as he moves to the taps. I see the door at the far end of the bar, presumably leading to the back room. The place we need to take a look in.

The man fills a taller-than-usual pint glass with crisp, bubbling amber. He reaches down into the fridge for a chilled glass. I look back around the restaurant, to take in the employees. They appear mainly to be young girls and men, maybe international students, earning extra pennies. Nobody I would consider part of a security force for an underground criminal network. No: If this gang is on site, they are in that back room. And this barman will know either way.

He hands me a small, cold tumbler of clear fluid. I sniff it, and even its redolence burns the back of my throat.

'That's eight ninety, mate,' says the barman.

'Can I set up a tab?' I counter.

The man measures me with his stare. 'That depends on how long you were thinking of staying.'

'I'll cut to the chase then,' I say. 'Sparkles Chu. What does that name mean to you?'

The man laughs heartily, launching his head back. It's a dismissive gesture, mocking me. I don't like it.

'Is he here?' I follow up.

The man smiles and takes to wiping down the bar. 'Finish your drinks and be on your way,' he says, leering arrogantly.

'That's difficult for us, considering we have come to kill him.'

His expression changes instantly, his eyes dancing with rage.

'Why kill *him*?' he growls. 'What's he done to you?'

I put my glass down and lean in with a glare of my own. 'We have it on good authority that he killed somebody. Somebody he shouldn't have killed.'

The man thinks this through. Eventually, he lifts his t-shirt to expose his taut stomach – which is covered in small tattoos, each a variant on a theme. Little, crackling, point-edged sparks, about forty in total, spattering his torso. It appears we have been talking to Sparkles himself. At my fleeting recognition, he lowers his t-shirt, then walks over to the back wall. I stiffen, ready to reach for the gun in my waistband, but he merely reaches up and activates the wall-mounted fire alarm. A bell sounds loudly, a continuous, droning note.

I glance behind me, as ordered chaos engulfs the restaurant. The waiting staff usher the customers confusedly from the tables, unsure of whether this is a poorly timed drill or a real emergency. I notice four heavy, solid-looking men appearing at the door. They help usher the people out. After a moment, the bell abruptly shuts off, and the restaurant is empty. Food still steams on plates. The four new additions approach us from behind. I need to swing the balance back in our favour without delay.

'Stay where you are or Sparkles gets a new tattoo,' I shout, whipping my pistol out and training it on Sparkles' spite-filled mug. Jack pulls his gun out also, and aims it at the approaching men, who come to a stop at the sight of it.

'I don't know who you are, or how you got in here, but you need to get the fuck out, now,' says Sparkles.

'Not until we have the retribution this man needs.'

'This has been an ill-advised and ill-judged attempt at intimidation that is not going to work. You are both outmanned and outgunned.'

There is a matter-of-factness to his delivery that suggests he isn't pissing about, and a tremor in his voice that suggests a growing, deep resentment.

'Then avoid the bloodshed and explain it to us. All the details.'

Sparkles doesn't seem to want to entertain that.

'You don't know me. I'm not like who you usually deal with,' I say.

'And who do I usually deal with?' counters Sparkles.

'I'm a soldier. I don't have any interest in your business or your turf. I'm trying to help this man get a job done, and I'm bloody well going to do it.'

This seems to ignite some kind of recognition in Sparkles, which is echoed by one of the men behind me.

'He's the bastard that fucked up Channy,' one of the men says. I can't tell which one it is, but I'll stake the contents of my dodgy bank account on it being the guy who was waiting for my visitor in the car park at the Premier Inn. Channy must have been in a fairly bad state by the time he was found, poor son of a bitch. I give Sparkles a light nod to let him know that what's been suggested is true.

'He shouldn't have been there, end of story,' I say.

Sparkles must be about thirty-five, with a sureness that belies his years. If Felix Davison is a competitive soul, he won't like this young upstart in the city centre making waves that ripple out to his little empire in the Quays.

'We acted out of protection,' says Sparkles.

'My hairy arse,' spits Jack, as rage fully gets the better of him. He spins to face Sparkles, and fires, but he fires too early in the manoeuvre and the shot goes over Sparkles' shoulder, as Sparkles drops instinctively to the floor. A liquor bottle shatters on the bar, glass tinkling.

I'm livid with Jack for blowing his cool and our position, but there's no time to think – the guns are coming out. I grab Jack by the shoulder and heave him up off his seat. 'Over the bar,' I order, and we both dive over the countertop, dragging glasses and bar dressing with us, as the first shots rain over our backs. We land ugly and hard on the other side, glass and liquor flying, and as I try to get my bearings, I see Sparkles scrabbling on all fours through the door to the back. Jack is pulling himself upright, and I reach back up over the bar and fire a couple of shots back at our assailants, hoping to keep them back for a moment, but the situation has quickly gotten out of hand.

And then I remember the barrels.

I lean back against the wall and unload five shots into the barrels. Liquor begins dripping out, followed by stronger gushes, and before long there are five streams of fluid spraying onto the restaurant floor.

The gunfire over our heads resumes, and Jack and I return it as best we can. There is a shelf under the bar, and on it sits some cleaning products.

I grab some j-cloths and twist them to a point. Gambling my life between bursts of gunfire, and covered by Jack, I reach blindly above me for a bottle, thanking heaven when I discover it's Sambuca. Perfect.

I twist off the cap, stuff the point of j-cloths into the top of the bottle, and light that sucker up. I pause for a second to let the flames blossom. I turn to Jack.

'Keep covering me,' I say.

Jack nods, and we both rise in unison, firing. Looking out over the restaurant we see our bullets haven't connected with any of the targets. The men are down low by the first row of tables, two of them getting soaked by the falling spirit. I take aim at the most central barrel and throw the bottle. It sails, tumbling end on end, before shattering on impact – and with a loud, hot smash, fire sprays down onto the restaurant. The flames ignite the falling streams of *baijiu*, and suddenly the restaurant is engulfed in flames from ceiling to floor.

Two of the men are on fire, their clothes blazing like animated yellow and orange puffer jackets, and the remaining two are diving for the door. We don't have much time, and my attention turns to the back room. I tell Jack to flank the back door. Those barrels are not going to stay suspended much longer, and I don't really want to be there when they disintegrate and all that burning spirit comes down.

I kick the door open sharply. I was ready for gunfire, but not for the silence we are greeted with. I spin into the room, firearm raised – but the room is empty. It seems to be part office, part chill-out room, part industrial workshop. There is a mah-jongg table, an office desk with a phone and computer, then two tables arranged next to each other, festooned with industrial equipment. There are two metal black boxes, hooked up to a central computer hub, with thick wires linking the components together. The black metal boxes have transparent Perspex sides, revealing a little plateau inside, doused in blue light. The room's air carries a sharp bitterness.

'Where is that prick?' Jack shouts, as he peers over my shoulder. I look frantically for another exit from the room, then from back in the restaurant, I hear a deep groan, which echoes loudly over the crackling flames. There are a number of smaller fires, separate from one another, but all fuelled from above. The moan slows to a couple of creaks, and I realise it's caused by wood straining under weight. Suddenly, one of the barrels bursts, wood cracking and splintering, and gallons of *baijiu* fall to the floor and go up like a reverse waterfall of flames. The restaurant is swallowed and the whole boat is filling with smoke. Without question, we need to get out of here.

'Where is he?' shouts Jack.

Just as I'm about to say I don't know, I see Sparkles running along the far wall past the main windows, ducking to avoid the spitting fire. I was wrong. There must have been a secret exit in the back room leading straight out to the front. We set off in pursuit, hopping the bar like Olympic hurdlers but with far less grace. As we land, a second barrel explodes, showering flaming liquid. I dive to my right and wind up by the windows. Sparkles is almost at the toilets now, but he too was knocked over by the blast, and is clawing his way back up to his feet.

I can't see Jack. Panic shakes me, but then I hear him shouting. I stand and look for him, and through the orange haze I see that we are separated by the ever-growing fire. He's by the door. I can't quite make out what he's shouting, but then I get it loud and clear.

'*He's mine!*'

I jump after Sparkles in an awkward sprint. The heat is fast becoming too much to bear. I reach the edge of the corridor, and sail around the corner – straight into a shoulder charge. The impact is brutal, and knocks me to the floor. A savage kick to my gut brings tears to my eyes, and forces me to gasp for breath. I see white dots dancing in the corners of my vision and, afraid I might pass out – which would ensure an all-too-early ending – I bob sideways and weave away, then cover myself as I haul myself to my feet. Sparkles swings and I block it, then follow the momentum and throw what I hope will be a huge right, trying to put as much force into the blow as possible. I'd love to knock him out of his boots here and now.

The connection is good, but Sparkles is obviously a tough one, and he doesn't go down. He looks dazed, and takes two steps back for steadiness, but I'll definitely need to bring more. He comes forward in a head-down charge, and I let him, because he's given me his forehead, a target I can definitely use. I thrust the heel of my right hand as hard as I can at his brow, and it connects with a thick, solid thud, jangling his brain, bruising it against the bone walls of his skull, and giving him an instant concussion. His momentum carries him forward, and he hits the wall hard. Like a tree, he goes down, felled.

I bend down and push my knee firmly down on his solar plexus, then take the three fingers of my right hand and push them down hard into the crevice of his collarbone. His scream lets me know I've hit the spot. I grip fast, a climbing hold. It's a nasty move but one that brings compliance.

'We've got about thirty seconds to get out of here, so talk fast,' I say, forcing my fingers a little more deeply in behind his clavicle. 'The truth – now.'

All of a sudden, Sparkles seems keen to talk.

'You've got the wrong man,' he says, writhing. I keep my knee pinned tight and use my fingers like a tight leash.

'Explain that to me,' I say.

We're on the floor, but the heat is increasing by the moment and it's hard to breathe.

'We got a tip-off that a Jack Brooker was out to kill me, so I put out a hit to beat him to it. Of course, you know we found you instead.'

The flames are creeping down the corridor towards us, a crawling, arachnid pyre along the wall.

'Who gave you the tip-off?'

'It was anonymous.'

'And you took it seriously?'

'Turns out I was right to listen though, wasn't I?' Sparkles gasps.

I can't argue with that. 'You know why he wants you dead?'

'No idea. But everyone wants a piece of us here, there's big things going on.'

The workshop out back swings into mind.

'What about the berg?'

'Jealous, controlling bastards. Don't have much to do with them, but we have come into contact a few times.'

'To kill Royston Brooker?'

'Fuck, no. I don't know what you think about us, but we are not like them. They are a different animal, a bigger one, too. I wouldn't do that unless I wanted to cause a big problem.'

'Well, you've got a big problem on your hands now, haven't you?'

Sparkles seems sad, blood trickling from his lower lip. 'Like I said – you've got the wrong guy.'

The floor starts to tremble beneath our feet – this can't be good. I hear the faint murmur of sirens. I need to leave now.

And where the hell is Jack?

If Sparkles did kill Royston, I should leave him here, but the story does not seem that clear-cut. Yes, I'm interested in justice, but justice is reserved for those I'm sure are guilty.

'Come on,' I say, releasing my hold on his collarbone. I get to my feet and head back to the main restaurant floor, careful of the flames. The scene is a bizarre, melting, wooden belly of hell. There is still a little room to the left where the windows are, that isn't completely engulfed. Our only option.

I take out my pistol and run towards the windows. I fire the remaining bullets into one of the window panes, cracking them, then cover my face as best I can and hurl myself at the glass.

I fall through incredibly cool air and hit the freezing water of the Irwell. I've traded a very hot hell for an icy cold one, but it's a lot better than being cooked alive. Coming back to the surface, I breathe deeply. The ship is ablaze, now more like a Nordic funeral pyre than a Chinese merchantman, eager flames reaching out into the night air from every window, every opening.

I can't see Sparkles. Surely he won't have stayed on the craft, unless some twisted sense of duty meant that the captain had to stay with his ship, come what may. I refuse to believe it, as the great mast begins to crumble, and come loose. It falls, and smashes right across the belly of the boat, ripping the cabin roof in two. It is greeted by explosions, as the remaining barrels finally burst. Charred and burning debris starts to tumble down towards me, hissing loudly as it hits the cold surface.

I start to swim, my clothes tugging me down; but I press on with determination. Shit. Sparkles is gone, and so is Jack, as far as I know. But my central problem is that I need to get out of here. If I'm picked up by police, I'm done for. As blue and red lights bounce off the high buildings around the riverbanks, creating a two-hued art deco light show, I take a deep breath, and sink under the surface. I begin to swim upriver as fast as my bruised, singed body will allow.

14

The dark and cold feel unending, an uncomfortable dissolution of everything that humans need to feel at ease. My legs and arms are numb, my scalp burning. I'm freezing, but I can't stop moving. If I do, I'll sink to the bottom like a shark, and reluctantly expire with pathetic acceptance.

I flip onto my back and allow my face to break the surface. The air is so dry and bitter that it feels like acid on my cheeks. I breathe, gulping two mouthfuls of air, then sink again, hoping that I was subtle enough to avoid detection. I'm hoping Jack managed to escape the scene, but I'm unsure. He was so fixated on revenge that he may have hung around for too long, and ended up either dead or arrested.

I turn onto my stomach again and try to crawl. My fatigue is extreme now, the frozen ache in my limbs all but unbearable. Lactic acid has built up but will do nothing to warm me; moreover, it brings a furious nausea. I keep going, committed to my escape route. I always thought the water would play a part at some point, and instead of going maudlin over in Yorkshire, maybe I'd have been better off going to Toys R Us for a sodding blow-up dinghy.

I know my limits, and I'm fast approaching them. Training in the cold was never something I was keen on, nor am I used to its feel. I was never thrown into any freezing rivers in Afghanistan nor Iraq. I am more used to trying to regulate my temperature in the opposite direction. I need to get out of this water, and fast.

I angle my stroke left, and head towards the bank, feeling for concrete. I'm having trouble getting a deep breath, and I feel my torso, my very core, squeezed in the constricting grip of a quickening hypothermia.

My hand hits concrete, and I blink water from my eyes and quickly look around. To my surprise, I'm only a hundred yards from the boat, which is entirely aflame, huge fans of fire offering columns of thick smoke to the heavens. I must have only been in the water a couple of minutes, tops. My problems are not over, as I realise I'm stuck about twenty feet below the crest of the riverbank, with no obvious means of escape.

I scan the brick surfaces of the bank wall, and I can't see anything to grab, or pull myself out with. I'm too far down. I lean against the wall, trying to think.

The cold is clenching me, and I feel mentally numb – and dizzy and disorientated. My body has decided to conserve it's remaining energy stores by shutting down certain facets. I hold onto the brick wall, hoping that the sensations will pass, and I can have another go at escaping.

My hearing has gone now, and all I can hear is my own slowing heartbeat. I'm in trouble.

Usually, panic would take hold at this point, but it doesn't. I'm not prone to panic, but my eyes feel extremely heavy; each blink is like hoisting an anvil. I let them close for a moment.

Bad news. I can't open them again.

I can't bow out now. But it seems I have no choice. I will not go quietly, and will fight to the last... but even as I think that, I know it is a fantasy. I lose grip of the wall, my fingers scrabbling weakly, and I begin to sink.

Then my mind clears, and my hold on consciousness breaks free – and I let it. I float down, within myself, the lid closing in on me. I feel hands grasping at me, beckoning me to the afterlife. They grab me by the lapels, and pull me to the heavens. I go without protest. It is the end.

15

I hear a crackling, feel heat on my cheeks, and smell something charring.

It reminds me of old camping trips, dozing by fireside. I am snapped back into the present with the frightening thought that I'm still floating along with the burning Chinese junk.

I see flames, but they are small, and very close. Did I never make it out of the restaurant? Surely I did, I remember the tumble, then the cold…

My eyes adjust, and I see that the fire is encased in a white ceramic oval, a funnel over it sucking the smoke up to a chimney and away. I follow the chimney with my eyes as it reaches twelve or so feet to a glass ceiling. Bemused, I turn and see that the glass ceiling continues along and down, in a huge three-sided glass box enclosing the most ornate swimming complex I have ever seen. A kidney-shaped pool, with a bar at one end, with little paths routing from one end to the other, lined with ornamental foliage of all description. A little glass house – a conservatory of some kind.

Somebody saved my life.

I get to my feet, noticing as I do that despite still being dressed as before, my clothes are damp and I am draped in a towel. Outside the glass is blackness. I would immediately look for escape if it weren't for my rising curiosity, and the notion that whoever brought me here doesn't mean me harm – if indeed this is the home of whoever pulled me from the water. As I look out through the glass, I see an expanse of water, flickering along at a high, wind-driven pace. In the distance I see a huge edifice lit in neon, with blocky curves and all the hallmarks of modern architecture. It is The Lowry, in Salford Quays. And that must mean… I am standing in Felix Davison's house.

Well, that is not what I was expecting. Winding up here definitely adds another layer to this complicated unfolding onion of intrigue.

Before I can think any further, a voice behind me breaks the quiet – a low, soft, man's voice.

'He's up,' the voice says.

I turn to see a little old man approaching me. He's bald, with a soft ring of white fluff around the ears. He wears grey slacks, a white shirt and wide, round glasses. His face is ruddy, chubby and grandfatherly, and wears a kindly smile. I don't know whether to thank him or ask for a bedtime story. He must be no more than five and a half feet tall, and his back is hunched over a bit, suggesting at one stage he must have been taller. His belly sticks out like a small gym ball's stuffed up his shirt, and that, combined with a heavy tan, suggests he lives the good life. He looks to be in his seventies, but his face shows few wrinkles – moreover the skin is pulled almost tight by his impressive hanging cheeks. His eyes gleam out from behind the frames, positively beaming that there is plenty of life in this old dog yet.

'I am indeed,' I respond, playing along, not entirely convinced how to handle this. 'Felix?'

'Yes,' he replies, taking a couple of steps towards me. They aren't the most sure steps, so I instinctively walk forward to meet him. 'Jack said that he would leave it to you to make your own introduction.' A very slight accent dwells somewhere in his speech, but it seems clipped and well controlled. It is north European, but is buried well down, the only remnant now being the odd vowel out of place. I don't think he is English, but he has been here for some time.

'Jack's all right?' I ask.

'He's fine,' Felix replies. 'I had him taken home. He fared a little better than yourself, I'm afraid. I would have arranged for you to be dropped off home too, but I didn't know where that might be.'

Felix holds out a small weathered hand, and smiles, and I find myself reaching for it, still undecided. We shake. This is the part where I give a name. Do I go with one I make up, or do I go with my own?

I want to be honest, to be true to myself. I reason that even if Felix finds out my full name, it's not like he is likely to be too onside with police or anything.

'Ben. My name is Ben.'

'Ben. Thank you for looking after Jack. He is like his father, I'm afraid, a single-minded soul when he eventually works out whatever it is he wants.'

'He did me a big favour. I owe him, and I like to keep promises.'

'It's nice to know there's still decent men out there. He's going through a difficult time. Would you like some coffee perhaps?'

'Sure. Black, please.'

'Make yourself at home.' Felix slowly paces back towards the main house. I genuinely find it hard to picture that guy doing anything more criminal than parking in a disabled spot when he's forgotten his badge.

To my left is the pool, and a smart table with matching chairs. I take one. I am still a bit disorientated and I want to make sense of things. Is this man really Felix Davison? The feared crime lord that can pull whatever strings he fancies? Is Felix Davison all those things Jack says he is?

In a foreign or unfamiliar setting, my mind's default response is to source an exit, but here I find myself longing for answers. This situation is certainly more than interesting, especially now I have met the main man himself, and found that he is nothing like what I had imagined. It appears nothing is quite what it seems, and I have so many questions my head feels like rush-hour traffic jammed into a blender.

As I listen to the trickle and hum of the pool filter, and smell the chlorine, I feel more than a bit seduced.

Felix returns, bearing a tray with a couple of mugs on it. We appear to be alone, which amazes me. This old man, who some argue is most wanted and sought after, is hosting a perfect stranger in his own home in the middle of the night, alone. He must be confident. Either that or we are not alone at all.

'Are you warming up a bit?' Felix asks, placing the drinks tray on the table. His eyes radiate genuine concern. His precise, measured way of speaking seems pulled from the pages of a book, exactly how you'd picture someone of his generation learning a foreign language.

'Yes, thank you. I was beginning to think I wasn't going to get out of that river.' I grab the mug and squeeze it to stave off icy memories.

'You nearly didn't,' he replies. 'Would you like for me to call a doctor?'

'No, I should be fine, thank you.'

'Are you sure? Any painkillers or anything?' Even in the soft firelight, there is nothing in his eyes other than genuine care.

'No, really – I'm just happy to be out of the river.'

'If you are sure.'

'This place is lovely,' I say, gesturing at our surroundings.

'This house is far too big for me,' he says with a grin. 'Everyone gets old eventually. I've not been up to the top floor in at least two years, and even then it was by accident.'

'You live here alone?'

'Most of the time,' he replies with a sigh. He rubs the palm of his left hand with his big weathered right thumb, looking away almost apologetically.

'Are you married?' I venture.

'I was, but my wife passed away a while ago now,' he says. I sense no pain in his voice, just whimsical acceptance of what used to be and what is now left behind.

Felix stretches back in the chair and crosses his ankles out in front of him. We have got to that point in our conversation where the small talk is history and the elephant in the room needs dragging out under the spotlight. Felix apparently senses the same and takes the lead.

'I'm not going to take you for an idiot, Ben. I'll assume you know how I know your friend Jack, and why Jack dragged you over to that restaurant.'

Felix's vision fixes on a point in the middle distance.

'I knew that the people there were unhappy with his father. But I desperately didn't want to tell him that. He… just wouldn't take no for an answer. He threatened so much, and, in so many ways, I don't blame him. If I refused to tell him what I knew… I ended up giving in. I didn't want to, I just wanted to do right by him. Help him. Like you.'

The old man seems unwilling to acknowledge that that moment of decision has long gone, and dramatic, possibly deadly consequences have resulted. He comes across as an extremely understanding, friendly, empathetic sort, and allows me to lead the conversation.

'I think it would have happened the other way round if you hadn't have done so,' I say. 'I checked into a hotel as "Jack" yesterday, and a man from the Floating Far East tried to kill me, assuming I was him.'

'This happened yesterday?' he asks, softly put but with a firmer edge, like a concrete wall mere feet behind a film of mist.

'Yes. I think the paths of Jack and Sparkles Chu were going to cross regardless of whether you told him or not.'

'Dear God…'

'I don't think Jack is going to be troubled by Sparkles anymore.'

Felix's demeanour lightens a touch. 'No. I suppose not. What happened over there?'

'I don't want to betray Jack's confidence, given your complicated relationship with him, but, as you will expect, we went to confirm if Sparkles had indeed killed Jack's father. The encounter went sour, things got quite heated.'

Felix nods, but seems distracted. 'Jack says our relationship is complicated?' He seems a little hurt by that.

'That's just what I got from his description of things.'

'I… didn't know he felt like that,' he says. 'I care for that kid a lot.'

'I believe you were there at his birth. *The Baby And The Brandy*?'

Felix snorts.

'That old chestnut. People talk about it, misty-eyed and rose-tinted. They hear the story and like the romance of it all. The doomed love, the elation of new life when all seemed lost. It's the story that has everything. Nobody ever gives a second thought to how terrible it was. The *blood*, the hopelessness… The sheer scale of what was at stake. Seeing someone who means so much to you, struggle so fatally when doing something that should be such a simple, natural, *beautiful* act.'

'I know the main points of the story, but… what happened?'

'Something that doesn't happen anymore. It was the eighties – the clichéd era of excess. Men wanted it all, and they wanted it there and then. Sarah – Jack's mother – was a collateral casualty of that greed.'

I want to ask whose greed was the catalyst – Felix's, Royston's, Sarah's or someone else entirely, but the man is on a roll, and I leave him to it.

'She was just nineteen,' Felix continues. 'So young, and having a baby. None of us ever got over that.' He delivers his words with such sorrow now that it is very clear that this moment, this story, was defining in many ways.

The big question pops into my head, the answer to which will tell me exactly the extent of the power of the man who sits next to me – and how much I am to fear him, perhaps.

'What happened to the people that did it?'

Felix looks me straight in the eye. It wasn't intended to be a challenge, but it may have come out that way. His gaze softens almost immediately, as if he's read my thought and feels bad about giving the wrong impression.

'We never knew,' he replies. 'Royston was too preoccupied with losing his wife and gaining a son to concern himself with it. We are many things, Ben, but cold killers is not one of them. I never wanted Jack to go to that damn restaurant, I didn't want bloodshed to come from the death of my dear friend.'

'You and Royston were good friends?' I ask.

'It's an oft-repeated phrase, but he was more like family,' he replies. 'It was in the early eighties when a young mover courted my attention like a suitor. That was Royston. He had designs on an employment path that wasn't being fulfilled in other avenues, and he forced me to take note of him. I had no interest in working with a young man, but he was persistent. I gave him a chance, and grew to love the boy like my own. One Christmas, he even asked if he could spend it with me and my family, as opposed to his own.'

He keeps mentioning work casually, like he may have an office job.

'Royston's death will herald change for us all. But I know that he died because of his association with me, and even though he was a grown man, who made his own decisions a long time ago, I can feel the uneasy spill of blood on my hands.'

It is strange to watch a man I've never met before, reveal himself so candidly and intimately – his doubts and fears creeping around the edges of his character. He speaks easily, even poetically, but obviously imploring me to see things through his eyes. He may be taking the opportunity to clear his conscience of the things that dog him the most.

'We all are forced to make choices,' I say. 'Cicero said, "Any man is liable to err, only a fool persists in error." I think we are all allowed to learn from the choices we regret.'

Am I right in counselling this man this way? I don't know him at all, aside from the hint of a legend given me less than a day earlier. When I got up this morning, I hadn't heard of him, and now I'm sipping a late-night winter-warmer in his home, philosophising cack-handedly.

'I'm just an old man, Ben. An old man who was better suited to the fifties. You knew where you were back then.'

'Forgive me for saying, but you don't seem to be doing too badly.'

That elicits a slight smile, quickly followed by a question of his own. 'And you? What is your current place in life?'

I should be able to answer the question immediately. Maybe it's the late hour, the easy conversation, or the fact that I almost died only hours earlier, but somehow the honest answer seems like the right one. I want this man to trust me. Trust brings answers.

'I was a soldier,' I say. 'But I'm not anymore. I've struggled to find my place ever since. I've got a skill set the country has no use for, but it's the only thing I know.'

'And… forgive me, but when Michael brought you here, you were a bit confused. You were talking quite a bit, but your eyes were only fitfully open.'

I hesitate. Christ knows what choice details I've blabbed while out of it. I try a light approach: 'Nothing bad, I hope?'

Felix seems troubled, as if perhaps he's brought up too delicate a subject. 'You mentioned Strangeways, amongst other things.'

'What other things?'

'You were agitated, mostly. You said that "he" would never find you.'

When I hesitate again, only for longer this time, he says with apparent genuine concern, 'Are you ok, son?'

'I'm fine,' I reply, too wearily.

'Is there any trouble I can help with?'

'Not at all,' I say. 'I suppose it's just been a hell of an evening.'

I really didn't want these people to ever find out about my trouble with the law, even if what I wondered earlier – that if they were in a mood for a bargain, an escaped con would make a very nice negotiating tool – was a good idea. Doesn't seem so at the moment.

He leans back into his chair, relaxing again, and I respond in kind.

'Please stay here tonight. The spare room is made up. It's far too late to head back out into town, and it's the least I can do after how much you looked after our Jack. You kept him alive, and I won't forget it.'

Suddenly the fresh, opulent setting in which I sit strongly suggests there is a king-size bed somewhere upstairs with my name on it. I can only think of sinking into it and wallowing in the luxury. I don't know what to make of what is happening, and frankly I am too tired to make sense of it tonight.

Accepting his offer may be dangerous, but I just don't sense any immediate threat from the old man. We seem to be alone, and he seems to have placed his trust in me. If he wanted me dead, he would have had his associates make sure I never got out of the river, let alone drag me out of it. I believe that if I want to learn about Felix, here will undoubtedly be the best place to do it, regardless of the other issues on my mind.

'If that isn't too much trouble, I'd be happy to,' I say.

'Excellent,' says Felix, rising carefully. 'Follow me.'

I do just that, tottering after him, ready to spend a night under his wing. The word of caution says: *keep your friends close but your enemies closer*. But confusion and fatigue are tempting me to let down my guard.

*

I'm besieged by awful images, vile creations that shred my peace. I'm lost, alone, in some pit of dark doom, while foul sights split my skull like an axe chopping through an old watermelon. A bloodless bullet wound next to a belly button. A leg landing at my feet, no shoe, the little toe twitching. A man screaming as he is doused with fire from above. Craggs stabbing Quince in the rec room. The silence of my old living room, empty of family and furniture…

I wake up in a panic, my skin cold and clammy and my brow burning. I feel skewed, nauseated, my breath coming in pants.

The fever I feel is surely a by-product of my narrow brush with hypothermia, and my body is fighting back. But my mind nags and claws – a familiar feeling. The doubts and depressions flood in, relics of those years after I'd been discharged, a period in my life I try hard daily to leave behind. I breathe, and take a moment to compose myself, and with such composure comes clarity, even a revelation.

That phrase. What I said to Felix downstairs. That Cicero quote. It's dragged itself front and centre. *Any man is liable to err, only a fool persists in error.*

What a hypocrite I'm turning out to be, because here I am on the cusp of making the same mistakes all over again.

Last time I took on organised crime was Terry Masters. He made me angry, and I made mistakes. I was on the run, looking for a purpose. He appeared on TV, looking like a repulsive caricature of criminal entitlement, standing outside a courtroom laughing after his trial for armed robbery fell through. His attitude was inflammatory, his treatment of a female reporter sickening. I made a detour to London, to sort him out.

Only I didn't sort him out. I went in half cocked, with a false sense of invincibility. He shot my knee out and forced me into a one-armed knife fight against his own son, who had wronged him with his own stupidity.

Masters decided to teach us both a lesson. His son ended up with a knife in his heart, while I ended up in handcuffs on a murder charge.

I clearly haven't learned that lesson, because here I am again. Vulnerable, charmed almost, by the very people who should stand as my opposite. Too close, too stupid.

Someone could have crept up here and slit my throat, easy as that. Downstairs I had reasoned with myself that he clearly didn't want me dead, but when blood is involved, things change in a heartbeat. I've walked myself into danger once again.

Why?

Deep down I know. It happens when I'm alone. Rudderless. It didn't happen in prison because someone else was in charge. It didn't happen in the army for the same reason.

It's down to fathers and fatherhood. I honestly thought I was stronger than this.

I've always fought introspection, something that was aided by the strictness of the military. I hop up in the darkness and look to the window. The night outside is deep and distant. I cross the room and peer out at the blocky glow of the Manchester skyline and the ebony water down below. I feel like I'm on a cruise ship moored on the edge of a distant city.

My chain of command is missing vital links. Above me? I've been abandoned by my parents, adrift. Below me? There is a darker chapter, one I still can't bring myself to address properly, even though I know it accounts for so much of my unease. Of a fling, a pregnancy ended without my involvement. *My* child, stripped from me before I even got the chance to properly feel its presence.

I almost became a father. Almost. So close I felt a flash of joy, the elation, the lighting of an irrepressible torch of love, fulfilment, and purpose. But a flash was all I got; a moment. I would have changed everything about myself to be a dad – a good dad.

During my training, I had a fling, and it resulted in a girl getting pregnant. Stephanie, her name was. We were head over heels in that way that feels so all-important at the time, but life threw us an early curveball that showed how different we really were. She rang me one evening and casually told me how she'd found out she was expecting. Six weeks gone.

And in her next breath, she told me she had got rid of it.

My child. Got rid of.

It was a loss that I have never really finally come to terms with. I never knew how important being a father was to me, until I tasted it for those brief seconds. Stephanie never knew what I would have given up to make that situation work – the army, my entire military career, whatever was required.

I went away a mess, and whenever I came home, I knew I was visibly different, a difference augmented a little more every time by the horrors I was witnessing on my stints abroad, and the tensions and stresses that went with it. I was performing well, but grim resolve was my fuel. I was obsessive, meticulous, and organised, with a cold, determined manner of execution: the recipe for the perfect soldier. Hence my success in my country's service.

Enter my father, that stone-faced Yorkshireman who covered his abundant compassion with as much grit as he could manage, who tried to counsel me, in his own way. Something we had in common in those days was the spectre of children that would never be; but this was largely unspoken. I was an only child, the only reason for which being physical complications in my mother. My parents would dearly have loved more children, but their only son would have to do.

What a massive let down I'd been. And now they're gone.

I'm adrift again.

After leaving home, the next time I saw my parents was at my murder sentencing. I had taken a guilty plea, to keep the prosecution from digging too far into my past, where they would surely find more nails with which to fasten my coffin shut. They barely looked at me, crippled, I assume, by what I had become. But I detected something else there, too. Guilt. I thought they looked as guilty as me, only I was the one in the dock. By the time of the trial, in their eyes I was beyond saving. Our family was fractured irreparably, and its sole son was sentenced to seventeen years.

They didn't have to accept what I did, nor who I have become. But I hoped in a way that they would learn to live with it, just as I have. I hoped they knew me more than most, and would know now that there's no murderer in me, just a lad trying to do the right thing.

My mind blanks immediately, so conditioned by the upset that it now censors it out on autopilot.

Bottom line: I've got nothing and no one, nothing to anchor me, nobody to give me purpose or guide me.

And that's how I get in these messes. All it took was kindness from Felix, and the caring tone of his conversation – and I was willing to let my guard down.

No more. I may have daft issues. I know that seeing my empty childhood home has made them so much worse. But that's the last time I'll acknowledge them. I'm going to take these thoughts and bury them down deep. Somewhere I won't find them, or at the very least, somewhere they won't jar loose under pressure. Last thing I need on this new lease of life is the dregs of a life I should be putting to bed.

I reach to the bedside table, for the sandwich bag that contains my phone. I check the time: 4:37 a.m. Nothing else on the screen, no attempts to contact me. I'm surprised not to have heard from Jack, and I'd like to know where he has got to. Felix told me he had looked after him, and I can only take his word.

Sparkles' words are echoing in my head, his vehement denials regarding any involvement in Royston Brooker's death. Did he get out? If he did, there's a loose end out there, and I don't like loose ends one bit, particularly with their uncanny ability to return and haunt me.

16

I am awoken by a roar of laughter. It snaps me alert, and in an instant I remember where I am. The sunlight squeezes through the gaps in the blackout curtains. Sitting up in this bedroom, while people downstairs are having a good time, reminds me of when I was a moody teenager, hiding upstairs in my room on family get-togethers, deliberately late for their arrival for God-knows-what reason.

The mist of bad dreams and disturbed sleep hangs heavy for a moment. I scatter them instantly with activity, and bury my mind in the present, right where it should be.

I smell pretty appalling. I notice a white plastic bag over by the closed door. I get up, not as easily as I might, thanks to a few dull aches and pains, particularly in my ribs. I don't feel too bad, but not one hundred percent. I check the bag and find a red t-shirt and some check board shorts, which strikes me as a little strange, particularly as the tags are still on them.

There is an en suite over in the corner, which is a mighty relief; at least I can get washed up in private. I take my hastily purchased beachwear and hit the bathroom, to scrub the smoky exertions of last night firmly off my person.

*

Five minutes later, I am inching open the door, decked out in my assigned costume. I can still hear the unmistakable sound of voices from downstairs, both male and female. The upstairs landing is a cream-carpeted luxury zone, with a series of doors along the landing, and opposite, over the staircase, a vast window overlooking a sun-bathed Salford Quays and the Manchester Ship Canal, with the gleaming, flat crest of the conservatory roof just visible below the sill.

I descend, stuffing my old clothes and shoes in the recycled plastic bag as I go. The benign veneer of luxury is everywhere, from the spotless carpets to the hint of cleaning products in the air. The staircase is wooden, but as I reach the bottom I am deposited into a marble reception area, just off what looks like the front door, which in itself is a huge mahogany piece that looks as if it could stop a medieval army. Life has been good to Felix.

I follow the voices, walking down a couple of perfectly appointed passages and then through a gigantic, spotless kitchen, which looks like nothing has ever been prepared in there. In fact, the feel of the house is one of immaculate disuse: there's no trace that anyone actually lives here. No family photos, no family muss – nothing. A shell, in which a man can live and then abandon at a moment's notice, perhaps.

I pass through the kitchen in the direction of the conservatory and find myself in the midst of a poolside family get-together. I see a child, about six years old, floating merrily in the pool, with another of a similar age careering along the ornate pathways. There are three men and two women reclining on the chairs around the table I had sat at under moonlight just hours earlier. Starbucks cups are on the table, and a couple of brown food bags. Strong sunlight blazes in through the glass.

I recognise two of the men, Michael and Samson, and they too look ready for a day at the beach. I'm wary, and the sensation grows. I'm really in the lion's den here.

'Ben! He's up!' shouts a voice I recognise as Felix's. As faces turn to look at me, I spot Felix in the pool, bobbing along under a blue floppy sunhat. 'Michael, give me a hand, will you?' he says.

Michael hops up. I head towards Felix, and a man from the table snaps to his feet and offers me a skeletal hand. He has a thin moustache, a tall but lithe frame, and a classic Lego haircut. I recognise the man from my earlier investigations – Leonard Freund.

'Had to say hello. Ben, is it? Leonard,' says the man rapid fire. He is a man of coiled energy, encased in unlikely seeming holiday clothes.

'Pleased to meet you, Leonard,' I reply. I haven't worked out how to play this yet, so I keep it light and amiable.

'Saw the smoke in the sky last night, could see it right out here. Never seen anything like it. You need to tell me everything,' he says with grinning conspiracy, as if he wants to hear all the juicy details of a date I went on last night and get on with it too.

'Leave him be, Len,' chastises Felix, who is now being hoisted out of the water in a disability harness, the support crane for which is being manned by Michael.

'Sorry,' Leonard says smiling, as I walk past him. 'Just impressed, that's all.'

'No, it's fine – I'm sure there'll be time,' I say, as I walk to the poolside.

'Arthritis. The docs said that a pool would be good for me, help me day to day,' Felix says. 'They said it would be exercise without the mental commitment of exercise.'

'I can see the appeal,' I reply.

'Ben, you couldn't grab my robe there, could you?' Felix says, pointing. I grab it and bring it to him. He pulls himself up, with Michael's help.

'Sleep ok? I see you found the little package to make you feel a bit more comfortable.'

'Yes, on both counts,' I reply, lying through my teeth about the former. 'I believe we met briefly yesterday – Michael, is it?'

I extend a hand to Michael, whose demeanour has changed entirely since yesterday, his suspicions apparently erased and replaced with a warmness so similar to Felix's that there is no mistaking him being his son.

'Bang on. Great to meet you proper.' His accent is pure Mancunia.

'Michael pulled you out of the river last night,' Felix says, fastening his robe. 'He said you were in a bit of a state when he got to you.'

'Then I need to thank you, Michael. God knows I wasn't going to last much longer.'

Michael shrugs, and smiles. 'Hey, one thing I know from growing up over 'ere, is that the water's bloody cold, and it's not gonna be much different a coupla miles away in the city centre.'

'Thanks all the same. Is Jack ok? I haven't seen him since it all started getting a bit hairy.'

Felix looks troubled, his eyes drifting lower, but Michael dives right in.

'He's fine. I took him 'ome, made sure he was ok.' We start walking to the table.

'Everyone, this is Ben,' Felix says, gesturing toward the people surrounding the table, and I am greeted enthusiastically. 'Here you have Samson with his girlfriend, Tina. I know you've met Leonard and Michael, and this is Michael's wife, Carolyn. Those two kids are Mike and Carolyn's, for their sins, poor buggers.'

That brings a laugh. When Felix speaks there is an expectant silence, as if his next words might be pure auditory gold. But I suspect it is simply respect.

Samson, rises, as does Tina. The man formerly known as Mr Sportswear shakes my hand. He is tall, well-built, tanned, stubble-cheeked, and decked in a vest and shorts. He looks like a Mr Universe contestant, albeit with a cruelly broken nose between dark brown eyes.

'A pleasure, mate. Thanks for looking out for the young lad last night,' he says. His voice is engine deep with a southern accent, not quite cockney but certainly home counties. Something must have brought him up north at some point.

'Hi,' Tina says, pecking me on the cheek.

Tina looks like she just walked off the set of a music video. Blonde and toned, packaged tantalisingly in a bikini and sarong, she is stunning, even if her heavy make-up gives her skin the muddy pallor of builder's tea. That peck on the cheek, though, twinned with the soft whisper of a heady perfume, would send butterflies to the stomach of any man. Tina: the ultimate arm candy, suited perfectly to a Mr Universe.

Carolyn appears at my side, and I'm passed from one soft embrace to another. 'Hi, Ben,' she says. I've not been close to a woman in nearly a decade, and the last three seconds have been a pretty stark reminder of what I've been missing. Carolyn, too, is intensely beautiful, but in a more refined sense. More vintage Hollywood to Tina's MTV. Long chestnut hair framing a face of delicate, classic lines, and dressed much more modestly, in a long linen dress, but still packing a visual punch. She is older than Tina, and carries herself as such. More mature; warmer.

'I've got a mocha, a cappuccino, or a tall black?' says Michael, pointing at the cups.

'Tall black, please, if that's ok.' I take a seat.

'Spot on.' Michael slides a cup over.

A few moments pass in which nobody says anything at all, while Felix settles into his own chair between Michael and Carolyn, the latter whose eyes are fixed on the cavorting children. When he is settled, he looks like a squat, doughy oracle, the way we all face him.

The atmosphere is unmistakably jovial, like the preamble to an all-day party. I'm expecting to be offered a G & T with a twirly umbrella any second. Suddenly Leonard rises. He'd only just sat down, but he moves with such decisiveness that I'm convinced he has somewhere urgent to be. Instead, he replaces the chair at the table and then leans against it. Felix has pulled a little plastic contraption out of his robe and is clicking it apart.

'Sleep all right?' Michael asks.

'Really well, thanks,' I say, transfixed as Felix begins to count out different coloured pills from what I see now is a daily pill splitter, containing all his medications counted out ready to go.

He speaks as he counts, having noticed my stare. 'One for high blood pressure, two for high cholesterol, one for low iron count, one for the joint pain, one for the muscle pain, cod liver oil to send it all swimmingly, and one for good luck. Everything a juddering old man needs to keep going.' He grins, and throws the lot into his mouth, just as one of the children appears at the table, the blond-mopped boy of six or so.

'Grandpa, you promised I could help you count them,' he says with disappointment.

'So I did!' Felix says, and opens his mouth to display the pills jumbled on his tongue. The boy gasps in delight, giggles, and starts to count. 'Eight!' the boy shouts, and Felix grabs a cup from the table and washes the lot down with an over-the top-gulp.

'He'll be a doctor!' Felix exclaims.

'Or at least some kinda pharmacist,' says Michael, ruffling the boy's mop with pride, before planting a kiss on the top of his head.

The boy goes back to the pool and Michael asks, 'Got any sprogs yourself, Ben?'

'None, I'm afraid,' I reply. *Fuck off*, I seethe inwardly.

'Best job in the world,' says Michael.

I smile but inside it's a grimace. Leonard sits down again, animatedly pulling the chair out and dropping himself in. It's quite dramatic and off-putting, a thought which Leonard himself seems to recognise.

'Not one for keeping still, I'm afraid,' he says. 'Felix isn't the only one with a few bits and pieces not working right. OCD, ADHD, and a sense, ah, sense…'

'Sensory modulation disorder,' finishes Felix.

'He needs constant stimulation,' Samson says. 'It keeps us all busy.'

Leonard hits me with a lopsided grin. 'What can you do? My glass is always half full.'

'It's over-bloody-flowing,' Michael quips.

'Repetition, order, routine, and sensation are all big parts of our Leonard's life,' Felix says. 'It keeps his world turning.' He turns to face me. 'Ben, just to be serious for a moment, from all of us, thank you for looking after Jack last night. His father meant a great deal to us all, as does his son. I didn't want to bury two Brookers in one week, never mind one.'

'I'm sure Jack could have got through last night by himself, but two heads are always better than one,' I say.

'You are too modest regarding your own efforts.'

'Jack is a very determined, capable young man. He'll get where he is going, eventually,' I say, and pick up my cup, which is only slightly warm to the touch.

I decide to up the ante.

'I assume from the tone of this conversation, and in light of recent events, that I can speak candidly.'

'Just spare the grim bits,' adds Michael, with a slight smile, gesturing to the two little ones, the blond boy and an equally blond and bubbly girl. He's like a slick, redux version of his father.

'I was there to help Jack. I owed him a favour, as I've told Felix. He wanted to avenge his father, and he was going to do it anyway. He told me that this is where he got the information, and that's about it. And as pleasant as all this has been, with the greatest respect, I'm not sure why I am here, or who you are.'

My words drift into the middle of the table, and the men glance at one another. Felix's voice grumbles in like an old steam train, but softly.

'In what feels a previous life, I worked in a joiners in Gothenburg, the city of my birth. Seduced by your Queen, I caught a ferry out into the North Sea, seeking my fortune on these fair shores. I loved Sweden, but I felt there was nothing for me there, and I had no family to speak of. Usually one finds an element of hardship in such a move, but for me it was indifference.

'I was unmotivated, but still in search of something. I started in London, but London was too harsh. I tried to find work, but in post-war London I found that as a young Swede, honest work was hard to come by. Our country had passed through the devastating war years in a position of rigorous neutrality, and because my country hadn't erred on the side of Churchill and the Union Jack, I was frowned upon. I was hungry, and had to take jobs I didn't want in order to keep any sort of money coming in. If you show up in the same dark recesses of a city long enough, those who dwell in those recesses will have something to offer.

'London was full to the brim of cockney wide-boys and sneering mob bosses. There was no room for someone who had the desire and the ambition to grow into his own. But I made friends down there, and retain good standing today.'

As Felix speaks, I feel a twitch of awareness. London, connections, crime. I see my past and present double helixing into one, a dovetailing of purposes both new and long-standing. Masters.

'So I moved north, settling here. I saw the potential then of this very spot where we sit, and I still see it now. It became the centre of my own business. Davidsson became Davison, but in Sweden, we have the word *berg*. In English, *mountain*.'

He points to the other men at the table, one at a time, with pride.

'*Väktare*. Compass point, or direction.'

He inverts his fingers to point at himself.

'*Toppmöte*. Summit. The old Swedish businesses in the south of the country used to refer to the inner workings of a business as the berg, with

101

the *väktaren* acting at the behest and protection of the *toppmöte*, with mutual gain in mind. Like a company with executives and a chairman. You'll notice that there's only three men here,' Felix adds.

'Because Royston was the other *väktare*…' I venture.

'Exactly,' he says.

The men are all looking at me with stares that show evident pride but seem to ask for understanding as well. I decide to push in. I probably know far too much now, what more can a little extra do?

'What areas are you involved in?' I ask.

Michael answers. 'Import-export is top of the list. The Quays are a big help. We've got our central warehouse and dock, over the water there, and of course there's this place here. With the right palms greased, we are in a very good position.'

'You have some kind of police immunity?'

'Not fully, but enough local help to leave us safe as houses on these waters. We also have a scouser in Merseyside who, for a fee, helps us onto the international shipping lanes, letting us dip into Europe.'

'What commodities?' I ask.

They are really giving up the goods here. But why? Are they really this candid? I need to keep this momentum going, as everything that is coming out here is of extreme value and interest.

'A mix of things, but we focus on a few key areas. Cocaine is one. We've a factory just south of Cork, in Ireland. Arms is another. Not for, like, equipping a militia, but we do manage to transport arms to those that will pay good money for it. That's been a bit quiet recently.'

A look passes between Samson and Leonard, a glance laced with meaning. Michael continues.

'Third is, sadly, heroin.' He hurries on. 'It's not the best, and we're not crazy about it or anything. It's been happening since the dawn of time, we didn't start it. Might as well make something out of market demand, and provide that market with a safely available, pure product.'

Slick, I think. *Slicker than eel shit.*

'Number four, is the one that started it all…' Michael turns to Felix, who is grinning sheepishly.

102

'Siamese fighting fish,' Felix says. '*Betta splendens*. An exotic species that is quite small, extremely beautiful, and very aggressive. The males are the worst. If you show a male his own reflection, he will get so worked up he might die of pent-up anger. In underground circles it is fashionable to bet on which will survive when you put two males in a tank together. The very best are so hard to get hold of, but we have an unrivalled source of the finest.'

'And Sparkles, last night. Where does he fit into things?'

Felix clears his throat, and puts his palms on the table, like he's drawing the words themselves from the wooden tabletop.

'The men, down by the river, have been working with us for some time. Sparkles' uncle before him, too. We help them with getting things in on the ship canal, in exchange for some distribution rights in their parts of the city. All in all it worked well – for a time. Then Sparkles decided he wanted to change that, and he made a direct threat to Royston, saying he'd kill him if he ever saw him in that restaurant of his again. We believe Royston wanted to make amends. A healthy union with the River was important to us, and I think he felt responsible for our arrangement with the River going sour.

'I know that the night Royston died, he was going over there to try again. A street pusher saw him going in, but that same pusher didn't see him come out. Next thing, he is found dead over at the airport.'

Felix clearly is very hands on with his business, and very little gets past him. 'Do you know why they would take him to the airport?' I ask.

'As far away from their patch as possible, perhaps, but an anonymous place – a number of parties could have been responsible,' says Leonard, cutting in with heat. I get the feeling that there are no slouches here; all are on point, and all on the ball.

'Sparkles is a clever man,' Felix carries on. 'But even I didn't think he would do anything like this. Something that has ended so terribly for all parties. It's sickening, really.'

'I spoke with Sparkles last night,' I say. 'He has a different version of events.'

That puts the cat amongst the pigeons, as looks are exchanged once more.

'Of course he would,' says Tina. She has an accent of her own, one altogether more exotic. Eastern European maybe.

'Ben, you keep talking about Sparkles in the present tense,' says Samson, and I turn to look at him. 'You think he's still alive?'

'I have no idea, but I definitely didn't see him dead,' I reply. 'And that usually counts for something.'

'Doesn't matter, doesn't matter at all,' Leonard cuts in. 'Business is sunk, down down down with his boat.'

Before any other voices can chime in, Felix holds his hand up for silence.

'We didn't want any of this. This is not the way our business is conducted, not now, not ever before. If this is to be viewed as a sensible, well-run business, then it needs to at least behave like one.'

'With my actions last night,' I say, 'I certainly meant no disrespect. I was merely doing what it took to keep my friend and I alive. My concern is that Jack's desire to avenge his father will continue since we have no guarantee that Sparkles is dead, never mind a guarantee that he was responsible for Royston's death in the first place.'

Felix looks like he is trying not to bristle at that, but I catch him and eye him carefully.

'I mean no disrespect in that either, Felix. It makes no odds to me who killed who in this, however, it certainly matters to Jack. It depends on what he believes.'

'Not anymore it doesn't,' replies Felix, with authority. 'He's had his go, and I want no more bloodshed associated with us.'

This attitude, this careful renunciation of violence, seems at odds with the stories that Jack told me about the berg. Where was this ethos, for example, when they apparently applauded Jack for running a man off the road? It doesn't add up. There is something not right about it all.

Felix speaks again.

'Ben, you have learned a lot about us. Please tell us a little about yourself.'

I frown, unsure about how much I want these people to know. I want them to respect me, and be interested in me enough to have me around for a little longer. The longer I am about, the more dirt on them I can amass. Regardless of how they doll up their business, I am in the central nerve centre of a top-level criminal gang, and they are exactly the kind of shit I want to eradicate. But here I am, barely out of prison, in the deepest of deep ends. This is a dangerous turn of events but one that, if I am to remain true to myself, I mustn't let slip by.

'What is it you'd like to know?' I ask.

'Where on earth you picked up the balls to do what you did last night, for a start,' fizzes Leonard, his enthusiasm becoming even stronger. 'Tell, you have to tell us.'

If I give them information, personal details, about myself, they will surely use them against me if I choose to wage a visible war against them. But sometimes, the truth is actually better than fiction. Or at least some of it.

'I used to be a captain in the Welsh Guards, Her Majesty's Royal Army. I was trained all over the world by the best in hand-to-hand combat, demolition, survivalism, weapons and tactics. I served for nearly a decade in Iraq and Afghanistan.'

That shut everybody up pretty quickly.

'Shit,' says Leonard, the briefest sound he's made since I met him.

I survey the other faces and see eyes widening; it is good, after my descent, to have someone to hear my background and regard me with respect and admiration, even if they know only part of the story.

'Were you in combat?' asks Carolyn, in a quiet, well-spoken voice.

'Caz…' Michael says, frowning.

'I've seen my fair share,' I reply. 'Oddly, those parts were the bits I seemed the best at.'

'Is your tat from your army days?' Samson asks. 'I'm a tattoo man myself – yours is nice.' He draws the word *nice* out like a heavy elastic band.

My tattoo. I'd completely forgotten about it. I always do. I should have picked a more covert place for it. It consists of writing, in an ornate script, on my right forearm, below the crook of my elbow.

'What does it say?' Tina asks.

'It's something daft,' I reply, hoping to brush it aside.

'It's Oasis,' Michael says. '*The Masterplan*?'

'You know your music.'

'I know my Oasis. Hard not to round 'ere twenty years ago. *Sail them home with acquiesce on a ship of hope today, and as they land upon the shore, tell them not to fear no more.*'

'Sadly, like most mistakes, at the time I thought it was the coolest thing I'd ever done.'

That gets some chuckles. I'm glad to have deflected it. Truth is, I had it inscribed on me in simpler times. It spoke to me of hope, and gave meaning to the military madness around me. It made me think of Britain, and how I'd been entrusted to spread goodness in the East. I was a messenger of light, of a better way. Of salvation.

Later in my career, as the weight of a decade of service twinned with what I'd seen began to show, it became a melancholy verse of yearning to get the hell out and go home. The tattoo changed with me, as I grew older. And now? It seems like Noel Gallagher himself was telling me all along that I should never have fucking bothered in the first place, that it was only ever going to end in tears.

'Why did you leave? You still seem so young.' Carolyn asks.

'I felt my time was up. I'd done my duty,' I say, gritting my teeth, the bitterness I harbour deep down throbbing with each made-up sentiment.

'Bad memories?' asks Michael, joining his wife after his initial attempt at respectful reticence.

'Too many. I've seen enough, put it that way, and done enough things that I can't undo.'

I say no more, knowing the more I say the closer I get to revealing my undoing. The reason I'm not a soldier anymore. The promise I made to my friend Stephen over a beer, the same Stephen that was Kayla's husband and Joshua's dad. Where I failed my friend, I won't fail my country. I can't.

'It is what it is,' I say, shrugging, trying to bring the sombre mood back around. Besides, I want dirt. Incriminating, solid, unashamed dirt. 'Anyway, tell me a little more about how your business works.'

That seems to do the trick, as the atmosphere brightens immediately.

Felix looks at me with a smile. 'What area interests you?'

'Well... I take it you have other employees aside from those sitting here?' I say, but before I can follow it up, into the conservatory walks Jack Brooker. Last time I saw him was through a haze of flames, smoke stinging my eyes. He is still dressed as he was last night, only with heavier bags under his eyes. Lack of sleep is clearly this guy's enemy at the moment, and he doesn't look best pleased. In fact, he looks thoroughly pissed off, his eyes narrowed and his jaw set.

'Jack!' exclaims Felix. 'Come and join us.'

The other people at the table turn and wave, but they look far less welcoming. Nevertheless, Jack approaches, and as he gets closer, I realise his eyes are fixed on me.

'A fucking tea party, perfect,' mutters Jack.

'Calm down,' Felix soothes, smiling. 'How did you sleep?'

'I didn't.'

The atmosphere has changed, with the other people seemingly wary, on edge. Jack pulls up a chair and perches on a corner of it, like he might spring up any time. In terms of nervous energy, he's even outdoing Leonard. 'Is Sparkles dead?' he asks.

'Calm down,' Felix says again. 'We don't know yet, Jack.'

'We've just been talking it over,' adds Michael. 'You two did quite a number on that place!' Michael gestures to me with a smile.

I feel strange, like I am in the middle of a disagreement I can't really comprehend but that I had a great part in creating.

'I don't care about that *boat*. I care about Sparkles,' Jack rasps. 'Is he dead?'

'I don't know,' I say, trying to convey with my eyes that if we can get a chance to talk, I can tell him what happened, and how Sparkles asserted his innocence. 'I got off the boat just before it collapsed. I didn't see him get off, and I know there was no other way out. My guess would be that he is dead, but I have seen no body. No confirmed kill.'

'You knew he was mine,' says Jack, giving me a black look. It occurs to me, not for the first time, that, in this mood, Jack has a very limited sense of perspective.

'Jack, whatever you think, I didn't kill him. If he died on the boat, you know the boat went under thanks to both of our actions.' Sort of a lie, but it might placate him a little. 'If it is his blood you want on your hands, you might just have it already.'

That satisfies him a little, and I see his shoulders loosen.

'Here. Have a cold mocha,' says Samson, sliding one of the coffee cups over to him. 'We can break out the hard stuff in a bit, and have a good old drink if you want? Turn today into a wake or something.' Again, nothing from Jack.

107

Tina gets up from her chair and rounds the table to him. 'I know it's hard, but chin up Jack, yes?' she says, and she leans down to hug him. He says nothing and accepts the embrace in silence, without returning it.

Felix speaks up.

'Jack, you are carrying yourself around with the air of a broken man, and I understand that. But you have had something that so few in your situation get – the chance to look into your enemy's eyes, and tell him what you think of him.'

All I can remember of what Jack told Sparkles was related to his hairy arse, but I get Felix's point.

'Whether you killed Sparkles or not, by destroying his business, you have taken more from him than taking his life. If he is still alive, you have destroyed that which he has built, and left him with nothing, a fate which I am sure he would view as at least as bad as death, if not worse.'

Jack just looks at him, and Tina takes her seat again. Felix continues.

'You have a chance to move on, you have a chance to leave what happened behind—'

'And join you?' Jack interrupts. The outburst hits the atmosphere hard, charging it with electricity.

'I loved your father,' Felix says, his expression no longer benign, rage darkening his eyes. 'Don't you *dare* forget that. You may not have agreed with what your father wanted, but you are missing the plain fact that it was indeed *exactly* what he wanted. He came to me, of his own volition. You need to accept that that was precisely the way it was. And when things went wrong, *you* came to me, and I helped you after you begged for information. You emotionally blackmailed me into setting you on a course I know your father would have disapproved of. And then you march in here disrespecting the very same group of people who are equally broken by your father's death. After everything, how dare you speak to us in this way? Your father was like a son to me, he was a brother to Michael, and he was family to these men and women.'

Jack looks down, the strength of Felix's speech and stare too much for him to repel. Now there are tears on Felix's cheeks, as he struggles to keep it together, anger and grief bubbling to tipping point. I look away, and catch movement by the door.

An unmistakable peroxide bob – a woman, in a jumper and jeans: Zoe. How long has she been there? She wasn't there before. Her expression is anxious as she watches at a distance, unseen by the others.

'What about you?' Jack says, and it takes me a moment to realise he is talking to me.

'What about me, Jack?' I say. I don't want to make things worse, and, despite my interest in the criminal faction we are sitting with, I feel a pang of loyalty towards him again. 'Look, let's go.'

Felix is still staring Jack down, but Jack isn't taking him on.

Time to go. I get up.

'It was a pleasure meeting you all,' I say, and start circling the table to Jack's side. 'And I appreciate you putting me up last night, Felix.'

'It was my pleasure, Ben. I would say look after him, but I know you will. Is there anything I can do for you, before you go?'

It takes me only a moment to remember the one thing I badly need.

'There is something I could do with. A new identity. Completely new. I'm looking for a new passport, driving licence, national insurance number, employment references, medical history, the whole lot.'

Felix raises his eyebrows, as if surprised.

'My name is associated with failure,' I say. 'I want to leave it behind, and start a whole new life. I am finding it hard to do that with my current… social standing.'

'I've got a guy,' Michael says. 'He might be able to help you out. Gimme your phone number.'

'I'd appreciate that a lot,' I reply. I don't like the idea of giving out a contact number, but the phone is a pay-as-you-go so I could drop the sim card in a bin if needs be. Plus this is all give and take. Michael hands his phone over, and I look at him blankly.

'Just type it in so I can save it,' he says.

When I've done so, a smattering of goodbyes rises from the table, as finally Jack rises also. We begin heading back towards the kitchen, when Felix speaks again.

'Gents, if you fancy a pint tonight, we are having a drink together over at Lumen, about eight o'clock. It would be really nice if you could both be there. A social occasion to put these sadder times to the back of our minds.'

'And I'll look into that business for you,' says Michael.

'I appreciate that,' I say. 'Perhaps see you later then.'

We leave, and as we go we pass Zoe, finally going into the group. She looks at Jack with concern, and smiles at me weakly. Her role is still unclear to me, and I don't get her involvement. If the men are *väktaren* and Felix is the *toppmöte*, what is she? Is she another ingredient to this criminal recipe, or something else entirely? As we walk through the kitchen, I think of how close I was to getting some specific answers – some detail – as to the extent, scope, and scale of Felix's business, details that I could use to my advantage. So I think showing up tonight is a must.

We pass through that grand wooden front door, into the driveway, and almost before we've stepped off the porch, Jack combusts.

'What the fuck were you doing in there? Playing house and happy families?' he spits out, pointing back at the house animatedly.

'Jack, calm down. I know it's a stock phrase, but: it's not what it looks like.'

'Fuck off. I'm sick of people telling me to calm down. Didn't you listen to anything I told you about them? Didn't it mean anything to you?'

'Every word, and of course it did. *Calm. Down.* Let's talk somewhere else, ok?'

'I asked for your help, not for you to get seduced. They are not what you think.'

'I am a lot of things Jack, but I'm no fool. Is your car here?'

'No, I assumed you still have it. Zoe brought me.'

We start walking down the driveway, which widens and becomes a long bare road along the waterfront. When we get a fair way from the house, I speak up again.

'We need to talk about Zoe. She's the only piece of this puzzle I don't get so far.'

'Get fucked. I'm not telling you shit. You're shaping up just like the others.'

'Sparkles said he didn't do it.'

Jack abruptly stops walking. I continue.

'He said that we had got the wrong impression, and that he did not kill your dad. He said, just like Felix said, that he doesn't do business that way.'

110

'He's lying.'

'Perhaps he is, but why? Why would he lie? Aren't crime bosses supposed to take pride in the amount of blood they have shed to get where they are? Nobody here seems to want any dirt under their fingernails whatsoever!'

'He's lying. I know it. He's a fucking liar.'

'Jack, I have done my fair share of interrogations, and believe me, I am good at putting the squeeze on another human being. Interrogation can sometimes get physical. In those moments, I have seen a lot of men lie their arses off before they eventually tell the truth. You always know the moment they've turned because they always betray it in some way. You can see it coming, and it becomes very hard to miss. Sparkles, last night, never did so. When he protested his innocence he carried the hallmarks of it, too.'

'So you're a bloody psychic now, too?'

'It's not infallible. But I wasn't usually wrong with these things. And I don't think I am now.'

'So, what… Felix is the liar?'

We resume walking, but more slowly.

'It's a possibility, but perhaps he was misinformed. We are talking about a criminal underbelly that, however flashy and glamorous, is still a criminal underbelly, as full of the lowlifes, cheats, and scumbags as any other. Who knows what lies are being told about your dad's passing.'

Jack doesn't like hearing that, and if I heard something like that about my dad, I wouldn't either. Jack wants answers, but every answer comes layered with doubt. Nothing simple is rising to the surface. No wonder he is hacked off.

'Jack, I want you to listen to me.'

I take his silence as my invitation to continue.

'My loyalties here lie with yourself, so please don't be twisted about that. I have a purpose and intentions. But my main concern at this point is Sparkles. If he is innocent of your dad's killing, and he is alive, he is going to be one pissed-off individual. He's willing to fight dirty, if pushed; he proved that by sending that killer to the Premier Inn to take you out. We just obliterated his business, and I can only imagine he will want retribution. So then there is the problem that your dad may have been killed by another party altogether. I think it's worth checking out. We need to go back to the beginning because, for now, the info from Felix doesn't lead anywhere. That's what I'm going to do today, and we are going to that get-together tonight.'

'Fuck that, I'm not having a little shindig with those creeps.'

I think about it, and he's probably right. I don't want him to blow it for me.

'Understood, Jack. You don't have to. I must ask, though. What loyalties do you have towards the people in the house we just left?'

'What do you mean?' Jack asks, burying his hands in his pockets, as if to keep them from fidgeting.

'Before you asked me to help you, I had an agenda, and now I'm going to tell you what it is. It involved a man in London who had put me in a very sticky situation that saw me arrested. While I was in the slammer, I changed. I pity the society that put me there, but I won't give up on it.

'I engineered an escape plan that got me out and let loose on the quiet, with an insurance policy in place that would give me at least fifteen years to get shit done.'

'What do you mean?'

'I'm a soldier, Jack. I have specific skills that allowed me to fight for my country, and now I feel my country needs me more than ever. I was on my way to London to get started, but first I'm going to do my part by putting the berg out of business. So tell me, and don't mess me around: What loyalty do you carry towards the berg?'

'None whatsoever,' he whispers.

'Good. After we find out who killed your father, they are next in my sights. I intend to put them out of business, for good.'

I've finally managed to jolt Jack into silence. He looks down, like the very ground might quake and crumble, and drop him into an abyss.

'You… are using me?' he mutters.

'No. What I've told you is for after we have found your dad's killer, not before.'

Jack doesn't respond.

'Jack… I'm back in the country that I have given everything to protect, but this country doesn't want me. I've been discarded by my superiors, hated by my peers, and sneered at by society. My family want nothing to do with me. I can hardly believe how my life has turned out. I am asking for nothing from you, Jack, only that you let me continue. The social niceties back in Felix's house, the evening drinks… it's all about gathering intel for their downfall. Don't believe, for one minute, that I am being suckered. I know what I'm about.'

Jack eventually looks up at me – a cold look. His trust and faith in people has taken a battering. I feel bad for him, because the hand he has been dealt was not what he hoped for.

'Zoe,' he says.

I look at him. The peroxide mystery rears up for examination.

'What about Zoe?'

'When you… put an end to it, will it be violent?'

'Violence is always my last resort, but some people only play with fire, and fire is the only way to address them. I actually don't see that with the berg.'

'Zoe,' Jack repeats.

'Loyalty?' I ask.

'Not loyalty. It's complicated.'

'How complicated?'

'I grew up with her. She is…' He can't finish, so I try to tease it out of him.

'You and she have something together?'

'We grew up together. Back before I knew anything about this. I had always had this hope… Well, you know.'

'I don't, but I'll pretend I do. What is her involvement here?'

'Accountancy,' says Jack.

'She keeps the books?'

'Yes. She keeps everything in line, way in the background.'

'Christ.' So she's not just a little helper, she's an integral cog. Her importance on my radar balloons.

'Are you going to hurt her?'

'I've no interest in hurting her, Jack, understand that.' I leave out that now I have to take her down too.

Shit.

113

If Zoe is their bookkeeper, she is also a rich source of evidence: all their dealings – profits, expenditures, jobs, employees, bought-off officials. The power of what is locked in her head is surely massive. And I might be forced to get that information out of her, one way or another. Jack wouldn't like that one bit and I sincerely hope that his mind isn't racing to where mine is. That would deeply upset him, and would definitely turn him against me – if I haven't managed that already.

'How old is Zoe?' I ask.

'She's twenty-four, same as me.'

'How did she become involved?'

'I don't know the ins and outs, but Felix took her in. She was very young when her parents died, leaving Felix to pick up the pieces.'

Interesting. Felix, the crime lord with a heart of gold. Sensitive, loyal, caring: caring enough to take a child in out of the cold – and then use her.

I would imagine that Zoe's loyalties are fiercely attached to the grandfather who put a roof over her head when her parents passed away. I know mine would be. So whatever I want from her will be hard to get.

But the issue of Jack's father is pressing, as is Sparkles' fate. If he isn't dead, we are marked men.

'Let's head to your place, Jack. I have a few things I want to look into,' I say.

Jack shrugs. He seems quite beaten down by the hopelessness of the situation he finds himself in, and it doesn't help that he's also exhausted. I worry about him. Last night he was all gusto, and today he seems a strange mix of jaded and fraught, like his world is ending.

Maybe it is.

'I don't mean to exploit this position, and the information you have given me, Jack. But when it comes to the things I broke out of prison to achieve, this is an opportunity that is too good to pass up. If the berg are everything you say they are – and it seems they are exactly that – then both of us will be doing this city and this country a favour.'

We need to get off the streets, and do some digging. And that will be harder. I can see my afternoon getting busier and busier – if we can stay alive long enough to get anything done, that is.

17

We take a cab back to Jack's house, a ten-minute ride. When we arrive, Jack jumps out immediately and wordlessly, while I am left to pay. I don't quibble, I just pay the man.

I follow Jack as he unlocks the door and enters, slipping his shoes off as he crosses the threshold. I do the same. We head into the kitchen where Jack embarks on that great British tradition, brewing a pot of tea. When the kettle's on and the Yorkshire teabags are safely in the pot, I walk to the fridge.

'Can you show me the safe?' I ask.

Jack walks over and gives the fridge a sharp yank from the wall, after which it slides easily along, leaving a gap I can poke my head and shoulders through. The safe is a rugged beauty, black brushed steel. It looks as if it could withstand just about anything, and I can imagine a nuclear strike detonating right here, wiping Manchester off the face of the earth, leaving nothing behind save for this perfect ebony box in the middle of a gigantic, smoking crater.

Jack sticks his hand through the gap, and I hear gears whirring. Then a clunk, and a creak. He steps back to allow me a peek.

'The only thing I moved is the gun,' says Jack. 'The rest is exactly how he left it.'

I glance around the corner and see a square opening a couple of feet across, with the contents on three shelves, lit by a blue neon LED. There are a fair few things in here, suggesting that Royston was not expecting anything to happen to him anytime soon.

Top shelf: three mobile phones, each the same model of iPhone; a blank space, presumably where the handgun used to sit; and some documents. Will need sifting through in detail.

Middle shelf: four five-inch cubes, each containing beautiful little fish in exotic colours. Each cube is separated by a black piece of card. Felix's little side-earner, the one that started it all. The fish all look fine, save for the one on the end that's floating belly-to-the-heavens, its eyes milky. Next to the cubes is a little pot of fish flakes and a second plastic container full of brine shrimp and red worms.

Bottom shelf: cold hard cash filling the whole shelf, stacked up and along. They all look like fifties, and fast maths suggests there may well be close to a million quid in there. *Bloody hell.*

I leave the money where it is, and take out everything else, placing it on the kitchen countertop. Jack slides a hot mug across to me. I turn all three phones on, one at a time. Opening the lids on the cubes, I sprinkle in some shrimp for the fish, which eagerly smash into the falling crustaceans like tiny, ornate piranhas – except for Milky on the end there, poor lad. His ship has sailed.

The phones sing to life with a happy little jingle, and all look at me brightly, ready to do my bidding. I take the first one, while Jack sits on the counter opposite me. I look at the screen and try to navigate the interface. I had seen one of these before, but had never owned one. They look nice. Thanks to my brief relationship with my Samsung, I get the hang of things pretty quickly, and open up the contacts.

I figure that it's only the extremely unlucky who get killed by people they don't know; by accident, or by psychopaths. Royston's line of work was one tinged with inherent dangers, so that now, as the contact list gives me a modest seventy-odd names, it reads like a menu of extra suspects. I'm pleased it's only about seventy; it's a number I can conceivably tackle, given time.

I scan the names. Bolt, Brian, Christian, Delores, Eustace, Gloria, Grieg, Happy, Harry… None mean anything to me. More than that, none of the names I already know are showing up, like Leonard, Felix, Samson, Michael, and so on, but that doesn't really surprise me. Any one of the names in the contact book could be a pseudonym. Or Royston purposely left some names out: fewer footprints.

I do the same task on the second phone and the third, checking contacts. The second one is far more interesting, in that it contains a simple alphabet: twenty-six contact entries labelled with only a single letter. And no email details either, simply mobile numbers. Much more promising.

The third phone's contact screen is blank. Nothing at all. In fact, the whole phone is empty. No pictures, no apps, no calls placed, no nothing.

'Jack, did your dad know a Delores?' I ask.

'Yeah, she was his cousin. My kind-of aunt. Not seen her in a while though,' Jack replies, while staring out of the bay kitchen windows.

'And Bolt?'

'Umm… I think he was a guy he used to go to the football with. A Bolton fan. Yeah, that was it.'

We go through all the names quickly, and Jack identifies each one as one of his father's friends or family members. He can't identify a couple of them, but the picture is already clear. The first phone is for personal use only – a useful tool for organising the dualities of the life he had chosen.

That poses the inevitable question of the twenty-six names on phone two. Call signs or numeric pseudonyms for twenty-six people who clearly got the special treatment. How best to find out who they are, though? And of course, what was that third phone used for, if not for business or personal? That makes me question if there's a fourth, that perhaps he had one with him when he was taken. I could ask Jack, but all three phones are identical. '*IPhone 4S*' in black, '*32GB*' it says on the back of each. There's no telling them apart. Even the home screen wallpapers are the same.

The phone I'm holding beeps, and a little microphone icon appears. I can't see any way to exit the screen.

'Do you know what I have done here?' I ask.

Before he can answer, a robotic voice speaks from the phone.

'*I'm sorry, I didn't catch that,*' it says, amiably. It's kind of freaky.

'That's just Siri,' Jack says. 'You must have accidentally pushed the home button for too long. Just press it again to get out.'

'Who's Siri?' I ask, regarding the phone with suspicion.

'It's a voice recognition command system for iPhone. You just tell Siri what you want.'

'Umm, like what?'

Jack takes the phone. He presses the home button and it beeps.

'Siri, where am I?' he says.

After a second, the robot voice speaks. '*Blantyre Drive, Worsley, Greater Manchester.*'

'Thank you,' Jack says.

'*Don't mention it,*' Siri replies.

'Jesus,' I say. 'That's impressive. Weird, but impressive.'

Lightning strikes in my mind. I grab phone number three and activate the Siri character. 'Where was I on Thursday night?' I ask.

The screen blinks to a calendar page for the month of October – entirely blank.

'*I have no appointments entered,*' Siri replies.

Fantastic. It's no help yet, but still encouraging.

I continue interrogating the phone.

'Who did I last call?'

'*079775550981*' Siri answers. The number is on the screen, and I type it into phone one, since I have no pen or paper handy.

'When did I call?'

'*Call took place Monday, October 24th at 23:42.*'

The night of Royston's disappearance. All call logs have been erased, but Siri's individual memory hasn't been wiped – the robot is the spy in the camp.

I try to think of something else to ask. While I think, Siri handily offers suggestions.

'*Would you like me to place a call to the number, or send the number a message?*'

Siri, you genius.

'Send a message, please.'

'*What would you like it to say?*'

I speak loud and clear, enunciating every word. 'I'm still here.'

'*Should I send the message?*'

'Yes, please.'

'*No problem.*'

A little tinny *whoosh* through the phone speakers lets me know the message has been sent. Fantastic. And that should be enough to tease out whoever Royston spoke to that night. I feel one step closer to answers.

I notice the other phone is on, however – phone one. The keypad is up, the mobile number I just typed in is on the screen. But this phone already has that number entered into it, assigned to a contact, and that name appears in faint lettering below the number: Nigel.

'Jack, remind me who Nigel was again?' I ask.

'That's a bloke Dad had round here a couple of times, mainly in his office. He said he was a colleague at Quaycrest.'

A colleague at a fake company? And so another suspect emerges. Who is Nigel? What does he know about Royston's murder, considering he spoke to him just before his disappearance?

I get a quick idea, borne from the grim stir that hasn't left me since Felix mentioned the capital earlier. I take phone two, open the contents, and view all at once, the simple letters and their numerical counterparts cascading down the screen as I scroll. I'm looking for area codes, one in particular. And I soon see that two of the contacts feature what I'm looking for.

The area code 020. London. Two of the numbers in here are London landlines.

'You have a pen and paper?' I ask Jack, who glances over from out of his pensive fugue.

'Come on, mate, get with it,' I say.

He shakes off his mood, unclips a little magnetised pad from the fridge door, which has a dangling pen on a piece of string, and slides them over to me. I jot, tear, pocket the scrap.

And with that, phone three beeps, announcing the arrival of a text message – a reply from Nigel. It is one word, in block capitals:

EXPLAIN.

18

In Royston's office, I ask Jack for some time alone with the computer. I don't have my laptop with me – I'm still in bloody beachwear, for Christ's sake – but I need to follow something up. Something that's been nagging me.

I walk into the beautifully furnished, wood-clad office, and sit at the desk chair. I glance around, trying to let the mood of the room seep into my senses. I try to imagine what the dead man used to do in here.

I fire up the computer. I can imagine spending plenty of time in this office, this man-cave. It has that solitude to it that I am attracted to. Dark wood shelves, dim lamps, books. A little womb away from the hurly-burly.

The computer reveals, curiously, nothing. Empty. It's an outdated PC, which I'm grateful for, because even I know how to access the C drive. But there's nothing there. Has it been wiped?

It has Internet Explorer, however, and I get a connection. I don't want to log into anything of any note here, because eventually, the berg will go down. And when it does, Royston's computers will probably be seized by the authorities. Last thing I want to do is leave digital breadcrumbs leading back to me.

The MSN home news page loads in the Explorer window. What I've learned in the last forty-eight hours is that being a one-man band can only get me so far. I have the hankering for an ally. I don't mean backup. I mean someone on the other side of the legal looking glass. It's risky, but with trust and a relationship based on equal benefits…

Could be achievable, but has to be strictly on my terms. No names shared, only a way to reach each other to swap intel. I need information that police networks gather using their sophisticated infrastructures and algorithms – information designed for both surveillance and gathering sensitive material, but all presently unavailable to me. Google will only get me so far.

But I think I have the right man for the job. It will take a degree of sensitivity in approach, but it will be worth a go.

In the search box I type the name from the newspaper article I read yesterday, *Jeremiah Salix*.

Up pops, unsurprisingly, very little, save for that same newspaper article. I scroll down, find a link that looks far more promising, click it, and I'm given a simple web page with text and a picture. The picture at the top is of a wheelchair basketball team, the text below it being the roster. It appears this Jeremiah Salix is the shooting guard of the Tameside Tomahawks, in the North West Regional Wheelchair Basketball Association. There's a league table too, and it appears they are doing quite well. He's also the coach of the Stockport Royals, a youth team.

I click through to them, opening the page in a new window. Scrolling down, I see a fixture list – and as luck would have it, they are playing tonight, at Reddish Vale Basketball Centre. That's south of the city, about ten miles out. I look back at the first page, and find a team photo at the bottom. Following the caption names, I see my man. Sitting there in a bright yellow basketball shirt, thick dark hair curling across the top of an unshaven face. His expression serious. In a wheelchair. Seems they got him good and proper.

I bet he'd like a crack at who put him in that chair.

I back right up to the Google search screen. I take the scrap of paper from my pocket, and key in the first London phone number. It comes back with nothing I can immediately decipher, just its listing in a series of phone number banks, all ex-directory.

I try the second number, and strike gold.

It's the number for a pub in Tottenham, north London. The Old Tupenny. Google handily provides me a picture of the pub itself: red brick walls and black and white eaves... and my skin crawls so fiercely it seems to try to make a break from my body. The Old Tupenny is where I made my grand folly, and got my knee shot to bits. It's the authentic Tudor front for Terry Masters' entire operation.

Felix and Masters were indeed in cahoots, but to what extent I don't know. Christ, it's a small enough world, but it seems the criminal world is even smaller. If Masters is top dog down south, does that mean Felix is his northern counterpart?

I shut down the computer and consider turning the office upside down, but I suspect that all I'd find is further evidence that this office is fake.

Back in the kitchen, Jack is still drinking his tea. He has barely moved since the moment we got back.

'Jack, can you think of anything about this Nigel guy? Anything at all?'

'Not really,' he replies, distantly. 'I met him once or twice, but it was, like, for a split second.'

'And?'

'Nothing interesting. Bit of a fatty. Bald. Really ordinary. He had a nice car, though. Whenever he was here, they just went through to the office.'

'How did he seem with your dad? Were they comfortable with each other, was there any tension?'

'I only saw them together for a second, like I said. I didn't pick up anything wrong. There wasn't like a hierarchy between them. It was all just dead ordinary, dead normal.'

'I'm going to text him again, see what happens.'

Jack gives me a look I can't interpret.

'You've got a problem with that?' I ask.

'Nope.'

'Ok.'

I take phone three from the countertop and bring up the message strand. The screen shows me precisely what's been said and by whom.

Beneath *EXPLAIN*, I type: *You tell me*. I press send, and wait.

The response is almost immediate, announced by a buzz of vibration: *I'm on my way over*.

That's not what I want yet. In time, a face-to-face will be right, but not now. *Don't. Not the time*.

I hope that works, and the next response reveals that it has.

Have it your way.

I don't really know what that means, but then again, maybe I'm not supposed to. After all, I'm not actually the ghost of a dead gangster, regardless of what this Nigel believes. I go on the offensive:

I want answers.

A response doesn't come quickly. Five minutes pass, and I half expect the doorbell to ring. Eventually, the phone buzzes.

None of this went how I hoped. I can promise you that.

Fantastic. He knows. And it's shedding a little light onto what happened that night. The questions about Nigel are mounting, his importance in our crude investigation rising higher by the minute. I decide that keeping on the offensive is the way to proceed, as I have obviously caught Nigel off guard.

Not good enough. Send.

The response is quick as a flash this time. *You pushed it. You made it turn out the way it has. It was your own fault.*

This is the right direction. I'm even close to a confession here. If I press a personal button, I might just get it. I take a deep breath on this one.

Betrayal. From you. One of my closest friends.

Again, the response is damn near immediate, and its rage leaps off of the screen.

YEAH? HOW DID THAT BULLET FEEL, YOU FUCKING PRICK.

Wow.

I glance up at Jack. He is looking out of the window, still faraway. Just as well, for the moment. I'm not ready to reveal this to him. Not yet. That text could push him into another rampage.

On the phone, I type: *Tomorrow morning, 10 a.m. Piccadilly Gardens. Let's talk it through.*

No response, but I'll take it as an affirmative.

I look at Jack again, and notice that he's actually looking down at a creased photograph. I shuffle closer behind him, so I can see clearer. He is so engrossed in looking at this aged snap that he doesn't catch me seeing it. Two kids, on a beach. Buckets and spades, a boy with a Luke Skywalker haircut, a little blond girl with soaked pigtails. They are building a dam in the setting sunlight, happy as all hell. It can only be Jack and Zoe as kids.

This must really be hurting him, but I've got to snap him out of it.

'Jack,' I say quietly, 'I'm gonna take these phones and documents with me, is that ok?'

'Whatever, Ben,' he says. This battle is taking its toll on him, leaving him groggy and jaded.

'And tonight?' I venture.

'You go alone,' he says. 'You go do what you've got to do.'

'Jack, can I ask you something?'

He raises his eyes once more, and I see from his expression straight away that my assumption is right. 'Go on.'

'A lot of men would have crumbled way before getting to this point. But, are you in over your head?'

'Christ… I feel like I've been drowning since yesterday,' he says. 'I took that shot in anger at Sparkles, and everything went to pieces. I can't do this. I want it all to go away. I might think I'm strong enough to deal with this, but I'm not. It was just me being stubborn. I want out.'

I feel for him. He's been pushed and pulled in so many directions that he doesn't know which way is up.

I find myself taking the second chair in the window. 'You're a good man, Jack. Good men all do things they wish they could change. That's what makes them *good*.'

He looks at me as if unconvinced.

'Do you know why I was kicked out of the military?' I say.

He shakes his head.

'I murdered my friend,' I say. If he's feeling repulsed by what I just said, he's doing a damn fine job of hiding it. 'It was a night op, a pretty simple building clear-out. It had gone well. Our transport home was a Puma Mk2. A chopper. Orders came through on the way back to do a flyby over Lashkar Gah, Helmand Province. There'd been a lot of recent fighting there that had only just settled down, and the feeling was that fly-bys reminded the insurgents we were there.

'All it took was one guy trying to be a hero, for it all to go charlie foxtrot.'

I can see Jack doesn't follow.

'Clusterfuck,' I say. 'Bloke took a potshot at us with nothing more than an AK, bullet ricocheted through the cabin and buried itself through the pilot's visor. Even now, I still can't believe how unlucky that was. With no pilot, the chopper ditched itself right into the market district. All crew and passengers died except two. Me and my communications officer. Stephen, was his name.'

It's the first time I've spoken his name out loud since the court martial, and it still catches in my throat.

'The town blew up, everyone wanting a scalp. Turns out there were far more insurgents there than our superiors thought. We fought like vermin to get out. We managed to make it to the sewers – only he, Stephen, was gut-shot. Soon, he couldn't move and we were stuck there, on a ledge over a drain basin, the town over our heads pulling itself to rubble looking for us, while he began to die slowly and horribly, sepsis eating him from the outside in and back again.'

Jack's complexion takes a much darker hue.

'He begged me to end it for five days straight. On day six, I… did. He'd never have survived the sewer. I took my chances and threw myself into the drains, and by some sick miracle I survived. I was found by a local on the banks of Helmand River, and traded back to my superiors for chicken nuggets and diesel. I told them everything. They didn't see it the way I did; they said I was a murderer and they gave me the stiff treatment. I thought my record would rescue me, but turns out they were quite happy to get rid of me. The mission out there had changed, the army was changing, and it seems I wasn't enough of a *yes* man in their eyes. I came out angry, got drunk and caused trouble for a couple of years, then ended up in prison.'

Jack looks as morally confused about the whole story as I still am to this day.

'The point I'm trying to make is this. I made a choice that nobody would understand – that I *still* can't understand – because my friend asked me to. He *begged* me to. Said it was the one thing he truly wanted from me, and watching him suffer I could see why. In the end I wrecked my life to give my friend what he needed. Nobody understands how tough things can get when you're in deep. Nobody giving the orders or watching on will ever truly get it. But you do. You're in it. *You* get it.'

I lean forward to him.

'It hurts because you care. You know that choices are hard, but you know that the situation commands it. You know it's not easy, because you are a *good man*. Do you see?'

He nods.

'Now you know how far I'll go for my friends. I'll call you in the morning. A night off might do you good. I'm gonna keep the car another night. Is that ok?'

'Thanks Ben,' he says. I give him a nod and start for the door, when a phone rings again. There are so many phones in here, I can't work out which one it is, so I check all three quickly. None are bleeping for attention, and it takes me a second to work out that it's my own phone. I grab it, seeing that the number is an 0161 Manchester area code.

'Hello?'

'Ben, hello, it's Felix.'

'Hi Felix,' I say, after the door has shut behind me.

'Do you have a free hour or so?' His tone is hard to read.

I check my watch. Not really, but dare I say no to this guy? No chance.

'Sure, what can I do for you?'

'I have an investment project ongoing, but it's more community based, totally legitimate. I'd like to show you another side to me. It's going to be something I think you'll really find interesting.'

'Sounds good.'

'I'd love to show you it. Can you get to Irlam train station in say an hour or so?'

Irlam isn't far, maybe six miles.

'Yeah, I'll aim for it.'

'Great, thank you,' Felix says. 'I'll see you there.'

Shit. The lid on my fears is rattling, like a saucepan about to boil over. They told me a lot before, almost too much. Felix didn't sound sinister or threatening – far from it. But I suppose people never do when they want to corner you and kill you. You always whisper to the wasp when you're about to smash it with a newspaper.

126

19

Still concerned that I might be riding to my death, I board the train from Worsley to Irlam. Through the streaked windows of the carriage, I watch the city in the distance, shifting as we peel around it. I find it hard to take my eyes off it, and, feeling watched, check for the Glock. Right where I left it, easy against my right hip, although I have to admit, it's no real comfort.

The train switches tracks with an audible *clackety-clunk*, and we abruptly turn away from the city, towards the countryside and, somehow, sunshine. Ironic. The scenery takes on a different slant, becoming leafier for a moment, but it is short-lived. Tired houses begin to crowd the rail track before opening up again into daylight, as we begin to slow, the journey a strange microcosm of Greater Manchester's modern predicament: urban exhaustion bleeding concrete onto the green surroundings, which have held on like an obstinate rebel faction under siege.

It looks in parts just like any other northern station, but there is a magnificent two-storey Victorian station house surrounded by high building partitions, and the detritus has been stripped and painted. It looks fresh, the casual erosion of its surroundings having clearly been given some recent TLC.

I hop out, and try to work out what I am to do next. I see that further down the platform, Leonard is getting off the train also. No wonder I was feeling watched. He walks straight over to me and extends that same near-convulsing handshake.

'Hi, where are we going?' I ask, as I attempt to crush his hand in return.

'Follow me,' he replies, as if doing his best not to say anything more. There seems no pretence at all to him, no suggestion that him being on the same train as me, perhaps following me, is anything out of the ordinary. Truly, these are men who are used to having things just their own way.

We walk along the platform, then exit the station and head into the car park, but Leonard turns immediately left towards a set of blue-painted iron gates, beyond which I can see plant vehicles – yellow diggers, a dump truck, and neatly stacked building materials. Just through the gates, as we pass through, I notice among the construction paraphernalia a gleaming black SUV, parked next to the near-completed station house. The car park surrounding the building is not quite there yet, and is just a dusty track awaiting the firm hand of concrete.

Leonard holds the door open for me and I slip through, stepping into what seems to be the hollowed-out shell of the building before improvements get under way. Dust covers everything. The walls are bare brick with wires hanging down like veins. It feels like I've walked in mid-dissection.

'We're in 'ere,' someone says down a brick corridor – Michael? – and I follow the sound with Leonard at my heels, out into a high-ceilinged cavern, with dusty concrete floors and high windows. And there sits Felix in an unfinished bar area. Michael stands on the other side of the bar, as if he's waiting to take Felix's drinks order. They both smile, as if they are enjoying a lovely day out. I'm aware that Leonard is behind me, and I don't like that, nor do I like the fact that I can't see Samson, who, I'm assuming is here as well.

'Ben, thank you for coming!' Felix exclaims. He's bubbling almost as much as Leonard.

I haven't seen him out of his house before, and he wears a long heavy raincoat despite the dry weather, which enhances the impression of the senior citizen on an excursion from his nursing home.

'What do you think?' he says, gesturing widely.

'It's fascinating,' I reply. 'This building is really something.'

'It is, isn't it,' Felix says, shifting his weight away from the bar with the help of a black walking stick. 'It had been closed for twenty-five years, this building, and it fell almost to pieces. The man who we got it from used it as a chicken shed, if you can believe that.'

'Lucky chickens,' I say. Leonard moves quietly around me and walks towards the bar, and I feel less cornered.

'The building has stood here since 1880. With the help of one or two local authorities, we've managed to secure enough funding to get things up and running for a revival. We hope to open sometime in the next year.'

'This is a bit of a departure from what I was expecting.'

'Like I said, it's a project. And it's nice to do something positive for the community. Changes certain people's perceptions.'

'Plus, it's very helpful when it comes to the accounts,' Michael adds, as he crosses the floor to some large wooden boxes, big enough to fit people inside, lined up against the far wall. 'These'll be booths, in the shape of old carriages. Quaint, don't you think?'

There's an edge in his voice. 'It's a nice idea,' I say. They are bare wood, with pencil markings scrawled across them.

'The one on the end,' says Michael, pointing. It's an order.

Shit. These boxes could be big coffins, and what better place to do someone in than at your own deserted building site? I turn to Felix, and give him an '*are you serious?*' parting of my hands. Felix smiles and nudges me forward with a nod.

I edge towards the cabin, and peer through its empty doorway, only to be both amazed and disconcerted by what I see. Two benches face each other, with a table in between; and on the right-hand side sits Samson, the missing man himself, smiling almost merrily. Opposite him, wide-eyed, wrinkled, and looking in need of adult diapers, sits a man I had hoped never to see again.

Harry Tawtridge, chief warden of HMP Manchester.

A million thoughts try to cram into my mind at once. Tawtridge, somewhere in his late fifties, is a large man, five or six stone overweight, and he looks strained, tired, and agitated all at the same time. His jowls wobble just above the lapel of his ill-fitting light-grey suit, his bottom lip hanging with a wet dab of saliva. His green eyes look just how I remember, set in a brow of challenged entitlement. He's not used to what's happening to him.

We stare at each other, both seeming to swap the thought, admittedly through a veil of mutual hate, that we shouldn't be here, in this room, together. He should be at home, or in a restaurant somewhere, verbally rough-housing some young waitress. And I should be under his control, still locked up in my cell at Strangeways, with Craggs nattering away in my ear, boring me to tears about what an alleged hard nut he is. We shouldn't be looking at each other, the devil teetering in both our eyes.

'The other night, Ben,' Felix says, as he lays a hand on my shoulder, 'you were mumbling about prison. I didn't really think too much about it at the time, then I remembered another word in there. *Tawtridge*. I put the two together, with you speaking about prison and all. It seemed like you needed to settle something with this man.'

'How do you know him?' I ask. Tawtridge regards us grimly but says nothing.

'Some of us, at one time or other, have had brushes with the law's hospitality. And in the times that has happened, more often than not, it has been in the care of this man. So you could say we know each other a little.'

I look around at the men, who all stare at me with unconcealed enjoyment. They like having Tawtridge here, trapped like a rat, the tables fully turned.

Michael holds my gaze. 'Thirteen months,' he says.

I glance at Leonard. 'Six months.'

I look at Samson, who glares at Tawtridge with his jaw set in a clench. 'Seven and a half years.'

The moment floats, while Samson's words echo off the bare walls. I half expect Felix himself to offer a number of his own, but he doesn't.

Tawtridge finds his voice.

'Nice to see you reformed yourselves, boys,' he says, with an attempted cool that does nothing to disguise the quiver in his voice. His grey comb-over is straggly and slick with sweat, like an old heron's feathers after a storm.

'Pot. Kettle. Black.' Samson's voice feels like concrete.

'You did your time,' Tawtridge manages, 'which is more than can be said for this *fuck*.' He spits the last word at me, spraying the space between us with flecks of spittle.

'Harry, this is a civilised conversation,' Felix interjects, with a teacherly sternness to his voice. 'Please let's try to keep it that way.' Felix is cool, even when this place could go up in violence at any minute – but by his side, with his guidance, things feel like they will be ok. He gestures to Samson, who slides out from the makeshift booth.

'Ben, I thought that if I could get you two together, there'd be a strong chance that you could put whatever has got you both so upset behind you,' says Felix. 'Would you give it a try?'

I don't know what to say. I'd like to leave Tawtridge in the rear-view mirror of my past. But… Felix might be right. My breakout has caused all manner of problems, not just for me but for decent people like Freckles and his wife. Maybe I can get Tawtridge off my back once and for all…

'Ok,' I say, and move to where Samson was seated.

'Harry?' asks Felix.

'I'm here, aren't I?' Tawtridge replies, regarding me blackly.

'We'll leave you two alone for a while,' says Felix, ushering his *väktaren* away with his cane. 'Take all the time you need.'

The men disappear off into the bowels of the station house, leaving me alone with the man I blackmailed into giving me freedom. I expect brimstone from Tawtridge, but he slumps slightly.

'What in God's name are you doing with them?' he says. 'You really know how to pick your friends, soldier. I pictured more from you.'

'Harry – I'm going to call you that now we are out in the big wide world and not in your little social experiment of a prison – pull those fucking sadists you call guards off Freckles.'

Tawtridge smirks ugly in response.

'You and Freckles, that soft little shit. I knew you two were into something together. Nattering away all the time, like you're at a fucking knitting group. You asked him to look after something for you on the outside, and I heard all about it.'

I don't think he's an idiot, but I'll try to play him as one anyway.

'Those conversations were never exactly secret, but they weren't in any way incriminating. We could have been talking about anything.'

'No, no, of course not…' Tawtridge's face hardens somehow, his wrinkled cheeks suddenly tightening. 'But remember how you came at me in my office just a few days ago, during the riot, and demanded my clothes and your freedom? You were carrying a bag. A dark-coloured duffel bag, and you were squeezing it like your life depended on it. It takes no brain surgeon to know it was important.'

'Fair enough,' I say. He looks at me with such smug, sleazy knowing, and I picture him giving the same look to a cheap stripper as he fixes to put pennies in her G-string. I peep around the corner of the booth to see if any of the berg is in earshot. The coast is clear, the room quiet. I lean into Tawtridge quickly, catching him off guard.

'Quince. Remember him?' I ask.

'How could I forget? It took us ages to mop him up after you left. The riot smeared his blood all over the place.'

'I know what happened to him. I'm asking, what do you know about him?'

'He was a wrong 'un. A nonce. Caught with a hard drive full to the casing with kiddie porn, half of which he'd made himself.'

'And?'

'Rumour has it he had done some pretty grim stuff at a boys' school in Whitefield, but he took a guilty plea of possession rather than dragging the sexual assaults through the courts.'

'But?'

'But *what*?' A snarl.

'We all know he did it. He bragged about it.'

'Well, yes he did. The sick little puppy.'

Tawtridge actually smiles, and something in his pupils flickers what could be a debased enjoyment. I feel my fists clench.

'What about Craggs? Before what happened,' I say.

'Just a street scally who got into gang culture and couldn't get out. Wrapped up in the ideal.'

'He always had a point to prove, didn't he?'

'Yes, you could say that. Where is this going?'

'So you can picture it didn't take much to push him over the edge… say, to push him into doing something he might regret.'

Tawtridge blinks a couple of times, and leans back with a sharp inhalation.

'You put him up to it. You put him up to killing Quince.'

'Not something I'm proud of, but Quince's crimes deserve the roughest justice imaginable. Her Majesty couldn't give him what he deserved but I could, by hook or by crook. All it took was telling Craggs that Quince was chatting shit about him behind his back and it was only a matter of time.'

Tawtridge's face displays a mixture of displeasure and lascivious enjoyment. 'Craggs would have fucking loved that. A paedo too – it's perfect for him. He wanted a murder on his rep, and you gave him the perfect target.'

'He loved that he was cellmates with me, he'd tell everyone he could about it. He got what he wanted.'

'Oh, you're all about making people happy.' Tawtridge grimaces. 'But I don't see how this has anything to do with your bag.'

I find myself smiling, enjoying this repugnant worm on my hook. The berg have given me the chance of a clean break here, and I'd be insane not to take it.

'Would you say I was a good boy in prison?' I ask.

'Right up until orchestrating that little murder, you were a proper solid-gold suck-up choirboy.'

'I enjoyed volunteering. I wanted to help.'

'Yeah, as if you were going to get out on good behaviour, a con with your charge.'

'What do you remember me helping with?'

Tawtridge hesitates. He knows he's being dragged down the rabbit hole, but he has no choice but to play it out and see where it leads him. A train hurtles by outside, its roar muffled by the solid walls around us. 'Kitchen duties. Laundry. The infirmary. So?'

'Do you see it as perceivable that I may have got my hands on some guards' shirts?'

'No, no. They are always done separately, you can't fool me there.'

'Do you think your idiotic staff members were following protocols? They were as jacked up on power as you are.'

We lock eyes, neither one budging to give the other ground. I hold firm. Eventually, he relents.

'So you've got some shirts. Big fucking whoop,' he says, crossing his arms.

'Do you remember the blood drive?' I ask, tightening the noose. He frowns.

'Yes.'

'Do you remember me helping?'

'Yes.'

'Good. I was helping in admin, wasn't I? Well, it didn't take much for me to nick a bit. You can picture that, can't you, in that fucking zoo you call an infirmary…'

He just looks at me, pissed off but baffled. He doesn't like where this is going, I can tell. I'm loving it – I've waited months to get one over this bastard.

'So, for argument's sake,' I continue, 'let's say I've got five guards' shirts covered in blood. That's not very good, is it?'

'Proves nothing,' Tawtridge replies petulantly.

'Yeah, but… if the blood was that of a dead man? Say, a very recently dead man, killed in a riot only days ago. Five guard shirts soaked in a dead prisoner's blood, a man who died under mysterious circumstances.'

'Quince. You stole Quince's blood… But the murder is on closed-circuit TV. It will show it wasn't any of my men.'

I smile again. I can't help it. 'You remember where Quince was stabbed, don't you?'

'The rec room.'

'*Where* in the rec room?'

His silence tells me I've got him.

'The northeast corner,' I say. 'Where the CCTV misses.'

'You know it doesn't.'

'Don't be stupid. I watched the rotations and measured the viewing field. I know it, you know it, Craggs knows it. All the video will show is your guards storming the corner, and all hell breaking loose.'

Tawtridge's nostrils flare, and he knows he's done. I line up the final nail in the coffin.

'Your way out is this. You forget all about me. You forget I was ever there. You do whatever it takes to cover me, and I've no doubt you can do that, I'm sure you've done it before. And you leave Freckles alone, because he doesn't have the bag. The bag is with me, safely locked away in a secure location, should I ever need it. If this doesn't happen… I break out my insurance policy. The bag and its contents finds its way to the authorities, with all the information about its relevance.'

Tawtridge stares, his mouth hanging open.

'They will come crashing down on you like you'd never believe, and your prison will be put under the microscope. Stories will come out. I've been there, I know what goes on behind closed doors. The gambling, bribery, prostitution, abuse and torment. It would ruin you.'

Tawtridge looks away. I have no clue whether the blood and shirts would hold up to any rigorous forensic scrutiny if it came down to it, but it's merely the thought of all those questions, all those probing investigations into his prison, that will have Tawtridge wound tight with panic. He knows he has to do what I say, but I have one more way to drive the point home.

'And… you don't want these guys knocking on your door again, do you?' I throw a thumb in the direction of where the berg were standing.

Tawtridge slumps, beaten. He puts his palms on the table and takes three long, rasping breaths. He is sweating. After all the hurt he has caused, all he's done, it feels like justice to see the tables turned.

'We're done,' I shout through.

The berg reappear, first Samson, then Leonard, Michael, and finally Felix, who approaches the booth directly.

'All sorted?' Felix asks.

'Yes, I think so,' I say, then turn back to Tawtridge. 'Is that right?'

'That's right,' he says hoarsely. 'I'd like to go home now.'

The look on his face is one I'll remember, and I can't help but revel in this small victory, not only in terms of seeing this swine get his comeuppance, but also for what it means to my freedom and my future plans. Once I have a new identity in hand, I can move forward without looking over my shoulder.

'Well, let's get going,' Felix says. 'We can all come back when the bar is open properly. Maybe even you, Harry.'

The berg have helped me so much here, and while I don't want to owe them anything, their charity has left me deep in the debits column. It feels wrong – but I'll never forget the look in Tawtridge's eyes when I first came in. Evil punctured by fear. The comeuppance that makes it all worthwhile.

20

I can hear the *squeak-squeak* shuffle of sneakers on hardwood. It's a reas-suring sound, free and fresh, as opposed to the smell of the disabled-toilet cubicle I'm standing in. I don't think they are used very often and they are seemingly cleaned even less.

I am at the basketball centre, hiding. I have been here a while, and even caught a bit of the game. It was quite a good standard. I used to play a little on Bastion, and enjoyed head-to-heads with our American comrades whenever they came to town. I'd always felt I was a bit handy at basketball, but this lot here in this Stockport suburb would've smashed me and all my army pals into the paint.

I'd seen Jeremiah immediately, and recognised the sad resignation in his eyes – the look you carry when you've had something stripped away from you. We know our own. I reason that the toilets are the best place to get a private moment with him.

On the way here, I stopped at Supercuts in Stockport for a shave and a haircut, and am now much better presented – and not just from the neck up. I am wearing good clothes, jeans and a shirt, and feel a little overdressed to be hiding behind this bathroom door, clutching the light cord. Waiting, my speech rehearsed. I hope the man has access to the networks that interest me, and I hope that he'll want what I can offer him in return. Considering he's about to come into contact with someone who has been in contact with the berg and is willing to share that info, I will likely be both very popular and valuable to the police.

I realise that being here is a gamble and there are no guarantees, but he's the best hope for the kind of ally that I want to recruit. He may, in fact, no longer be a policeman, but my instinct believes otherwise. The police are known for looking after their own, and have been so low on numbers for such a long time that I am sure they will have done what they could to keep hold of an officer in need.

What the berg did to him might have started a grudge that he was prepared to carry forward. In which case, I am hoping he has angled his career to put himself in the best possible position to bring the berg down. And now, with eight further years on the force, he should be in a decent enough place to help me.

I hear voices outside. I pray it's him; any longer in here and I'll be heading out for a drink wearing L'Eau du Old Piss for cologne.

The voices come closer. I can't make out individual words, but it's the rising boom off the polished gymnasium floors that gives away the approach.

Suddenly, with a soft pop and click, the door opens. I hear the tread of wheels on the old linoleum floor, and Jeremiah is in here with me, facing away. As soon as the door swings back into place, I hit the lights, and we are doused in a smelly, inky blackness.

'Jeremiah. I'm sorry to do it this way, but I need to speak to you. Please don't alert anyone I'm here.'

He doesn't speak. Even though I can't see him, I can sense his stillness.

'I feel we could have an arrangement that would help us both. I have intelligence I'm willing to share, in exchange for information from your resources.'

After a moment, he speaks.

'What information could possibly interest me from some pervert who jumps me in the toilets at my local rec centre? Unless, that is, he's come to offer me an Olympic-level point guard with a mammoth field goal percentage...' he replies, with a deadpan coolness.

'Fair point. Whatever it is you think, I promise you I'm well placed to deliver. And my intentions are completely genuine.'

'A lot of bad things come from good intentions, my toilet-dwelling friend.'

'True. I have come back from some time away to a country I don't recognise. I see what's wrong, and I want it to stop. I assure you I have both the resources and training to pull it off. I am committed.'

'An ex-serviceman,' Jeremiah says. 'With the tenor of your voice I'd say you're not that old. Forty, tops. The fact that you don't want me to see your face suggests a rap sheet, maybe an outstanding warrant for arrest. Your identity is being significantly whittled down the longer we talk. You sure you want to carry on this conversation?'

Christ, he's good. He's even more than I hoped he would be.

'I have inner-sanctum access to a group I think you have an interest in. The berg.'

The bathroom seems to chill. I press the point home.

'In fact, I'm meeting them for a drink after I leave this bathroom. I'm taking them down. If you want them gone, help me succeed. If you are my help from the outside, I'll give you everything you need to expose their whole operation. I assume you are still in the police force?'

'No.'

'Oh,' I say. *Shit.*

'I am an officer of the Organised Crime Command, within the National Crime Agency. We are a fairly new unit. We provide intel to the police in the fight against organised crime operations.'

What a result – he's more perfectly placed than I could have hoped.

'You will be the NCA's golden boy,' I say.

'I don't give a shit about being anybody's golden boy, mate. If you are saying the berg can be taken out, then indeed you have me interested. But I need assurances at my end.'

'Of course.'

'I need to know who you are.'

'I can't give you that. My success depends on my anonymity.'

'You expect me to go along with that? This isn't the first time someone has offered me mutton dressed as lamb.'

'I want to prove both my loyalty and that what I say is true. And then if you feel you can help me, let's take these fuckers down.'

I let that sit a moment.

'The berg,' he says, his voice distant and detached, 'made me watch the changing of the doors.'

'What is that?'

'It's an unwritten rule between police and criminal gangs, in a given city.

The police witness a symbolic act that illustrates a transference of power from one group to another. The power, in this case, was the turf rights to sell drugs in certain pubs and clubs across the centre of Manchester. The berg took me, a young copper, and this dealer from a rival drug-running gang, and beat him half to death in front of me, to show me that they now had "the doors". Problem was, I protested. I kicked and screamed, I even tried, foolishly, to arrest them all. Being young and new to the beat, I didn't know that I was actually supposed to witness it – I didn't understand the significance of the message. It's a practice that has been going on between criminals and coppers in this city for years. It makes sure both parties know where they stand.'

'I know what happened next, you don't have to tell me. I read about it in the *Manchester Evening News*.'

'It didn't mention that Michael Davison put a brick in a pillowcase and beat me with it, did it?'

I'm sickened. Michael Davison, the father of those two fun-loving kids, and the husband of that beautiful woman, is a man of secret and bloody premeditated violence.

'No, it didn't.'

'That was around the time of the Commonwealth Games in 2002. All the crime statistics were buried so that the city would seem nice – respectable. Approachable. Manchester refused to wake up to the horrors of what was really going on, and it's still happening now. The men in charge would rather pretend, or they don't have the political will to face the truth.'

It's a sad but common story. The berg changed this man's life forever, twisted it out of shape, just because they wanted to sell drugs in a particular bar. And I'm going for a drink with them shortly.

'Then work with me, Jeremiah. I know the central NCA offices, in Birchwood, about thirty minutes from here. I'll have something for you tomorrow. A package. It will be irrefutable proof that I am what I say I am. Open it alone. I really hope you'll get on board, Jeremiah. Now listen…'

When I've finished, Jeremiah says nothing, but nods, and I know I've got his confidence. It's too bad I've had to remind him of things he might prefer to forget, but it's the only way.

Time to go for a pint.

21

The Lexus is purring. Rain has just started to spit from mucky clouds high above, and the wipers have come on automatically. I like this car, its luxury is a welcome, if momentary, distraction.

I make the journey back into Manchester on the M62, which is nothing more than a stop-start crawl. Over to my right, I can see Manchester's skyline, winking and twinkling.

Manchester is a proud, progressive city, less susceptible to the navel-gazing of other elite cities. Things get done with less self-importance; it's what attracts big business, and it must be what also attracts illegal business. Come to think of it, I often feel there isn't a great deal of difference between big business and illegal business. They both swim the same way, in the same direction, just with different preoccupations. Both seek financial reward, the universal bottom line.

As I move slowly along the ring road, I remember that it was probably around here where Jack ran that thief off the road, and everything changed. There had been a metaphorical fork in the road, with two destinies splitting off for him to choose. In so many ways, he chose poorly. His future was augmented, his character altered in a fundamental fashion. A boy no more. A moment in which a certain kind of manhood was sealed.

I know those moments well. I have stood by many boys as they turned into men, fire and brimstone whipping over their heads, forcing life-defining reaction and decision. I have presided over many of these transformations, like an observer at an exorcism, only in those instances, it was the evil coming in, not going out. You can't take back what happens in these moments, no matter what. And Jack is not unlike these boys.

The big difference is, the squaddies picked their scenario, their path. Jack was born into it, very literally. Born right into the hands of organised crime.

I turn off the motorway and feed down through Stretford, near Old Trafford again, which now looks even more imposing under the night sky: a red neon coliseum, albeit smudged by drizzle. I hang a left as I pass, and swing down towards the Quays. There are three high residential towers that look like the sails of a gigantic metal and glass yacht, and I keep them in my eyeline as a point of reference. I know roughly where Lumen is. I'll figure out parking as I get there.

As soon as I think about it, a square blue road sign emblazoned with a capital 'P' presents itself, below an arrow pointing left. I take it, and swing down along the waterfront.

I would imagine that for the twenty to thirty days a year, maximum, when Manchester actually has good weather, this would be a lovely place to hang out, socialise, spend time. A little taste of a more luxurious, continental, marina lifestyle. Like a really, *really* shit Monte Carlo. I see the lumbering hulk of The Lowry, squatting like a metal-clad beetle by the shore. I remember when it was first built, it seemed so ahead of its time that it caused offence, Manchester's residents clamouring for a more conservative continuity to the architecture of their centrepieces. And then, when planning permission was granted, more and more similar, forward-thinking buildings were built in the city, not to mention my old pal, Beetham Tower.

I am directed to the arse-end of the beetle where there is an opening for cars. Within a couple of minutes I am parked up and marching to the entrance of a fancy waterfront bar. Lumen. As in lights. As in illuminate. I hope to be both illuminated and enlightened in the course of the evening.

I can do this.

I am sucked through glass revolving doors, from a cold, neon night straight into a warmer, moodier one. The place is softly lit, warmly arranged and pretty empty. Piano music tinkles from somewhere within, providing a ghostly, intimate soundtrack. A huge glass bar rests at the back, with tables and low candelabras in front. Booths line the sides, each with their own locked fridges. Stylistically the bar resembles an antique shop in Valhalla,

141

with its concoction of fur, wood, and vintage. Is this cool? Christ knows.

The patrons look relaxed, their Saturday night just beginning. Perhaps some are pre-show at the theatre opposite or perhaps enjoying the fourth or fifth drink of a post-matinee sup. That beer I've been fantasising about looks ever closer. I don't want to dull my senses, but one can't harm.

Then: 'Ben!' I hear a shout over the rolling ivories.

I turn to the direction of the voice, and see that one of the booths has a couple of inhabitants I missed, buried at the back. Dolled up, one for glamour, the other for sophistication, are the two women I met earlier in the day. Tina and Carolyn. I head over to them, feeling a little prod of nerves. Have I missed the company of the opposite sex that much? I think the answer is *yes*, if these butterflies are anything to go by.

I'm nervous around women, anyway. Save for that period that got me in a proper bind, I always have been. I had a period of confidence, right at the start of my army training, when I was being groomed and readied to be all that I could be, and I certainly felt like it.

The last time I was in a bar, chatting with the opposite sex, was a decade ago, over on Canal Street. It has literally been more than ten years since I've been with a woman in any sort of romantic or sexual sense. I swore off them after the whole near-fatherhood thing, burying my head in the sand, dousing any romantic desires with unwavering duty.

And here, ready to join them at their table, in this sensually lit bar, I can't believe what I have been missing.

'You want a glass of champagne?' Tina asks me as I slide into the booth, opposite them.

'Thank you, if you don't mind, that would be great,' I reply.

'Of course,' says Tina. 'The guys are on their way over. We thought we'd come and get a head start.'

'And why not?' I say, as a bottle of bubbly and a fresh flute is taken from the lockbox. 'This place is smart.'

'Of course. It belongs to Felix.'

The fizz is passed over to me. I should have guessed that Felix would own something like this; if protection is a primary concern, you can't have a pint just anywhere.

'Cheers. It's surprising what a quiet afternoon can do for you. I feel like a new man.'

'Well, the guys are all very impressed with you,' Tina says, replacing the bottle. 'They've been talking about it most of the day.'

I catch Carolyn give Tina a sideways glance, as if to suggest that perhaps she shouldn't be talking about this with me.

'I'm afraid Jack won't be joining us this evening,' I say. 'It's been just a… a hell of a few days for him. I've told him to get some sleep and take it easy.'

'That's probably a good idea,' Tina says.

Tina is very confident, very assured. She wears glittering silver eye make-up that looks like crushed gems placed carefully along the lateral angles of her eyes, giving her face the look of some kind of exotic, historical princess. However, her long, flowing, purple dress negates that impression, and the look ends up more Ibiza nightclub than ancient Egypt.

In contrast, Carolyn wears a black turtleneck jumper and thick, dark eye make-up, an altogether more subtle ensemble. She looks at me as if she still doesn't know what to make of me.

I remember what Jeremiah said her husband Michael did to him. She looks so much younger than Michael, maybe as much as ten to fifteen years. She is far quieter in character than Tina, and if her reaction to what I said earlier is anything to go by, easily the more sensitive of the two. She seems a little nervous, more than a touch agitated. Perhaps, like Zoe, these two know something I would find of critical value. Best keep them talking.

'Besides, we might as well enjoy our night out while the kids are being looked after, right?' Tina says. Carolyn smiles quietly, as if well-practised in the art of putting up with Tina's brassier moments. It's easy to see that they are not the most conventional of friends. In fact, they seem to be polar opposites, and it is very much like they have been thrust together by this situation, and expected to get along – the difference being that Tina appears genuinely to love it, while Carolyn is a bit more put-upon.

If that's the case, it must have been something juicy. Let's see if I can wangle it out of them, but before I can, with the suddenness of teleportation, Leonard appears at the end of the table. He is dressed snazzily, with a white blazer and pink shirt more fitting to a Wham music video than a night out in Salford. That pencil moustache gives me the creeps, wriggling and cavorting while he talks, and his eyes fix me with unnerving intensity.

'Ladies and Mr Mystery, nice to see you all!' he says. 'Does the lockbox have enough in it, because I feel the call of the bar!'

We say hello, and Tina checks the fridge. Leonard does a quick sweep of the bar, his eyes roving.

'No Jack?' he asks me. On closer inspection, his eyes are pinpricks. He is high as a bloody kite.

'No, I'm afraid not. Getting a well-deserved early night,' I reply.

Leonard seems thoughtful at that, his dancing eyes glazing a touch. 'A shame,' he says.

They are strange men, this group. Fettered by secrets and shrouded in mystery, despite my earlier open conversations with them, and what I have gleaned from my other sources. I don't know where I stand, despite the pleasantness. All I know is, I am alert for any eventuality, and I must stay that way.

'It depends what you are up for tonight, Len,' Tina says. 'We've got enough for a couple of rounds of champers, but after that we are down to bits and bobs of vodka and mixers.'

'Well, that will simply not do,' says Leonard, putting his hands on his hips theatrically. 'We must show our new friend the utmost hospitality, in all its possible manifestations.' His mannerisms are pretty weird, and he seems to have taken on the guise of a jaunty character from *Mary Poppins*, albeit one jacked to the bollocks on class As.

Behind Leonard, a shadow looms, approaching our booth: Samson, Michael, and Felix. The two younger men flank Felix, guiding the elderly man to the table. Seeing Michael makes my spine itch, after what Jeremiah told me.

'Sorry, everyone,' says Felix, walking slowly. 'I'll get there in the end. Seems to take me longer to get back here every time we come!'

'Felix, what can I get you?' Leonard asks, his tone settling into a more respectful lilt.

Felix sits slowly on the same bench as me, and slides down next to me. I'll be between the wall and a mob boss – not completely dissimilar to a rock and a hard place. Bad start, Ben.

'I'll have a mineral water, please, Leonard, with a small vodka cranberry to wash it down,' he says.

Satisfied, Felix sighs. In the dim light, he looks very old, his face a mask of soft crags and wrinkles. He catches my eye and smiles.

'Good evening, Ben. Thank you for coming,' he says. He extends a hand outwards to the women opposite. 'And ladies, you both look beautiful.'

The women smile, and Tina even blows a kiss. Carolyn's pursed smile still carries that worry, that preoccupation. Felix catches it.

'The children, Carolyn? I know what you are like,' he enquires.

'You know I can never fully switch off when I'm not with the kids,' she says.

I'm intrigued by her. The doting mother. The gangster's mol. The classic beauty. So many clichés, yet none seem to fit.

'They will be fine – good stock,' says Felix. He smiles warmly, and she thaws a little.

'That solid Swedish stock?' she says.

'Exactly,' he replies, before pulling a blue medical inhaler from his jacket pocket, taking a lungful, then settling.

Samson takes a place next to Tina, pecking her on the cheek as he does so, and Michael sits next to his father, who turns to face me, his body language secretive. His voice lowers, and he speaks to me with as much privacy as one could get in a booth with six people.

'Young Jack… He is not here, is he?' says Felix.

'I'm afraid not,' I reply. 'He sends his apologies.' Not true.

'Such a difficult time for the boy. I feel so deeply for him, but I can't reach him. He shuns me, he shuns us, and I can understand why. But it cannot stop me caring for him. His father was so important to us all, and we feel indebted to Royston to keep an eye on his son, if his son will let us.'

'How honest would you like me to be here, Felix?' I ask.

'Very,' Felix replies.

'Jack and I are both concerned about Sparkles. About no body being found… and another suspect has come to light.'

Felix listens intently. His eyes meet mine.

'Who?' he says, with a touch more firmness than before.

'A man named Nigel has turned up, and he's definitely a suspect. I'm going to look into it.'

Felix looks away. He may be wondering if his own information hasn't been deemed reliable.

'I think the question is,' I continue, 'how confident are you that Sparkles did it?'

Felix leans back. When he replies, it's to evade the question.

'I wish you could have met Jack's father. He was a very loyal, kind man, despite what people think about what we do. Violence was not something he was interested in, and neither was making enemies. Sparkles took very unkindly to something that Royston said, and believed that his honour had been provoked. A provocation of honour is a cross-cultural danger, because gestures can mean something different between societies, you understand?'

'I do,' I reply.

'I think Royston might actually have unwittingly offended Sparkles, in this sort of misunderstanding, and it got out of hand. Sparkles made a death threat to Royston, and that's the only time I have ever heard of that happening where Royston was concerned. He didn't look for trouble; that's why I am sure it was Sparkles. I dealt with Sparkles' uncle prior to dealing with his nephew. He was an unpredictable so-and-so as well, with a very short temper. I have seen little difference in dealing with Sparkles.'

That seems to make sense. He was certainly very quick on the draw last night, and had his team well-drilled in enacting a prompt lethal defence of his floating fortress.

'So this other lead, Nigel. You don't think it's worth following up?' I ask.

Felix mulls it over.

'It's not that, Ben. I think you're astute enough to handle yourself, and smart enough to make your own judgements. But… I've never heard of a Nigel, least of all one that had a problem with Royston.

'Further to that – how do I put this… I do know we are an entity of considerable scale, commanding citywide respect – there are only a few people who would dare murder Royston, and most of them are no longer with us.'

Felix is like an old man talking about his World War II experiences, rather than inter-criminal politics and conflict. Perhaps that is what happened: while most men of his era were fighting abroad, like I did, he was waging a defence at home of his illicit business. It's a rare admission of the violent side to his activities. He carries on:

'One of those people I considered capable of such an act was Sparkles Chu, and more than that, he actually threatened it. He said he would kill him if he ever saw him at that place again. Royston went back, and was next seen murdered. It makes a lot of sense to me. If I was a betting man, I'd be stacking my chips against his name.'

'When you put it like that, it seems the most logical explanation,' I reply.

'For Jack's peace of mind, however, it might be right to follow this Nigel figure up. But I honestly believe Sparkles did it. They even tried to take out his son, for Christ's sake.'

He makes good sense. If it weren't for the strange text-message conversation earlier with Nigel, I'd shut this investigation down right here and now.

The drinks arrive. Leonard pulls up a chair to head the table, and takes off his jacket, folding it neatly over the chair back, straightening the cuffs and wiping away specks of lint. The curious obsessive-compulsive aspect of this guy, which, twinned with the seemingly bottomless battery of his energy, gives his personality an almost pathological slant. And his appearance only accentuates my overall impression. He carries himself like a fully fledged nut job, and this man, especially, is beginning to make me feel uneasy.

Suddenly, Michael speaks, raising a pint of ale.

'To our dear mate Royston, and his son, Jack. We miss you, pal,' he says. His eyes are lowered but fixed. He doesn't seem like a man dominated by emotion; there's an economy to him, a well-managed control. Which makes his reported actions all the more unnerving.

Everyone drinks, and I finally get to the fizz I was offered earlier. The champagne is sharp, sweet yet dry, and it feels like an electrical charge has been set off in my mouth.

'And one quick one to Ben,' he says, gesturing his glass to me. 'For looking after Jack and for settling the score.'

Drinks are drunk again. I don't know whether to smile, drink, protest – not a clue. I find myself nodding at Michael, who nods back.

'Ben, I've made some inroads into that thing you were after before,' Michael says.

'Really? How's it looking?' I ask.

'It won't be a problem. My guy just needs a name, a photo, and he'll do the rest. What do you fancy calling yourself?'

'Sean,' I say. 'Sean Miller. I've no idea why, but I've already started getting used to it.'

I can feel myself dangerously brushing that fine line between playing my cards close to my chest and over-sharing. That's the name I'm checked in under at my hotel.

'Ok then, I'll let him know. Should be ready tomorrow. Face me,' says Michael, holding up a camera phone. I sit up straight. The flash goes, and he pockets the camera, his precision of movement evident even in such a simple, mundane action.

'Blimey, that's fast. How best to settle the balance with your guy?' I ask.

Felix pipes up between us. 'I'm taking care of it, Ben. As a thank you.'

Gaining a totally new identity lifts a big weight off, but… favours last night, this morning, this afternoon, and now…

'What are you going to do with your new identity, Ben?' Felix asks. 'What future plans do you have?'

What a question – one never asked of me, by so many people who should have done so. The mother of my unborn child didn't. My army superiors didn't. My parents didn't. How best to answer…

It hurts, but the question echoes in my head: *What do you want, Ben?*

'I… don't really know,' I say. 'Whatever it is, I want to start afresh. Put my skills to use in whatever way I can. I've long since given up thinking I can serve my country, so a blank page is what I'm after.'

'Here? Abroad?' Felix continues. He sips his cranberry through a short thin straw.

'Doesn't really matter,' I reply. 'As long as it's different.'

'Would you consider staying in this city if there was work for you here?'

Hang on a minute.

'I haven't thought about it,' I reply. I suddenly feel very trapped in this little booth.

He stirs his drink with the straw, and I understand what he's about to say. 'Think about it. You need a fresh start with a new identity. I could do with another man close to me, to add to this inner circle. You can handle yourself, you are a man of honour, you are a gentleman. In my eyes, you are the ideal candidate to fill the hole we find ourselves with.'

I wonder whether Jack heard a variation on this speech. For crying out loud – I came out to crush people like this and all I've managed to do so far is convince them to try to hire me.

'We discussed it today, after you left,' Felix continues. 'We are most impressed with the way you handled yourself last night, the way you cared for Jack, and the respectful way you carry yourself. I am on the lookout for one last *väktare*. That's the way this business works, and that's the way I intend it to continue.'

This is the first full glimpse I have had of the man behind the myth, of the serpentine game-player that dwells inside the body of a quiet, well-spoken old grandad. You don't get to the top of any trees without having a cut-throat competitive streak. His career must have been built on opportunism, seizing moments, taking chances, and making the most of unexpected circumstances. And here he is, doing just that. For the time being, I decide to play along.

'I'm flattered. Very,' I reply. 'I wasn't expecting that.'

'Would you, at least, just take the time to think about it?'

I remember Jeremiah, and what he needs to trust me. 'Tell me,' I say, shifting my position, 'for argument's sake, what the position entails. All the details.'

Silence. Felix looks at me, and gives a smile so gentle I barely notice it. I think he enjoys my caution. It seems to prove he was right to approach me.

'I'll take this,' says Michael. 'We're in charge of the main operations of the business, top to bottom, but strictly in a management sense. Final say on everything is Dad's. As you know, the business is already up and running – the infrastructure is already there. Our days are usually about delegation and problem-solving.'

'Can you give me an example?' I ask. I really want to hear something incriminating.

'A simple example would be this. You won't find us on the street pushing the dope, but if we lose a pusher we've got to find a replacement.'

'Is that an area of the business I would be expected to operate in?'

'As *väktaren* we cover all areas of the business, so that would be the arms dealing, the heroin, and of course the meth. Felix likes to handle his fishy side-project on his own. Frankly, I wouldn't know where to start on that score.'

'I have my sources,' Felix says, winking.

'Where do you distribute and what is it you distribute in those areas?' I ask.

The more information I can provide Jeremiah with, the better. The men are looking at each other, while the girls are riveted; it seems we are having a conversation that they have never been privy to.

'You want a PowerPoint presentation?' Michael asks sharply. It takes me aback but I try not to show it. It's the first suggestion of any menace I've had from any of them.

'Look, in order to make an informed decision, I'd like to know. We can speak on this more privately, if you'd like?'

Felix sets his jaw and merely nods, signalling Michael to continue. Michael gives a quick glance around for any listening parties, before speaking again.

'Everything is based on respect.'

Still extremely vague.

'So which territories do the berg operate in?' I ask. I want to force that issue, and skin this beast.

'Can I?' interjects Samson, leaning in enough so that his ample forearms actually dim the brightness of the booth.

'Go for it,' replies Michael, relaxing a little. They have gone all in here, showing their hand, and Michael especially seems to know it.

Samson proceeds to give me a rundown of UK locations in which their narcotics trade operates, the precise details of which will be of huge interest to Jeremiah – but I'm fixated on the size suggested here. Their influence, clearly, is *nationwide*.

He then goes on to summarise their strong history of arms dealing, how they had three quarters of the country in their pocket at one time – and how, after a recent blip, things seem to be on the up again. He leaks a wry smile, which seems contagious – Leonard sports it too.

I don't know what that means, but I need to keep them talking.

'You're sure?'

'I would say that the change is definite,' says Samson.

Is this all genuine? Would they give all this up so easily, just to recruit me? I have a nagging doubt that screams 'smokescreen', but the more questions I ask, and the more seriously I take this conversation, the more revelatory the answers are becoming. I press on with playing the role of careful investor.

'Any guarantees of that?' I ask. That seems to impress Felix who almost giggles to himself.

'Wise sailors never want to join sinking ships,' laughs Felix, smiling broadly. The other men echo his amusement. I'm detecting a smugness that I was unsure existed, a self-confidence that I was waiting to experience for myself. It's here all right. It just took the right environment for it to present itself. I suppose all parents are proud of their babies, and the baby in question here is a criminal empire.

'It's for definite, sure,' says Leonard, through his grin. 'Nothing to worry about there.'

'And on the front of the Siamese fighting fish…' Samson continues, 'Felix has all of Europe in his pocket.'

'You… make a compelling case,' I say.

I need to buy some time. My intention to take them down is stronger than ever. But not yet. I need to squeeze more juice out of this one first, and learn all I can about other people of interest, not least of all the true identity of Royston's killer. But if I say yes, they might take me out into the city right now and order me to do something compromising. I don't want that. On the other hand, if I say no, they might decide I know too much, and find a quiet hillside upon which to silence me for good.

'I'm very, very flattered,' I begin, 'and I'm going to take your offer very seriously.'

'But…' Leonard says.

'No buts. I would like to sleep on it. Is that a possibility?'

No answer there, and it seems like I have liberally pissed all over their parade. I get the feeling they don't hear the word *no* very often.

'Look, I found myself helping Jack as an old friend who was in need of some assistance, but now, I… I don't want any loose ends before I start the next thing. When I work out my next move, I want to commit to it.'

What a stack of vague bullshit. Why didn't I pick a seat at the end of the table? I bet this was the plan all along, to corner me like this.

I must remember that if I'm to get out of this situation alive, I need to be single-minded, cool, unbending, and without hesitation. I put my champagne down, supposing that that's a start.

'I am very flattered, and I can almost certainly say that my answer will be yes. But my father always taught me to sleep on big decisions before I make them, even if my heart is set on it and there is no chance of it changing. Felix, will you let me have tonight, in good faith?'

'Of course. Your clear-headedness and calmness is something I admire, and one of the many reasons I open the door to you in this way.'

I see an opening for an exit, and take it.

'Thank you, very much indeed. For the offer and the time to consider it,' I say, beginning to get to my feet. 'I would like to buy everyone here a drink, as a small token of my own thanks – no arguments.'

If in doubt, ply with booze. Nobody can turn down a free drink. Everyone smiles, even Michael shows a cheerful face, and he and Felix move aside so I can slide out of the booth. This has bought me some time, but I don't know how much.

'May I come to the house tomorrow, to see you?' I whisper to Felix as I go past him.

I knew Felix would like that: that I seemingly have such respect for him already that I would seek a more private audience with him. The man enjoys the more archaic ways of doing business, and if I can keep playing to that, I can keep everything floating along for a bit longer.

'Of course. Let's aim for around lunchtime,' he says, patting me on the arm.

'Thank you,' I reply, 'and thanks again.' To the rest, I say, 'I'm a bit lost for words. Is it the same again for everybody?' My question is greeted with affirmatives.

I head for the bar, and take a deep breath, the oxygen reinvigorating me like smelling salts.

I arrive at the bar, and the barman approaches.

'Same again,' I say.

'No problem,' he says.

As I stand and wait, I consider the gold mine of information I just have heard – intel that could turn to evidence. Evidence that could turn into prosecutions.

And I hope in the name of everything holy that the microphone in my inner jacket pocket has picked it all up.

The small flash memory dictaphone feels ok in my underwear and the wire seems intact. I ratcheted up the sensitivity of the mic as far as I could take it, so there may be a fair amount of static and rustle, but that should be fine to get a decent enough recording.

It's amazing what a trip to Argos will get you. I have tried this one once before, when I tried to rumble Terry Masters. He spotted it a mile off, and made me pay for it, big time. This time, I thought it would be worth another shot, considering I'm already kind of classed as an insider. I'll send the whole lot to Jeremiah Salix, first thing in the morning, with a note detailing how to reach me.

My senses tingle, and I feel an approach from directly behind me.

'That's quite the offer, isn't it?' I glance over to see Carolyn joining me at the bar. Instinctively, I glance back to the booth, but everyone is engrossed in conversation. I turn back to her. The apprehension is still there on her face.

'I seem to have done something he approves of,' I reply.

I am suspicious of her, as I am suspicious of all of them. But there is something about her that I can't pinpoint, a side that seems half buried. She must have seen some things, as Michael Davison's wife. I wonder what she used to be like, in the days before all this. Before Felix came along with all his trappings.

'You are certainly the flavour of the month,' she says. 'Keep it up, golden boy.'

Her words could be flirtatious, but her body language is stiff. She turns to go, and trips, losing her heel in the process. I reach out to steady her, briefly amused that she is tipsy. She reaches for my outstretched hand, and bends to put her shoe back on.

'Whoops! The bubbles, you… know how it gets…' she says.

I feel it immediately: in my hand, between mine and hers. It is revealed by a tickle on my palm. A sliver of paper, or something similar.

'No, of course, it's ok,' I say, supporting her, playing along. She straightens up, and makes her way back to the table, suddenly surefooted.

I turn back to the bar, as my heart thumps in my chest. The drinks have started to arrive and I take my wallet out of my pocket, open it, and drop a ripped-off corner of paper towel in alongside the notes. As I take out a sheaf of twenties, just before I close it, I read what's written on the tissue, scrawled hastily in biro:

'Please help me
07772 389082'

22

I don't sleep. Not a wink, all night. So much to do.

It's 6:30 a.m., and I am sitting in the Lexus at an unassuming office complex in Birchwood, watching a low mist rise spectrally off a pond in front of the glass front door. Birchwood itself, on driving in, seems to be nothing more than a few blocks of houses interconnected by a series of roundabouts, all of which are completely dominated by the huge office centres that line the circular ring roads.

I'm waiting for the arrival of… anybody, I suppose. I have placed a brown manila envelope by the front door, labelled '*F.A.O. Officer Jeremiah Salix*', for whoever next arrives to take in. It will probably go through the usual checks that packages at all governmental buildings go through, but it will pass with flying colours. Unlike myself: were I to appear at the offices of a UK-based central intelligence network, the digital flags would certainly start waving.

I should feel tired from lack of sleep, but I'm too wired by the crackling charge of the impending storm. Today is make or break, and I don't want to mess nor miss anything.

Earlier, at 5:30, I had gone to the rented storage lock-up in Bury that Freckles told me about after I left the bar last night. He said my bag would be there, and someone would be there to let me in. Sure enough, his wife, Stacey, was there, looking harassed and weary. She had been living amongst old furniture in a fifty-square-foot box of concrete and corrugated iron, in hiding until the danger to her and Freckles had passed. I took the bag, thanked her, and promised her that I'd get the money to her when I had a new identity cleared. Hopefully now she is on her way home to Freckles, while the insurance policy sits happily in the boot of the Lexus – and I work out what to do with it.

With that taken care of, I need to make sure the package gets inside. Next, I'll head over to Jack's to discuss the night before, and Felix's offer. Then, it's Piccadilly Gardens to catch up with this Nigel guy. If he's the killer – and I will definitely get it out of him – I'll take him to Jack. Then Jack can decide what to do.

From there, it's Zoe. Jack won't like it, but I need to know what the deal is with her, and I need her to empty her brain into something I can use for Jeremiah. By which point, if all goes as I think it will, he will have worked out whether I am genuine or not.

And then, of course, there is the tricky issue of Carolyn Davison. No amount of lying awake could help me sort that one out. Her note could be so many things and I mull them over as I sit and watch the package on the office doorstep.

It could be a ploy – a scheme to test my honesty and integrity. If I come to her all guns of chivalry blazing, they could tear me limb from limb for being swayed by fluttering eyelashes, and worse, *one of their wives*.

If it's not a ploy, and this woman genuinely needs my help, then that is just as dangerous. If I help her, and get caught doing so, I'm a traitor to the team before I even joined it. Retribution is sure to follow.

But what if she really needs my help? What kind of man would I be if I let her down?

Selfishly… she may know something. Something valuable and incriminating. She might know more than Zoe.

Jesus, it's complicated. And everything is coming to a head. The berg are waiting for an answer from me and the whole situation is fast approaching boiling point.

A security guard slowly opens the front door to the office complex; an overnight shift is just coming to an end. He has an unlit cigarette hanging out of his mouth like a cancerous stalactite. As the door opens, in flops the package at his feet. He takes it, shakes it, eyes it, then takes it inside.

I start the car, knowing that this day of days is properly underway. No turning back now.

The drive to Worsley is short, with the roads lightly frosted and empty. I listen to the radio for as long as I can stand it. After a lengthy discussion about various celebrities' Twitter feeds and their relative merits, followed by a summary of what happened on last night's episode of *Celebrity Love Triangle*, I turn it off. The cult of celebrity is somewhat new to me. Since when did everybody get to be so famous for doing so little?

I arrive in the cul-de-sac where the Brookers' house is, and crawl to the end. It is quiet, and I remember it's a Sunday morning. I park up and knock on.

Getting no answer, I knock louder. Still nothing. I head around the back, wondering if Jack's on another gin and juice breakfast. The back porch is empty. I peek through the kitchen windows. No lights on, nothing looking amiss. The fridge is back in place, in fact everything is as it should be.

The house is lifeless. I know I didn't tell him to stay put or anything, but I thought that his doing so would be fairly logical. I hope he's not got himself into trouble.

I begin worrying about Sparkles – about where he might be, and in turn, where Jack might be. I need some answers fast.

*

I'm arrowing into the city centre, and on the pavement as I come in I see a grimy old BT payphone and pull over. With my phone number saved, Jeremiah could get a fix on me in an instant if he chose to, with all that NCA tech at his disposal; no, a quick payphone call will be the safest way to reach him. The line is picked up almost immediately.

'Central switchboard,' a voice says.

'Jeremiah Salix, please.'

'Who shall I say is calling?'

'Royal Mail.'

'One moment,' comes the response. If in doubt, pretend you know what you are doing. It only takes a second for Salix to pick up.

'Ok, you have my attention,' he says.

'I'm very glad to hear it.'

'You just gave me more information than this department has been able to collect in an embarrassing amount of time. Our voice recognition guys are working on a copy of the recording now, but I know they have already confirmed Leonard and Michael.'

'The others will all check out, too. They were all there.'

'If it comes to a trial, will you testify? We can grant you anonymity and I can look into immediate witness protection.'

'I'm afraid I can't accept that.' Jeremiah seems surprised.

'These men are as dangerous as dangerous gets,' he says. 'I don't know how far back your dealings go with them, but it seems from the recording that it isn't that far. Look, regardless of what you have done, in exchange for testimony that could put these career criminals away for good, any past misdemeanours can be erased, within reason, or at least looked extremely favourably upon.'

If only he knew the extent of my past misdemeanours, he might feel a little different about such a generous offer.

'I'm afraid that won't work. I will give you them on a plate, but I need to be left out of it. I'm afraid if there is to be an agreement between us, Jeremiah, those are my terms.'

There is a silence on the line.

'Considering the value of the information you have just given us, I will accept that. You mentioned that this situation is to be mutually beneficial. What is it you are after from me?'

'I want to ask you some questions, and I'd like you to tell me what the NCA knows.'

Jeremiah is quiet again. Then: 'Ok, fire away,' he says.

'I'll set the scene. The fire at the Floating Far East, two nights ago. That was my doing.'

'Jesus,' he says.

'I was trying to establish who killed Royston Brooker, and I was led to believe it was Sparkles Chu. I challenged him on this, and he denied it. The situation got out of hand. I don't know whether he survived it.'

'He did.'

'You're sure?'

'Absolutely. As a person of extreme interest we monitor his movements. Facial recognition picked him up at Victoria Station. He didn't get on a train or anything, he was just moseying through. The vehicles we have him associated with haven't moved, either. The department believes he's still in the city, even though he hasn't come forward in association to the fire. Me? He's still here. Stubborn bugger like that's not leaving.'

Sparkles – still here. Brooding, dangerously, in a corner somewhere, no doubt. Licking his wounds.

'Do you think he did it? Killed Royston Brooker, I mean?' I ask.

'He's a candidate for sure.'

'What can you tell me about Royston's death?'

'Body found by a security guard at Manchester Airport – he called the police, the police called us. He was tied to a chair, single bullet wound to the chest. Still in his pyjamas, looked dragged out of bed. It was a strange one, but a lot of hallmarks of a mob killing. The chair suggested an interrogation, but there were no visible signs of struggle at all. The interrogation was verbal, we assume, and it looks like he didn't resist. Either he's a serious pacifist, or he knew his attacker, and didn't see it coming. I would say, knowing the type of people he did business with, that we are talking about the latter.'

'Was he tied up after the shooting, to throw an investigation off the scent?'

'It's a possibility, but the coroner didn't specify.'

'I have a contact I'm on my way to see. He spoke with Royston Brooker the night he died. They were friends, it seems, and I'd say, given what you have just told me, he's getting more important all the time. I'll let you know what happens.'

'I'd appreciate that. This is where I tell you not to do anything stupid, I think.'

'Then this is where I tell you to try to forget about it.'

'How bloody lovely.' Jeremiah's sarcasm couldn't be more obvious.

'In terms of the berg, I've got another avenue of enquiry that looks very promising. We are talking a shitload of evidence with this one. But we need a mode of contact – I can't keep pulling over to hit payphones, they are a dying breed.'

'Fair enough, if it applies both ways. I may need to grab you. But, before we go any further, I have a problem. I need to acknowledge your existence in a formal sense, or any of what you bring me is, however explosive, completely inadmissible. Information that could lead to extensive prison terms doesn't just drop out of the sky.'

'What are you thinking? My anonymity is crucial.'

'I'm thinking that a formal acknowledgement of yourself as an informant would do it but I need your consent to that. If I take what you sent to me to my superiors, and have it authenticated by another gesture of faith so that it's clear your first delivery wasn't a fluke, and my department knows about you, then what you've given me can be used to take these people down.'

I was always expecting something like this, and have had to reluctantly make my peace with it. I could just seek to deliver my justice my way and nothing else, but I know that, in the grand scheme of things, that is not enough by itself. I can't do everything. I don't have the manpower to tie up loose ends. I don't trust the police and the authorities, but I have a growing trust in Jeremiah, and if I can give him the foolproof evidence to take this villainy down, that will go a long way to having a real, lasting effect. Much more than I can do on my own.

'I can agree to this only if this is kept on an absolute need-to-know basis. That's you, and whatever superiors necessary, but no others. If you need to include court injunctions to make that happen, do so. My identity is never to be revealed. If that does not materialise, you will never hear from me again, and all the material I have to offer will go with me.'

'I'll see what I can do. You drive a hard bargain.'

'Get started on it. Tell your superiors that more is coming later today. That can be the leverage you require to prove I'm genuine. Then we can stop pissing about on admin and really get started.'

23

I see him.

He is sitting on one of the concrete benches, sunlight glinting off his hairless scalp. He looks fairly short and squat. His nerves, just judging from his erratic glances and leg-drumming, look to be ratcheted up to a lifetime high. Trying to see Royston coming.

Whatever I think of him, whatever connection he has to my clandestine investigation, he looks no killer. But I know too well that, more often than not, looks tell little.

I get moving from my vantage point a hundred yards away. I was simply leaning against a wall – Nigel doesn't know me, doesn't know I'm coming. He won't be expecting me, as I start walking across the frost-brushed stone square of Piccadilly Gardens, a little flat, concrete pocket that buildings press right up to, but don't infringe upon. There are a few trees, but they are more token gestures than anything. 'Gardens' is a very generous title indeed.

Nigel takes a bite of a doughy pasty – breakfast of champions. On closer inspection, he wears his hair in a ponytail, which droops down his back, fashioned from the scruff that hasn't left him yet. He brings the savoury morsel up to his mouth as I reach him.

'Nigel,' I say. The pasty hangs in mid-air, as his eyes divert to me. If I had any doubt at all that this was him, they are erased immediately by his reaction.

'Before you say anything, know this. There is a .338 calibre Barret M98B bolt-action sniper rifle aimed dead on the bridge of your nose. Don't look for it. If you answer every question I have, plus honesty minus hesitation, I won't have to give the kill signal. Are we on the same page?'

Nigel looks like he may have just filled himself, his eyes widening and the pasty jiggling. He nods slowly.

I take a seat next to him.

'As you've probably worked out, I am not Royston. I'm investigating his death. And you are my prime suspect.'

Nigel suddenly explodes into astonishment.

'*What*? But how could—'

'Answers only, please. Wait for my questions.'

This quiets him, and I see him glance to the rooftops in front of him warily.

'You spoke to Royston the night of his death. Correct?'

Nigel's gaze drifts from the distant heights to me.

'Yes. But—'

'The kill signal is a very simple one and my partner is so accurate you'll be dead before you even know I ordered it. Answer the questions only. That's your last warning.'

Nigel nods and looks at the ground, taking a series of long, forced breaths.

'It was me who texted you from Royston's phone, but you didn't seem pleased to know he was alive. Why is that?'

'He left me high and dry on a business deal. It fucked everything up,' he says, still facing the ground.

'What business deal?'

'I'd found us a good business – legitimate. A pub, in Exeter. We had one shot to go through with it, and he was going to transfer the funds. We were going to be partners, and I put everything on the line. Kitchen sink, lock stock, *everything*. All my savings, I fronted. And he quit on me. He pulled out at the last minute. I lost everything. All the money I put in has gone, turns out I can't get it back at all, and my family is flat fuckin' broke.'

'Why?'

'I dunno. I'm not happy he got shot, for Christ's sake, no, but it doesn't change the fact that he screwed me over royally.'

'Are you fully aware of what doing business with Royston meant? You knew what he was into?'

'Yes, but that wasn't the case here. This was his escape route – he told

162

me! He had been looking at getting out of the game for a while, maybe last year or so. I've never met the people he worked with, but I do know he talked to them about it. They weren't too keen, apparently, but he said they would respect his decision. He wanted to go legit, I'm telling you.'

This is an amazing revelation, if it is true, one that no other party has mentioned – Royston aiming to go straight. The berg certainly never brought it up, which has me concerned.

Nigel continues.

'It was all about his son. He felt the weight of what he was into every time he looked at his kid. Wanted to get out, and start a new, honest life, with his son. I fancied a new start myself, and his money joined with mine was the only way to get that opportunity. That's why we were going to be partners.'

Everything is changing. If Nigel is telling the truth, whatever I thought I knew about this situation needs to be looked at in a new light.

'Royston was a lot of things, but he was just hooked on his kid,' Nigel says. 'He told me that when Jack found out what he was really into, the shame just fuckin' destroyed him. He's been working on getting out ever since. His kid was saving him, even if he didn't know it. His kid was making him go straight.'

I am getting strongly convinced that Nigel is being sincere – and that Jack doesn't know this. In fact I am certain of it. Is this why the berg approached Jack? Because they knew Royston wanted out and they needed a replacement?

The whole story of *The Baby And The Brandy* clicks into stark relevance. Even though he didn't know it at the time, in handing Royston his baby son, Felix was giving him a reason to want out. It only took twenty-four years to kick in.

'Who knew of your exact plans?' I ask.

'Nobody. Just me and him.'

'Where do you fit in?'

'Apart from being jilted at the altar and losing everything? I'm an ex-landlord, I had a couple of pubs in Oldham. I met Royston there when I was behind the bar pulling pints and he was in there trying to get served at seventeen or so.'

163

'So you didn't kill him?'

'No!'

'You were *jilted* by him, you said so yourself. You have an excellent motive. I ask you again, did you kill him?'

'Absolutely not. Whatever you think… Look, yeah, I'm pissed off, but I am not a murderer.'

'Did you instigate his death in any way?'

'We had a nasty phone conversation that, for all the world, God in heaven, I wish I could take back. Like those texts yesterday. But I had nothing, nothing at all, to do with his death. I'm a pub man, and that's it. I'm not one of those people who he ran with, and that's why we got along. He made his choices and lived with them, but by the end, even he was tired of the life he had built for himself.'

I need to know, once and for all, whether it was him. I need that finality, before I take my investigation elsewhere, even if now I'll be damned if he did it.

'Last time, and with feeling,' I say, and raise my right hand out in front of me. I bunch my knuckles into a sideways fist, and stick my thumb out to the side, like Caesar making a life-or-death decision in the Colosseum. 'The simple signal is a thumbs up. My thumb points skyward, your brains exit your head.'

'I told you everything! I didn't do it!' Nigel starts shaking, his breath shredded and rapid.

'Keep still or my partner might miss, and hit something that will really fucking hurt, as opposed to something you won't even know about. It'd be the difference between an instant death, or a very slow, very bloody, very conscious grisly one.'

Nigel almost slips into a trance of panic, and I feel for him, in a way. Either way, for him, it'll be over soon.

'Did you kill him?' I ask, firmly.

'No. No! I swear. I swear on anything you'd ask me to swear on.'

Suddenly he turns and faces me on the bench. His eyes blaze.

'I never killed anyone! I mean it.'

I lower my outstretched arm and release my fist.

164

'I believe you. Thank you, Nigel.'

Nigel coughs, rattling snottily, then composes himself.

'I've been lied to a lot recently,' I say. 'It's only under extreme pressure that you see the truth sometimes. And today, I really needed to see it.'

'Are you with them?' he asks.

'Who?'

'His gang, or whatever the hell they are called. The berg?'

'No. I am not.'

'Thank God. He didn't trust them, is all. He told me, pissed up one night shortly before he died, that he wanted to run away more than ever. That when he told them he wanted out, they didn't take it well. *They take rejection messily*, he said. I think he feared for his life.'

And my jaw hits the floor. He feared for his life *from them*.

Everything I had come to bank on in the last three days falls to pieces.

24

My head is still spinning as I get back to the car, parked in an NCP a short walk from Piccadilly. I take a minute in the cool, echoing emptiness of the multistorey structure, to compose myself and to think.

I'm supposed to be going over there, right now, to tell Felix what I've decided. I need time to think – but not about his offer, because there is nothing to decide. I quickly text him, to say that I have a few loose ends to tie up, and then I'll be over.

The planets are aligning, and they are all suddenly pointing directly at an inside job. Was Royston Brooker killed by his friends, the men he trusted? It seems the strongest possibility now, after what Nigel said, and I need to let Jeremiah know what I have uncovered.

Zoe. I need to speak with her urgently. If this indeed was an inside job, she must know something. She has to – and Jack will know where to find her. But where is he? I take out my phone, and try him at home and on his mobile. No answer on either.

Suddenly, an urgent vibration signals an incoming call. I check the screen. Felix. He's called me back straight away. I have nothing to say to him yet, my brain too fried with what new possibilities are suggesting, to try to speak with him – the man who could be behind all of this.

I pick up, and try my best to sound cheerful.

'Hello?' I say, bright like a radio host.

'Ben, it's Felix,' he says mildly. 'How are you today?'

'I'm good thanks,' I reply.

'I got your message, but I wondered how you got on with this Nigel fellow. Are things any clearer? Is he someone we should look at?'

I'm inspired to take the line of least resistance.

'He's a nobody, Felix. Just confused and scared. Turns out he used to enjoy a pint from time to time with Royston, but nothing else. It was just by chance that he was in touch with Royston the night he was killed.'

The line is silent for a long moment, and I picture Felix weighing up the truthfulness of what I've said. Does he know about Nigel? I'd guess not.

'Ok, then,' he finally says, his tone giving nothing away. 'Nothing to worry about?'

'Not at all.'

Is Felix taking a genuine interest, or is he checking up on the things that could reveal his duplicity?

This can't be coincidence. The facts can't be chance. I don't believe in fate or luck. I believe you make both of those for yourself. I believe that coincidences exist, but there comes a tipping point – a pivot past which the scales are weighted by influence.

The berg's lies and the performances – how Royston's death was destroying them, all that – were impeccable.

'Good,' Felix says, his benign assessment cheerily puncturing my thoughts.

'Yeah,' I say, but I know my voice is cracking. I can barely contain myself. 'I'll be over shortly.'

I hang up before anything else can come out and tip him off that I'm onto him. I can only imagine he didn't like that, but I couldn't give a fuck anymore.

The devil is brooding inside me again, and I feel long, burning fingers of rage ripping deep. My darkness is returning. I'm feverish with hate, and anger, and it is all too reminiscent of an earlier me.

This rage will have to have its day. But not yet. I need to be certain. I need to be sure. But if I'm right, I will tear this fucking city apart to bring them the roughest justice I can deliver.

Manchester is not their playground anymore.

*

I drive erratically, my guts twisted like a badly arranged balloon animal. I need this moment of spinning hatred, because when it passes, focus will replace it. I need to reach that point of composure before I speak to Zoe.

Arriving in her neighbourhood, I realise I haven't a clue which house is hers, and I'm on an estate with sixteen houses arranged along one road, each one with a pleasant view over green pastures, the golf course, and Manchester, looming in the distance.

I cruise the Lexus along slowly, looking for any signs that would give away a double life. It's not as easy as I pictured. Middle-upper-class suburbia must be a petri dish of double lives, a landscape of distrust and competition. That's a pretty cynical thought, but I am suddenly feeling very much in that frame of mind. It'll have to be something pretty obvious to stick out.

And, suddenly, it sure is. By the front door of number twelve, are two bright red wellington boots, drying in the morning sun. I park up and hurry up the driveway, along a dark-blue high-end Mini Cooper, nice, but not too nice... *Nice but not too nice* seems to be these bastards' life motto.

I ring the bell, which chimes merrily somewhere deep inside the house, the first few bars of *Oh, What A Beautiful Morning*. It's about the twee-est thing I've ever heard.

I wait, and Manchester seems to watch me over my shoulder. Then I hear swift feet thumping softly downstairs, and the door is unchained. It swings open, and there is Zoe. Her bob is a little unkempt, her clothes very 'dress-down weekends', but she still carries herself with poise. Her blue eyes sharpen on me.

'Ben...' she says. Her jaw is set defiantly, and she doesn't look all surprised to see me.

'Zoe, can I come in?' I ask. I have no interest in physically harming her, but I have every intention of taking her down with the rest of them. I'm very worried that my element of surprise has been blown. That was an advantage I was carrying, but not anymore. Let's play nice to begin with.

'He's not here,' she says, still standing firm.

'I'm after you, Zoe.'

Zoe looks at me with suspicion. She mentioned Jack straight away; when I first guessed there was a spark of feeling between them, I was right.

'What is it you want?' she asks.

168

'I think you have an idea. I think he might have told you.'

'Who?'

'Jack. Your other half. Are you sure he is not here?'

The door swings open even wider, as if by its own volition, and reveals Jack Brooker, standing there, eyes just as fixed and unfriendly as Zoe's.

'It's ok, Zoe, I've got this,' he says, as he widens the door to allow me inside.

I wish he wasn't here. If he is acting as her protector, and I'm not careful, this could get very ugly.

'Go in the living room. Ben, sit on the sofa in the window,' says Zoe with authority. I don't argue, although the orders rankle, but I understand the desire for the positional upper hand. I have my gun with me, and I assume Jack has his.

I enter the living room: cream carpets and cream-upholstered sofas, a stone fireplace, and not much else. The room is so pristine, it looks like this is the first time it has ever been entered. I find my allocated sofa, and sit. Zoe sits on the sofa opposite me, and Jack mans the door.

'Your interests have always been my top priority here, Jack,' I begin, but he almost snorts at that.

'Yeah, yeah,' he says dismissively.

'It's true,' I say. 'Finding your dad's killer has pretty much consumed me. I've been able to scratch off a couple of suspects already today, and there is no question that we are narrowing it down. But Jack... I need some composure from you, because I don't think you will like what I have to say.'

Jack's face stills like granite.

'Spit it out then,' he says with a low rumble.

Of all the shocks and hurt he has been through, I don't want to suggest even more to him, but if he is going to be present while I get what I need from Zoe, I need him to be on my side, or at the very least, no side at all. I can't have him protecting Zoe.

'This won't be easy for you, but I think your girlfriend has some explaining to do. I need you to stay cool here, Jack. Everything I've discovered points to an in-house job. I think the berg did it themselves, and I think I can prove it.'

Jack looks at Zoe, his jaw hanging limp, and Zoe flushes crimson.

'No, listen,' Zoe blurts, but Jack cuts her off.

'Zoe, what does he mean?'

'Keep cool, Jack, we'll get to the bottom of this,' I say, knowing that it will be no use. I've seen Jack's rage, the fire with which it bares its teeth. It was his fury that started this whole thing.

'I didn't know!' Zoe shouts, tears starting. 'This is why I wanted to leave with you…'

'You wanted to leave with me? So that you could bury your grandad's dirty little secret?' Jack explodes. He paces back and forth as if caged, unsure what to do with himself but needing to do something. This looks to be one sting too much for him.

I stand up and grab Jack by the shoulders and stick him on the sofa I was sitting on. He offers no resistance, his brain occupied with other hurdles. I stand between them in the middle of the room.

'Zoe, you need to talk,' I say. 'Now.'

Her mascara slips down her cheeks messily with her tears.

'I need to get out of here,' Jack says, holding his head in his hands.

'No. Jack, you need to stay and hear this. You have been searching for answers this entire time and you're this close to hearing something that might hold a thread of truth. You need to see this one through.'

Jack takes a second, and his gaze cuts Zoe in half. I turn back to her.

'Zoe. I'll tell you what I have, then there'll be your chance to respond. If you help me it will likely look favourably on you in future.'

She nods, and wipes her cheek.

'I will try,' she says, 'but I don't know anything for sure.'

'I know what the authorities found at the crime scene and what they make of it,' I say. 'So much of the lower-level police is bought off, so I had to reach higher for the info, all the way to the NCA. They found your father, Jack, still in his pyjamas, tied to a chair with a single gunshot wound to the chest. The evidence points to a lack of struggle, and that he was tied up after he was killed. He put up no resistance, indicating he was either expecting what was happening to him and had resigned himself to his fate… or, and in my opinion most likely, he had known his killer well and didn't see it coming.

'And then there are the names we had in the frame. Sparkles Chu and Nigel. I caught Sparkles Chu, and had a good chat with him while his boat was falling to pieces around us. He swore he didn't do it. Said he is not that kind of person and they are not that kind of people. His business is destroyed, and he is underground in the city somewhere.

'I met Nigel this morning, and he spoke to Royston the night of his death. He swears he didn't kill him either. He told me that he and Royston were planning on getting out of Manchester and opening a pub down in Exeter. He said Royston wanted out of the berg.

'Your father wanted out, Jack. When you found out about the berg and his whole double life, it shocked him straight. He wanted to take you away from all this, and do his best to fix everything. Nigel was going to start a legitimate pub business with your father, and had fronted his life savings for the deal. Your dad told the berg, and the berg didn't like it. Nigel said Royston feared for his life, which caused him to pull out of the deal sometime before his death – and there was no sign of a struggle the night he died, not because he didn't see it coming, but because he knew his number was finally up. Nigel lost everything, and that's why he was pissed off with your dad. He'd left him high and dry.'

Jack eyes look like a newborn's, as if everything he has ever known was stripped away from him and he is experiencing things for the very first time.

'You said they tried to recruit you, Jack. I don't think your dad liked it at all. He wanted this new life for the pair of you. But when you wouldn't be recruited, I think they tried to force your hand. I think they tried to breed loyalty in you by helping you find Royston's killer.

'They gave you a name all right – the name of their direct competition. They wanted the River wiped out, and they knew you would make a damn good job of doing it.

'They decided to get rid of one employee, in a direct upgrade, for a younger, hungrier, meaner model – all in a clever plot that would get you in their pocket, doing their dirty work for them.'

I can see that this is hitting Jack hard; he's showing some classic signs of acute stress – rigidity, laboured breathing, glassy eyes. Zoe isn't faring much better.

'I'm nearly there, Zoe, it'll be your turn in a minute.' Then, to Jack: 'I believe they saw this as a great opportunity to take out the River, who were killing them on the arms front and growing in stature day by day'.

I take out my handgun, and Zoe gasps. 'Easy, easy, I'm just showing you something. This is a Glock 17. But it's not an authentic Glock. It's too lightweight. This is what I lifted from the guy that Chu sent to the Premier Inn. It's made of plastic parts.

'Jack, you know when we burst into the back room, at Chu's place, there was that workshop, and those box-shaped machines? They are trade-quality 3-D printers. They had two of them in there. They downloaded the specs of the Glocks, and were creating 3-D replicas. You can make damn near anything with these printers, I read about them, and they have chosen to make a dent in the berg's arms industry, by offering a cheaper, attractive, local alternative. Hey, you don't need to import guns anymore! You just build them in an afternoon, like an Airfix model. And the added benefits of these guns? Plastic doesn't show up on metal detectors. They were offering a superior product, on the cheap. No wonder the berg's own business was struggling, and I bet they didn't know about the printers. If they did, they could have just started doing it themselves, and avoided all this, but no, they needed the River taking out. And they played us to perfection, Jack. They had us go there, on the pretence of something entirely different, to take out their competition for them, our services bought by the spilling of your father's blood.'

Jack puts his head in his hands, and cries softly. I continue.

'And, I hate to say it, but… they may have done it before. Your mother's killers. Nobody knew what really happened to them… or who they definitely were. Maybe it was the berg all along.' Jack merely releases a low moan.

I look at Zoe, who looks into the distance, seemingly detached.

'What do you know, Zoe?' I ask. 'Now is the time.'

'I didn't know…' she says, her voice brittle and timorous, 'but I was always worried they might do something like this.'

Jack stops sobbing abruptly and glares at her.

'I promise, I know *nothing* about this, but they have been more secretive recently, more elusive. They haven't included me in the same way that they normally do. It was just… suspicious. I was just sure they were up to something. I just assumed they were closing ranks like they sometimes do.'

She crosses the room to Jack, and reaches out to him. 'Jack, baby, I swear

I didn't know anything about this. I promise. If I had known, I would have told you.'

Jack looks down again.

'Jack, please,' she says. 'You know what will happen if I don't go along with what they say…' She looks at him searchingly, but I myself am baffled.

'What do you mean?' I ask.

Zoe and Jack exchange looks, revealing something else slithering beneath the surface of this whole damn affair. What new betrayals lie in wait?

'They will kill me… I have no doubt they will,' Zoe says.

'What do you mean, Zoe?' I ask.

'Tell him,' says Jack.

'Felix is my grandfather. Michael is my uncle. But Felix had another son… my father. I was eighteen months old when he and my mother died. I never found out how. I was too young to know or notice. I was raised by Felix's wife, Theresa. She passed away when I was fifteen. It is partly out of respect for Theresa, and love, that I am still here. But there is another reason…'

I dread to think, knowing finally what these people are really like.

'You might think I am in a position of power here, but I am not. I wanted to go, but Felix said that if I went anywhere, he would kill me. He said there was nowhere else for me to go, and that I knew too much, and as the offspring of his *turncoat* son, I would spill. He offered to look after me and let me live, as he put it, in exchange for my compliance.'

'And your position as bookkeeper?'

'Theresa used to do it. And I used to help her in the later years, when she became forgetful. I was groomed in the inner workings of mob life from such a young age, so that by the time I was old enough to start thinking for myself, I already knew too much. Felix said he wanted to get his money's worth. And that way, if I kept working for him, I was becoming more and more of an accomplice. As long as I kept his books, I was just as much a criminal as he was. He kept my hands dirty, so I could never walk away.'

'That's a very skewed logic.'

'And a perfect one. Felix is a very complicated man, with an old-fashioned sense of honour and business. He believes that by doing what I do for him, he is getting his service, albeit late, from his dead son – my dad.'

'Zoe… is this the truth?' I ask.

'Every word,' she says.

'It's true,' Jack says.

I mull all this over. I can't help feeling sorry for Zoe now, all the pain that she has been put through, simply by a situation she was born into. It's no wonder that these two people see some sort of connection between them: they are in so many ways the same.

'Zoe, if I can fix this for you, will you let me?'

'Yes,' she says, without hesitation.

'Jack, I need to ask you the same question. You can't be here for the finale, not this time. You two need each other, and the only way out is if you both go now. I'll give you both a chance to walk out of that door and into a new life if you say *yes* this minute.'

They look at each other, and I see the glimmer of love between them. It burns bright on the back of a truth finally reached and revealed after being hidden for so long.

There is hope, salvation, and redemption for all of us here.

'Yes,' Jack says, and he and Zoe embrace, crying in each other's arms. It's a moment that warms me, but I'm not done yet.

'Zoe, I need everything you have. All the evidence. Everything. Any record of what you keep, on behalf of the berg, I need it. Now.'

Zoe pulls away, and looks at me, thoughtfully but with a little spark of joy in her eyes.

'Felix keeps everything at his house. I even have to do the books there, in old ledgers. We have a weekly appointment. I go over to his house and he fills me in on everything and I write while he speaks.'

'So there's nothing here?'

'No… well… yes. I always hoped this day would come. I made notes as soon as I came home, remembering everything I could. There's not a lot, in terms of volume, but the majority of the main transactions will be there. It's… a little book of hope.'

'Is there any evidence of yourself in there?'

'None. Penned by an anonymous author.'

'Or Jack?'

174

'Nothing. He never did anything official for the berg anyway, so never earned a cut. There's nothing there that could ever lead back to either of us.'

'That's perfect, Zoe. Well done. Get it quick as you can, so we can all get out of here.'

She runs out of the room, and I hear her pounding up the stairs. I turn to Jack. 'I'm sorry, pal,' I say. 'But this is the way it has to be.'

'What are you going to do?' he asks.

'I'm giving Zoe's notes to the NCA, to expose the berg and everyone who has done business with them. And then, I'm going after Felix and every single fucking one of the *väktaren*. I set out to exterminate scum, well, here's my shot.'

'Thank you,' Jack says.

Zoe re-enters the room. She hands me three slim, hardback A4 journals.

'It's all there,' she says, with obvious pride at her handiwork.

'Great. Now you two need to go, right now, before things get messy. You both have money put away?'

'Yes,' Jack answers. Zoe shakes her head.

'Felix keeps everything of mine. I have a card to an account which holds what he calls my *pocket money*, but it's in his name.'

'See if you can empty it en route.'

'I've got her covered, Ben,' says Jack. If he emptied that safe back at his place, he's not wrong.

'Good. You are leaving in one minute. Get what you need, and chop-chop.'

They sprint about, grabbing shoes and keys and phones. A laptop bag comes down the stairs, and Zoe even manages to change into jeans. I check the windows, then open the front door and usher them outside.

We enter sunlight as Zoe activates the keyless entry on the Mini. I open the boot, still holding the three journals under my arm, and Jack throws in the bits and bobs they are taking with them. Zoe had actually come out barefoot, and is shimmying into some trainers by the bonnet.

'Come on, come on,' I urge, nudging them that last little bit before they take flight on their own for the first time.

Jack shakes my hand again, looking at me with more meaning than words presumably could muster at this moment. Zoe comes around the car and hugs me. I barely know the girl, but I've been impressed by her since minute one and I hug her back with feeling. These two deserve better, and they are going to get it. I'll do anything to make sure of it.

Zoe pecks my cheek, and whispers, 'Thank you,' in my ear, before hopping in the passenger side.

Jack hops in the driver's side and I start walking back to the Lexus, which I suppose I can call my car now, parked on the pavement. I lift the journals, checking one last time that I have all three. Yes, all there. I am wondering what secrets are contained within, what cases can be built from the contents, and what scum can be rinsed from the streets with it, when I am shoved hard head over heels, pushed through the air on the blast of the explosion. I land hard on my back on the pavement, and the pain slams through me.

The quiet neighbourhood has been ripped in two. The explosion has literally sucked the surrounding air into it and for a moment it is difficult to breathe. Then I smell nitroglycerin and a stinging hint of household bleach. The hallmarks of an improvised explosive device.

I push myself up and turn to the Mini, which is engulfed in a blaze set off by an ignition-triggered car bomb. I sprint around the side of the pyre, getting as close as I can to the flames without scorching myself, and see that Jack and Zoe are completely beyond hope – dead before they even knew what was happening, their bodies blackening.

I back away from the intense heat as black smoke billows skyward. I hear a noise I realise is myself crying even though my ears are throbbing, just beginning to hurt. The flames are thick, like huge orange tentacles squeezing and engulfing the car.

I can't believe this. I just can't.

People are beginning to come out of their houses. I need to get out of here, before the authorities arrive. I feel my rage spilling over, dripping like hot wax down my arms, burning my muscles and making me coil. I will avenge them both, I swear it. They didn't deserve this.

I run back to the Lexus, scooping the journals splayed on the pavement as I go, while tears stream down my cheeks. I feel as if I'm going to explode, and as the emotion gushes out of me, I get behind the wheel. I scream long and loud, as if my voice can erase the images I have just seen, images which will haunt me till the day I too meet my own fate.

25

I need to get a grip, but I don't know how. I swerve in and out of traffic, not sure even which way to go. Driving like a madman won't help, and I need to calm down, but I just feel I can't, so I head back to my hotel, grab my things.

It's happening tonight. It's all going down when the sun does the same. There's no going back now.

My hotel is only a ten-minute drive from Zoe's house, and I make it in eight. I park up, and head for the lobby. I ask the young lad behind the front desk for the biggest envelope he has. It is big enough, just, for all three journals to fit in, but I borrow some parcel tape to make sure. I write Jeremiah Salix's name on the front, and the address of the NCA central offices. I take a piece of blank paper from the lobby bureau, and write a hasty note.

'*SHOULD CONTAIN EVERYTHING YOU NEED. ROYSTON'S MURDER WAS AN IN-HOUSE JOB. WHATEVER IS LEFT, BRING THEM ALL DOWN. THANKS FOR YOUR HELP.*'

I put it in the envelope with the books, and hand the lot over to the young lad, along with a twenty-pound note, making sure he understands that the package needs to get posted with the hotel's outgoing mail. I tell him to keep the change.

I trust Jeremiah to finish the job. It will probably make his career, but I know he's not in it for that. He wants his own personal revenge, for what they did to him. I will get it for him, and he can take the official plaudits.

I head up to my room, and pack. It only takes a second. I check the room one last time, before typing a quick text on my phone. Caution is going to have to go to the wind, it's down to the wire.

Leave with the kids NOW. I'll do what I can, B.

I grab my bag and head out of the room and within moments, I have checked out and I'm in the car again. I'm on my own, and I need to put together a plan for tonight. And that plan starts with surveillance.

26

The booming, sinuous swirl of the aggressive synth bassline hits me out here in the street. I am queueing to get into a nightclub, something I haven't done in who knows how long. It was frustrating then, and it's no better now. I am about ten yards from the front now, and started only a further fifteen yards back. I should be in fairly soon. I better had be.

It's Brink, a swanky-looking nightspot off Oxford Road. It seems busy tonight, with the line moving not too slowly. At the weekends it's a 'one in, one out' policy, the tired and bored replaced with the cold and eager, one at a time, but there are ways around that. The signs outside declare the place as '*Manchester's premier den of decadence, hip-hop and fine liquor*'. The clientele seem to have dressed for that exact vibe, with the men decked out like R 'n' B pimpstrels, the women like high-class prostitutes.

I wonder whether the theme was something that Leonard and Samson had a hand in. That would fit.

Leonard and Samson, I learned, thanks to more internet digging, make up one third of the ownership of this place. I couldn't ascertain how this deal fits in with their day-to-day activities, but why wouldn't it? Considering their nearly endless social-network stream of pictures plastered all over the web, all set inside these doors, I get the idea that they just couldn't help themselves to ownership of a *decadent* club. It's a status badge for them, and, as clearly the most image conscious of the group, it fits nicely.

And they are in there somewhere.

I'm so out of practice at clubbing, I have to think hard about how I used to behave, back when my social life wasn't so sparse. Drink ten pints of snakebite, try not to throw it all back up, have a bit of a banter, be generally hopeless with the odd girl unlucky enough to catch my eye... that about covers it. I feel a little bit beyond that these days, however I'm sure on another occasion I could give it a good go.

I have spent the entire day staking out Felix Davidson's house on Salford Quays. I changed my vantage point frequently, remained on foot the entire time, used my binoculars to keep a safe distance, and watched a lot of things happen – which allowed me to draw a series of interesting conclusions. Needless to say, I never went to see them.

It was a hive of activity. Lots of comings and goings. I wish I could have heard what was being said, but I was at too great a distance. I could see who was there and, broadly, what they were doing, but nothing detailed.

When I got to the long drive along the waterfront to Felix's house, I noticed street cameras where there were none elsewhere along the way. They were dressed up as council-approved-and-fitted security cams, but they increased in number in the vicinity of Felix's residence. Felix's doing. After all, councils rarely dole out free security networks for one solitary person or residence – if you can't get your bin emptied more than once a fortnight, surely that sort of service would be a bridge too far.

I saw Felix; he never left the house. I saw Michael, Leonard, and Samson. At one point they were in a kind of agitated conversation at the same table I was sat at with them all just a couple of mornings earlier. Leonard seemed preoccupied with his phone, which in turn seemed preoccupied with him. Samson seems like the heavy of the group. A physical rock which they all seem to like having around; their agitation slows when he is present. I get the feeling that perhaps he had something to offer to the group, something to bring to the table that others could not. Perhaps a business of his own, a specific expertise or perhaps a new customer. Who knows? It won't matter when I put a bullet through his eye socket.

Michael looks altogether different... An important cog to the machine, a vital *caporegime* directly beneath the don. He seems to be both the pivot and the counterpoint, the go-to. He was involved in all the day's discussions, never left his father's side, and, most tellingly, engaged in a number of private conferences with the main man himself.

I could see, and reaffirm, the dynamic of the group. Leonard and Samson are at an echelon, but not the echelon of Michael and Felix. There is a hierarchy within the hierarchy, with Michael seemingly elevated somewhere between *väktare* and *toppmöte*.

Felix still looks the same quaint, respectful gentleman he always does. Carefully pottering around his kingdom, never seeming flustered, always in control. What I would give to hear his thoughts. His character is so complex, and his duplicity is scary: one can only imagine the serpent coiled inside, a serpent so vindictive and controlling that it's a miracle his frail body can play carriage to its might. His eyes never gave it away, and neither did his conduct. A career criminal playing the role to perfection…

The queue moves, and as I shuffle forward I see a girl walking in the opposite direction, heading for the back of the queue while talking into her phone. She will fit the role I have in mind perfectly.

She is definitely what they call a babe. She is also alone, dolled to the nines, and perched on impossible stilettos. She must have been vacuum-packed into that dress, and the make-up she wears gives her face a positively ceramic look. Her hair is a voluminous bouffant.

I try to tune in.

'…you can't expect me not to ask that. That's exactly what I told him. They'll be inside there now, and he's probably flirting with that obese bitch as we speak.'

A charming specimen… Just what I'm looking for.

'Hey,' I say, looking hopeful. 'Want to come in with me? I'm getting VIP.'

'Oh, thank you, sweetheart!' she says. She pats my arm, swishes her hair nearly taking my eye out, and joins me in the queue, immediately linking arms with me and then shutting her phone. She is clearly used to getting her own way from men she knows how to handle – and being fawned over by them. Well, not this time, sister. At least, not for real.

I check my phone for the time, and realise I have plenty. My anger has given way to precision, as it always does when objectives are set. I have timings and a chronology to stick to, but everything largely is in place.

'That guy,' I venture, 'the one you were talking about on the phone? He hasn't a clue what he's missing.'

She likes that, a lot, her smile widening to reveal perfectly formed but discoloured teeth. It gets her talking again, but I tune out, and the happy couple move forward a few steps.

Early in the afternoon, Felix had texted me, asking if I was still coming. From my observation post I watched him send it, and watched him wait for my response, which, of course, never came. It resulted in him issuing what looked like stern orders.

I don't think they took too kindly to my silence and failure to attend. It was seen as exactly the rebuff it was.

I wonder whether killing Jack and Zoe was a punishment or whether they knew even knew about Jack and Zoe's relationship. Maybe Jack had started turning Zoe against the berg, and Felix knew it. Maybe he thought enough is enough – loose ends need tidying. Who knows what surveillance was in place regarding those two. Either way, Jack was never going to rest until he had exacted some kind of revenge for his father's death, and if it came back to him that Felix had something to do with it, Jack would certainly try to kill him. Maybe Felix just wanted to get in there first.

Another thing: Felix killed Royston to try to cajole Jack into joining them, with the promise of revenge. Surely he wasn't doing the same with me? I had asked for more time while deciding whether to join them or not, and Felix may think that Jack dying under mysterious circumstances might hasten my decision – and make me want to join them so as to get revenge myself. He knew that doing so would necessitate the murder of his own granddaughter, but that would helpfully remove yet another potential problem. If that's the case, there is nothing that this man won't do to further his own prosperity. Absolutely nothing.

His killing Jack to get to me, or to elicit some reaction from me, seems no longer simply a possibility, but a certainty. People are creatures of habit and routine, and the more psychotic the mind the more these character-istics are accentuated. It's habitual for Felix to use people in the way he has used me, Jack, Zoe, and Royston – and they're only the ones I know about. God *damn* it.

'Motherfucker,' I mutter.

'What?' says the girl.

'Oh… that guy… treating you that way,' I say.

I feel a wandering hand on my middle; the girl seems to have a bad case of the gropes. So this is how you attract girls: ignore them.

I don't really want her hand to wander any lower. Not because her actions have created a stirring in my loins, but because she will surely interpret it that way since I have the Glock wedged in the front of my underwear, alongside my manhood. Places like these, with their undercurrent of drugs and glamour, more often than not have metal detectors and sometimes a rough pat-down. I'm expecting both, given the organised crime connection. The only way to get my weapon in is alongside my other one.

I'm still not listening to her, but on the surface I am giving all the signs that I am. She looks half-cut, so the task is easy. I can feel her hand dropping lower, as feared. She grazes something solid with her fingertips, and, mistaking the handle of the gun for something else entirely, giggles. She pulls herself closer to me, angling up my neck, and I smile politely.

We are at the front now, and the bouncer, seeing our one-sided action, smiles at me. I wink back, and shrug '*c'est la vie*', getting him onside in an instant. Good. At least my little limpet is doing me a backhanded favour.

The bouncer gives me a nod and we move forward.

I put my arm around the girl's back, and usher her forward. She says something routine about me being a gentleman, but I'm already blueprinting the place for a layout, the VIP area and exits. A burly man approaches me, motions arms-up, and gives me one of the most half-hearted pat-downs I've ever experienced, as he clearly does it a few hundred times a night, never finding a single thing. Now the legs as well, the chest, and my arms. All done. No attention to the groin whatsoever. I suppose I wouldn't want to go fishing through drunkards' crotches every night either, but his oversight here will cost the lives of two of his employers.

We are ushered along the dimly lit hallway from the door. There is a little ticket booth up ahead, spotlighted, and the bass throbs even more. I take the girl by the waist, as I clock one fire escape door to my right, and further along, a large double door manned by two more thickset security men. I tell the girl that I've got this, and a hand flicks up to my chest again. I hear some garbled words of thanks, but I choose to ignore them.

183

At the ticket booth, I put a twenty over the counter and smile at a girl who looks the polar opposite of the one I have on my arm. Conservative, polite, naturally beautiful.

'It's twenty-five pounds,' she says. 'Each.'

Fifty quid? Bloody hell. No wonder my arm candy fancied a free ride. I smile and tell her it's no problem. I animatedly take a sheaf of notes from an even healthier wad, making sure they both notice, and hand over the money.

'I'm interested in some VIP action tonight, what can you offer me?' I ask. 'Just somewhere quiet to enjoy some champagne.'

My companion can barely contain herself.

'We have a private VIP bar overlooking the main floor, if you'd like that? I can call up and see if I can get you a table,' the girl in the box replies.

'Please do, that sounds fantastic,' I say.

My girl takes my lapels, tells me her name is Krystal 'with a K', and pulls me in for a kiss. Inwardly, I'm grimacing, but our lips meet. Oh God, it's a sloppy one. First kiss in ten years, and not at all how I'd envisioned it. Tastes like fags, old mint gum, and the muddy sweetness of weed. A classy dame, to be sure.

Finally released from her grip, I look back at the girl in the booth and shrug, smiling sheepishly.

'We have a table,' she says. 'Minimum spend for the table is £250.'

'No problem,' I reply. Ordinarily such a sum would churn my guts, but when I'm long gone I'll be leaving way more problems than an unpaid tab.

'Take this to the man on the door, he'll look after you,' she says, handing me a black, wood-carved stiletto. It's actually kind of a cool piece, perhaps best suited as a doorstop at the Playboy mansion. I take it, and thank her.

'Is there anyone interesting up there tonight? I hear you get football players in here all the time,' I say.

'No footballers tonight yet, but the owners are already knocking about. They usually say hello to the VIP guests, so you may see them,' she says.

Oh, I am sure of it. I tailed them here.

We get moving. It turns out the wooden stiletto is kind of an access-all-areas pass to this place, and we are ushered into the club with 'good evenings' and smiles from the security staff. We enter through the main double doors, and if the bass doesn't nearly knock me off my feet, the sight of the place does. It is really something.

It feels like an undersea kingdom. We are on a balcony overlooking a dance floor covered in thick purple smoke that drifts sensually between grinding revellers, a rich sheet of velvet, swirling slowly, caressing the ecstatic lovemakers writhing within it. Strobe lights dot the seascape like neon tetras, punctuating the eroticism. The balcony has stairways dropping down into the inky murk, and there appears to be a hefty bar directly below us. Hanging above it all, is a large Perspex tank holding chairs, tables, and a bar of its own. The VIP section. We head for it.

The reason I got this girl to come in with me was to deflect attention away from myself. It has worked very well so far, but now will be the ultimate test. I don't know where Samson and Leonard are, but I'm hoping that the first thing they see, or anyone will see if they're looking for me, will be this girl, not me. She is eye-catching, with a broad 'lads mag' style appeal. As we start descending the stairs, she does attract eyes, from both sexes. As a single man, wandering about in here, I may have looked conspicuous, but now I have someone with me who will draw attention actively away from me.

Nobody gives me a second glance. Krystal is stealing the show, as planned. All I need is to get up in that VIP.

I scan for green, the colour of exits. I find three, one by the bar, two either side of the back wall beneath the VIP tank, with another stairway between them, dimly lit. Security staff either side suggest we have found the VIP entrance. I direct us that way, and we continue to descend into the mist of the dance floor.

The girl starts to sway, moving her shapely body in perfect time to the heavy beat. My eyes are locked on the VIP, desperate for an ID of either of my intended targets. I spy security cameras, but that doesn't sway me in the least. They will be for the use of the owners and nobody else. There is no chance any of the tapes from here will ever make it to any official police avenues – I'm certain that Samson and Leonard use this place to peddle some of their illicit wares.

I begin to sway with the girl, taking part in my cover story.

My eyes are drawn to a column over on the far left of the dance floor that has a cage atop it, designed like an upscaled bird coop. In it there is a pole, with a bikini-clad dancer going through the motions. There is something familiar about the dancer, but I can't quite catch what it is. As I sway, and Krystal pushes into me, in a flash of reflected light I recognise her. It's Tina, Samson's other half, theatrically made-up like a burlesque goddess.

I pull Krystal in close and bury my face in her neck, pretending to nibble on her shoulder. If Tina is in on things, she will know I'm definitely not supposed to be here. My face is buried in her hair, and we look just like any of the other dancing couples. She grinds herself into me, and I spin her slowly away from the bird cage, so that our backs are to Tina, then usher her to the VIP.

'Champagne,' I whisper to her.

The stiletto gives us immediate access to the rear private stairwell, the bouncers' eyes roaming my companion without even glancing at me, and we are permitted to ascend.

'I've never been up here before,' giggles Krystal, while making heavy weather of the steps. The stairs double back on themselves after a short landing, and we enter the tank. I let the girl go first. Ahead of us are a few tables pressed up against the glass, and a bar to the left. There are a few people about, but, even though it's the middle of the night, it's still kind of early in nightclub hours. No sign of my targets just yet.

We are approached by an attractive girl, dressed all in black.

'Good evening. I'm Alice, I'll be taking care of you this evening. Would you like a table or a booth?' she asks.

So there are booths up here too. Where are they?

'Where's the toilet?' asks Krystal.

'Just past the bar.'

'I'll be right back,' says Krystal, as she scampers away.

'I'll just have a drink, please, and wait for her,' I say, motioning to the bar.

'Of course, I'll keep an eye out and you can decide when she gets back.'

'Perfect.'

I head for the bar, pretending to adjust my belt but secretly popping the butt of the gun up over my waistband, for easy access. I notice that the VIP has an emergency exit along from the toilets. Exactly as hoped for.

186

I see now that there are booths along the left rear wall of the tank, which I couldn't see from the stairs. They are slightly elevated, and dark. There are three, and I have to pass by each one to get to the bar. No one in the VIP is paying me any mind. The music blares from below, penetrating the glass in an auditory osmosis. The barman looks bored to tears, staring out and down at the dance floor below. My gun has a silencer, but considering the thumping bass, I could probably get away without it. I'm upon the first booth... I'm primed, I'm ready.

Empty. A leather wraparound bench with no occupants, its low, dim chandelier illuminating nothing but a menu card.

I press on.

Second booth: empty.

They must be in the third. Placing my hand around the grip of the Glock, I round the edge of the third booth.

Two pairs of eyes immediately look up from the bench seat, surprise etched on their faces. I'll soon make that surprise permanent.

Samson and Leonard, drinks and a dusting of cocaine on the table in front of them, look back at me, mouths open. Leonard has a sprinkling of white powder in his pencil moustache, like a kid who got at the icing sugar.

I draw and train the gun on them, not caring who sees. At this range, their fates are sealed, and they will die enacting their own ludicrous fantasy.

'I know what you did,' I say.

'Ben, Ben, Ben...' Leonard says, starting to rise, ready with his usual brio. I fire a bullet into his forehead and he falls back, his eyes still fixed on me. Samson sits arrow-straight, paralysed.

'Jesus Christ! We didn't know!' he shouts, pleading. It's funny to see a stacked man reduced to a whimpering wreck in a t-shirt six sizes too small. It will be his final indignity.

'Yes. You did. You knew about it all.'

I shoot him over his right eye, the bullet producing a neat, precise dot. He slumps heavily into the booth, against Leonard, and to the casual observer, it looks as if they have had one too many sherbets and are having a brotherly snooze. The staff might not even notice them for a while.

The minor *spurt* of the suppressed shots was muffled by the music. At the bar, the barman is still staring out over the dance floor, daydreaming while he waits for a drink to pour. The rest of the patrons are lost in their own little worlds.

I stick the gun in my pants again, and head for the toilets, reaching the doors just as Krystal emerges, smoothing her dress. I grab her arm.

'We need to get out of here, sweetheart,' I say, and usher her to the green exit door. She pulls back, protests a little. 'Why?'

'Someone came in the club a bit upset, it looked like something was about to go down,' I tell her. 'Best you not get involved. Let's go.'

She buys it.

We pass through a door and down a grimy staircase that looks like nobody has passed through in years. There is a fire door at the bottom. I waste no time.

We exit into a still and empty back street. We must have been inside no more than five minutes. Job done.

'You're on your own, darling. Go home. Clean yourself up, and I don't just mean with make-up wipes.'

She looks at me uncomprehendingly, as if I just revealed myself to be part alien. I don't think she gets the message, but from the look on her face, I can see she's about to deliver one of her own.

'You fucking *twat*,' she says, spitting the words at me.

I turn and start to walk, take out my phone and check it: 3:40 a.m. It's time for the next part. The first part has been an unqualified success. Word could reach Felix within minutes, about what happened here. I just hope I can get a fix on him in time. If I lose him now, and he disappears, I'll never get another chance.

I start to run.

27

I light the rag with one flick of a cheap lighter I picked up from an all-night petrol station just moments before. The flame is more than happy to take hold of the scrap I am feeding it, and it reaches out along the rag slowly, like a miniature human torch crawling hand over hand up a climbing rope.

I step back, and keep pacing in reverse. I hear a crackle now, as well as the soft, hot fanning breath of a live fire. It reaches along the wick to the silver bodywork, then angles into the opening of the petrol tank. A moment passes, and the Lexus rips from the inside out, a messy, bellowing convulsion of metal, rubber, glass, and upholstery. Goodbye Lexus, you have served me well.

I shoulder my backpack and duffel bag and start the one-mile walk to the waterfront. I picked this abandoned industrial estate on the edge of Stretford to be the car's graveyard, since it is only a short walk from Salford Quays, but far enough away not to be visible from Felix's vast windows.

I am supremely focused. Fixed on an objective.

I arrive at the waterfront in about ten minutes. I have already picked a secluded spot from which to begin my assault. I drop over a roadside barrier, shimmy down a gravel slope, and enter into some unkempt urban vegetation at the bottom. I hear the water, lapping in the darkness to my right. The sky is brightening in its furthest corners, as the sun begins its slow, steady ascent once more. The timing is fine so far, but I want to keep moving.

I search in the bushes, and find my hidden item with ease. When I was carrying out my surveillance earlier, I had pondered how to get over to Felix's house by water, considering the coverage of the security cameras over on the land route, and the possibility that he may have ramped up his protection given what I just did in Brink. Then I saw kayakers paddling about on the water over where the ship canal enters the Quays. I followed their progress to a small water sports club further up on this side of the water. I checked it out after dark, when everyone had gone home and the place had been locked up.

It was nothing more than a black shed with a side door sitting on a large jetty leading directly through two large double doors, locked, of course. Looking through the window, I saw kayaks, one of which I had intended to borrow; that is, until I got inside and saw the jet ski.

I pull the branches of the bush aside, and there it is now.

I take my duffel bag, containing my insurance policy, and open it. Everything is inside as I prepared it, the shirts all wrapped in cellophane. I'd collected some rocks earlier and piled them next to the jet ski; I now transfer these into the duffel bag. I stand with my back to the bush and pick a point directly opposite on the horizon over the water: the middle tower of an apartment block. Remember it. Never forget it. I lower the bag into the water, and let it sink to the bottom. It will be here, should I ever need it, safe on the bottom of the Manchester Ship Canal, here off this deserted bank.

I hope I never have to come back for it.

I grab the jet ski and push, lowering it into the water. I'm not really dressed for the part, in my jeans and shirt, but I hop on the back, make sure my backpack is secure, and find the ignition button on the handlebars. The jet ski roars to life, but at idle its small engine is remarkably quiet.

I have never ridden one before, and as I squeeze the accelerator tentatively, I realise immediately that I have been missing out. I am very familiar with boats, and the way they surge through moving bodies of water. The principles are identical with the jet ski, albeit to a different scale, and before long I am manoeuvring the craft along skilfully and easily.

I spot the twinkling lights of Felix's house across the water, the vast conservatory, and I accelerate hard.

Turning the jet ski, I angle into the current and the little boat bounces over the slight shift and swell of the water. This mode of travel is far quicker than a kayak, and I am on immediate approach within a couple of minutes. The lights in Felix's house are dim – night lights, it seems, not searching and bright.

Stillness all around. There is a little jetty that I hadn't seen before, to

190

the far right of the conservatory at the bottom of the short garden, which I proceed directly towards, slowly and quietly. I kill the engine and float the remaining few yards. Seconds later, the jet ski is tied to the dock and I am scampering up the jetty, my eyes alive to the possibility of being seen. *Keep moving, don't stop. Don't slow.*

The conservatory has a single glass door, which I check to see if I can prise open. It seems I can't without causing an almighty racket. Inside, the water in the pool is still, and the rest of the house is quiet. I keep following the edge of the conservatory around the side of the house, until I reach solid brick walls. I search for a window or vent, then notice that the kitchen window is slightly ajar. I check inside. Still nothing. Behind me, the sky is bleeding streaks of warm orange onto ever-lightening blue. I ease the window open, and hop in, directly over the sink. I have entered hostile buildings under the cover of darkness before, usually with a team behind me. I'm amazed how much easier it is when you are by yourself, but just how naked you feel without that backup.

I pause in the kitchen: Silence, save for the gurgling of the pool filters next door in the conservatory. I don't know which bedroom is Felix's. My plan is to kill Felix and wait for Michael. I make my way through the kitchen towards the stairs, the Glock drawn and aimed upwards in readiness.

I reach the landing. The door on my left is the spare room I stayed in, in what seems a lifetime ago. The door to the right is the one I suspect is the master bedroom, judging by the layout of the house so far. I cross the landing in the spot where I imagine Felix and Royston swapped the baby and the brandy, remembering that sobering story and how everything changed since that fateful night... and I stop. The huge window over the stairs that looks out over the rear of the house and the water beyond has framed something that's caught my eye.

There, out in the middle of the water, is a boat. A speedboat, just idling there. And on its deck I can make out three figures.

I squint, and strain my eyes to see in the near-darkness. And I can't believe what I see.

Felix. Michael. Carolyn. The men are standing together by the wheel of the sleek craft, watching the house – in fact, they seem to be looking at me – and Carolyn is on her knees at the stern, her hands bound and her mouth taped shut.

Slowly, Felix's arm begins to raise, and he starts to wave a merry goodbye.

My mind screams *SET-UP!* and my body reacts almost in that same instant. I sprint towards the view – I throw myself through the window, tucking my head down as much as possible, with my arms shielding my face – as an almighty explosion tears through the house. My shoulders take the impact, and I am in flight, fire and debris chasing me as I fall.

I fall nearly vertically, tumbling in a slow arc as I go down. Below me is the conservatory, and through the glass, just before I crash into it, I see the flames blasting through. I hit the conservatory roof with an aching, brutal impact, which only really slows me a touch. The roof gives way, and I rain down with the glass, straight through the fire, and into the pool.

The water is a cold shock. My clothes, instantly heavy and sodden, take me down, but I worry that I will be burned if I poke my head up just now. I open my eyes, which sting from the chlorine, and look at the surface. It's like an orange sky. I wait a few more seconds, and the orange reduces in intensity. My lungs are about to burst, and I have no choice other than to throw my head through the surface and inhale hungrily.

The air tastes boiling hot and dry, and I open my eyes to find myself floating with all sorts of debris, which cover the surface of the pool entirely. The conservatory is completely destroyed, with just a few struts of the metal frame remaining. Behind me, the house is pretty much flattened. There is nothing left. It's been a demolition job. An erasing of the evidence. An attempt to wipe a slate clean.

Through some kind of miracle, it seems I've broken no bones in the fall, though I can feel a dozen cuts – and the pain I know will come is still minutes away. I reach for the edge of the pool and hoist myself out. Wait, there it is – and God, it hurts. I look out at the water for the boat. I can't see it at first, but then I spot it heading off upstream, cruising at a solid rate. My fury doubles, but I temper that with how lucky I feel. That was the most narrow of escapes.

No need to find the door to the conservatory now, as there isn't even a wall, and I simply run through the wreckage out into the garden, and down to the jetty. The jet ski, fortunately, is untouched amid a floating rain of smouldering ash. I waste no time in pursuit, and guide the vessel away from the smoking, collapsing wasteland behind me on the bank.

I don't know if they know I'm following them, and I don't care. I have all my worldly possessions with me, and there is nothing else except the here and now. The past is left where it lies. The present and future are along the river in pursuit of those men and Carolyn.

I crouch lower, to make myself more aerodynamic and to avoid – I hope – being spied and shot at, and race after the speedboat, as the dawn light grows moment by moment. I make good progress, and I can see the boat more clearly now, about four hundred yards ahead. It is approaching a bridge, over which I can see a road, then it slows and pulls towards the bank, where a black SUV is parked.

Jesus, they are escaping. I see them pull up now, at a small wooden mooring, and Michael jumps from behind the wall to tie the boat off. They are leaving town, no question, and this looks like the enacting of well-laid plan.

I'm going as fast as the jet ski will take me, because if I lose them now, I don't know whether I will ever get another chance.

Michael is carrying Felix off the boat, to save his arthritic limbs. In evident haste, he just about throws him into the rear passenger seat.

At two hundred yards away, I'm closing in on them, but I'm worried it won't be enough. Come on. *Come on.*

Michael is back on the boat now, and throws Carolyn roughly over his shoulder. If both parents are there, I fret for where their children might be. Would Michael kill his own children? I don't think anything is off the table for these people, even something so horrific.

Carolyn is thrust into the back with Felix. I can only guess they have brought her along to act as a human shield or hostage, to be discarded when they have got where they are going safely.

Michael gets in the front passenger side, the car immediately kicking up dust as soon as the door is closed. Shit – there was a driver, ready to go. I'm still a good hundred yards away. What now? Try to moor up myself and hijack a car at five in the morning? Not likely.

The SUV moves up a dirt track to the road and turns left to cross the bridge over the waterway. I see Michael lower his passenger window, and the son of a bitch *smiles* as the breeze flicks his hair. The car picks up speed as it approaches the left-hand bank, a gravel slope leading up to the road itself.

To hell with it.

I turn sharply left and head for the bank, keeping my body low and my arms in tight. This is either the best idea I have ever had, or the worst. Either way, it's my last shot. I brace myself, as the jet ski, wound up and screaming, accelerates along the last few yards of water. It bumps and bounces sharply on the bank, skidding on the gravel. I hope my speed was enough, as the momentum carries me up the incline. Stones are spitting everywhere, and I am fully out of control now, my trajectory entrusted to physics. With another clatter and a spray of gravel, the jet ski lurches up into the road as the SUV passes. The two vehicles are yards apart, and the car swerves to avoid me, as I throw myself at Michael's open window.

My left hand catches the solid front wing mirror. I grab at the roof desperately, thanking heaven when my hand grips the smooth chrome rod of a roof rack. And I scrabble, trying to find something for my feet – and find it on the SUV's slim running board. I place my feet firmly, and hold on for dear life.

Michael and Felix and the driver are all shouting at one another. 'Get him off the fucking car!' I hear Felix roar. It's the most animated I have ever heard him.

Carolyn is sobbing through her taped mouth.

The wind is suddenly knocked from me as Michael hits me, hard. I want to double up, roll into a ball and drop off, but if I do that it's certain death. I hoist myself up, praying the rack holds, relying on the adrenaline still coursing through my arms, and climb up onto the roof of the vehicle. I roll onto my back, hands gripping the rack rods tight on either side, as the sky itself rolls by above me. I take a second, and breathe hard.

'Is he gone?' I hear a man say, a voice I don't recognise. It can only be the driver – another associate to deal with. You're next, mate.

I roll onto my stomach, gun in hand again, and peek down over the driver's-side door, then look up ahead, at where we are going, and I can see it immediately a short distance ahead: Manchester Airport, surrounded by high metal fences.

I lean down and over and point the gun inside, and with my eyes still firmly fixed on the airport, fire three shots in quick succession toward the driver. I look down over the front windshield and see blood up on the inside of the glass. I got him, and I got him good.

'Fuck!' bellows Michael, as the car begins to lose control at high speed. A common risk of shooting drivers, is if they were in the process of accelerating, they more than often carry on doing so, as their muscles contract and spasm. We are being driven by a dead man. The bouncing jolts the gun from my hand, which tumbles off down the road.

I throw my right arm down, through the smashed window, and grab the steering wheel, trying to direct us safely, while holding onto the front rod of the rack with my left. The wheel is tugged away from me, and I realise that Michael has had the same idea.

Before either of us can gain an advantage, the SUV crashes through the metal perimeter fencing of the airport. I hold on as tight as I can, bracing myself with arms outstretched, gripping the front of the rack. I close my eyes as the airport wall approaches fast.

If there was ever a time to pick a god to believe in, now would be that time.

The impact is all-encompassing, and the wall of the airport can't stop us. I am wrenched from my position and thrown from the roof out in front of the car as it crashes through the wall at high speed. I'm flying for a brief moment, not for the first time this morning. I see bright lights, polished tiled floors, and a great open space. The floor is coming up fast, and I hit it. It's an ugly impact, and I actually bounce: I feel like my bones are held together by my skin only, as I tumble to a stop on my front.

I feel rain, tepid, like a tropical downpour. I wonder if I am hallucinating. I open my eyes, and with great effort, look up.

It is a scene of devastation. There are clothes all over the floor, and suitcases. We have ended up in baggage reclaim, and the sprinkler system has gone off. The car is completely written off, still upright but crumpled horribly, covered in debris, cinders, and clothing, resting its rear wheels up on a conveyor belt. I don't think anyone else was hurt, as the room seems empty of anything other than that we just caused.

I see movement inside the car. I remember I don't have a gun.

I force myself to get to my feet. I'm going to hurt for days, but for now, I can't afford to care. Water runs down my face and over my body. I reach the car and see Michael, in the front seat, trying to undo his seatbelt. Blood is trickling down his forehead, and there are bricks in his lap that must have come through the shattered windshield. The middle of the roof is so buckled that I can't see into the back.

I throw his car door open. He looks at me, surprised, but his features transform to a face of unhinged contempt.

'Where are your children, Michael?'

'Fuck you,' he replies.

'Your own wife… Just another tool?'

'You don't know the half of it. Who knew she could be swayed by an ex-army nobody squaddie like you?'

He reaches for his jacket pocket, and I reach in, apply a simple wrist lock, disabling him, and put my own hand into his jacket: gun in a shoulder holster. Nice to get there first.

I release my pressure on his wrist, just for a second. We are inches from each other and I whisper to him.

'Goodbye, you fucking disgrace.'

With my hand still inside his jacket, I squeeze the trigger twice. He jolts in agony. A soft tendril of smoke leaks out from under his arm, rising up in between our faces. I pull the gun out in its entirety, and shoot him twice in the chest for good measure. Good riddance.

I hear Carolyn moaning softly in the backseat.

'Carolyn,' I say. 'Hold on, I'm—'

'*Wait there.*'

The guttural whisper, laced with hate, needs no introduction.

'I assume you just… killed my son.'

I turn slowly. Surely airport security will be here any minute, and I'll be in custody again, unless I get out of here as soon as I can.

'That's right, Felix.'

As I turn to face him, I see that the events of the last ten minutes have taken a serious toll on his elderly frame. His feathery hair is slick with sprinkler-wash, as the water smudges away the remnants of blood that is seeping slowly from a cut on the top of his pate. His dark coat is crumpled and sodden. There is a resigned look in his eyes, an emptiness; he is broken. Through his tears, he spits his hate at me.

'You took a legacy – a family – and stripped it from me. Who are you to judge us? Who the fuck are *you*?' he whispers, his words tumbling out, and that Scandinavian accent reveals itself more fully.

'You talk about family. What about the family you ripped apart? What about Royston?'

'You didn't know Royston... Don't get precious about Royston...'

'Believe me, I'm not. But all I've heard from you is talk about some grand mythical loyalty. Some loyalty you showed the Brooker family.'

'It's how it is supposed to be. It is what they wanted.'

'Not everyone thinks the way you do, Felix. Not everybody wants the same things. Zoe, Jack, Carolyn. Even Royston. And certainly not me.'

'Royston left me no choice! He took everything I did for him and tried to shove it back in my face. And he expected me to smile while he did it. He expected to walk away, but you reap what you sow.'

'Yes, you damn well do.'

I've had about enough of Felix, his clichés and the whole sorry affair.

'I don't know what it is you want,' he continues, 'or what I can tempt you with, but...'

He reaches into his pocket at speed. My reflexes act in response: I lower my aim in an instant and squeeze off a single shot into his right thigh. The impact knocks his leg out from under him and pitches him forward onto his knees. I approach him, and stick my hand into his jacket to disarm him – only I don't find a firearm. Instead, there is a brown envelope, which I pull out. The sprinklers have slowed, and the last drops from above speckle the manila. It is unmarked.

'Last chance,' says Felix, wobbling.

The envelope is unsealed, so I pull the contents out. First thing I see is a passport. Then a driving licence, both card and paper counterpart. Then some paper record: birth certificate, some inoculation certificates, medical records. All in the name of Sean Miller, bearing my picture.

My new identity.

'It's yours if you get me out of here,' says Felix. The old bastard, slithering to the last.

'It's equally mine if I put you out of your misery here and now,' I reply. He has no answer to that. 'On Thursday, I broke out of Strangeways.'

'I guessed as much.'

'And do you know why I did it?'

Felix stares, broken, panting now with pain.

'Simply to take down pieces of shit like you.'

I look at him without pity. Without his legacy, his empire, his surround-ings, he is just a frail old man. Nothing more. I could just leave him. Jeremiah will have everything he needs to put Felix away for good. But is traditional justice good enough for what he has done? The crimes he has committed? The lives he has ruined, at all ends of Manchester's society, from the drug users who fell too deep to the people whose deaths he has ordered?

No. I don't trust the justice that my country can give him. He'll hire the best lawyer and get off on some loophole or technicality. I'm not sitting through another sham trial. Justice is not supposed to be a 'tag and release' system. He will not be returned to the wild. Not on my watch.

He is poison, and this time around, I am the law.

I shoot him in the head.

He drops hard, face first, his heels popping up as his nose hits the floor.

Carolyn. I run to back to the car, pocketing my new identity as I go, and drop the gun. I round the side of the car and throw the passenger door open.

Lying on the seat, bound and trembling, is Carolyn, her eyes jiggling in their sockets. I tell her it's ok. I pull her upright, and untie her as quickly as I can. She rests her head on my shoulder, and I let my chin drop to her forehead. I get her out of the car, steady her, and with a sharp yank, remove the tape. She gasps and falls against me, putting her arms around my neck, and I hold her close. She sobs hard into my chest, an outpouring of emotion. She is safe, not just from the immediate horrors, but the life she was trapped in. She is free from Michael, at last. She looks up at me, her beautiful eyes filled with gratitude and tinged with an indebtedness that words would never be able to fully justify.

'Your children?' I ask.

The words unblock an even deeper relief which bleeds into her irises, deep amongst the sadness, shock, and hurt.

'They are ok,' she says. 'They are at our house in Eccles, locked in their bedrooms. He told them we'd be back in a moment. They're good kids, they'll still be there.'

I breathe a sigh of relief, still holding her, just to reassure her for a second.

'Stay and wait for the police. Tell them everything. Get your life back on track. I will be out there.'

I don't really want to leave her here like this, but she was strong enough to alert me, to begin the exit from the life she was trapped in. I'm sure she will be strong enough to start a new one.

I nod to her my own gratitude, and run, grabbing my rucksack as I go, and head towards the terminal. In the tattered clothes on the floor, I spot a baseball cap, which I grab and push down on my head. One glance behind me shows the devastation I leave behind. A battered SUV, bricks and masonry spread all around in chunks... and the bodies. It's a mess. And standing in the middle of it, her hands by her sides, is Carolyn. The hope. The good. The reason I did this, and the reason I will keep doing it.

I think of Jack. Of Zoe. Of Trev and Freya. Of all the people taken for a ride who didn't deserve it. Of the innocent. Of the evil. I know, in this moment more than ever before, that my destiny is set.

The Baby And The Brandy rises in my mind again as I slow to a less conspicuous jog. The expression has taken on a whole new meaning, and I believe that all those people who listened to the myth as a fable of retribution were wrong. It was never about messing with the wrong people. It was about being a parent, and the value and importance of that role.

Felix, Michael, and Royston weren't good enough, even though at least Royston tried. Their kids came second to their own desires. My own father could have done more for me, when I needed him the most. I'm not blaming him for what I have become, but I'm sure shrinks would argue that his actions formed a part of it.

And what kind of father would I have become, in light of all that and of the company I have recently kept?

It's probably best that I never had the chance, even though it might have prevented everything that has happened to me since. I'll never know.

Nevertheless, in that moment – when Felix handed Royston his defenceless offspring – he was faced with a choice, and he failed his son monumentally. That is what *The Baby And The Brandy* is really about. It is about making the right choices for your children, about standing up for your children when they can't. About doing the things your child needs you to do.

As I peel through the corridors and join the first travellers of the day heading for distant check-in desks, keeping my head down while members of airport security race in the opposite direction and somewhere a siren starts up, I realise that I have a chance now. I've got a passport, cash, and an airport's worth of outbound flights to choose from. The day is breaking in so many more ways than one.

I pull out my mobile, and flip through my contacts to The Old Tupenny pub and hit dial. I know it's early, and I'm half expecting it to go to answerphone.

With a click, and wet splutter of lips uttering their first words of the day, my call is answered.

'The Tupenny,' the voice says. It's a cockney gargle, broad vowels staccatoed through the earpiece. It's the same voice that rattled through that tin can on the Thames all those months ago. I can picture him there in his smelly bar, in a characteristically ostentatious dressing gown, leaning against one of the ale pumps. Masters.

'Live in fear, motherfucker.'

'…Who is this?'

'Your pals up north have just gone quiet. I wouldn't expect to do business with them anytime soon.'

'If you have any care for your own safety, you'll hang up right now and hope to Christ I don't find out who you are.'

'No, Terry, quite the opposite. You are the one that should fear for his safety. I would say change your ways and be spared, but you're long past that, aren't you, you greasy old shit… No, I've got business with you. I've just put a bullet between Felix Davison's eyes, and the next one is for you. You won't know when, and you won't know how. But I'm coming for you. Sleep tight, sugar, or die trying.'

I disconnect before he can say another word. I can picture him squeezing off a half pint of cask to settle his nerves. The very thought makes me smile. He'll get his soon enough.

Epilogue

I switch terminals from one to three, watching the commotion gradually fade the further I go, and as soon as I hit three, I search out the nearest bathroom. The bathroom I find has a shower cubicle, which I use to properly scrub the nicks and bruises and send the rust-coloured lot down the drain. I shave off my stubble with a razor, change into fresh clothes from what is in my bag, and emerge a new man. I know there are eyes everywhere, but the ball cap and the full change should have bought me a bit of time.

I find a cafe, where I can order a coffee and a bacon butty, and sit. As soon as the weight is off my legs, my bones flood with a tar-like tiredness that seeps everywhere and feels leaden, but there is a sense of satisfaction that remains. After a while, I spot a payphone in the corner, and feel one final grace note needs to ring out before I can call this one dusted. Salix, and the NCA.

When the time is right, I call, repeat my Royal Mail routine, and get through to Salix's desk, hoping he is there on a Sunday morning.

'Hearing about my post has got a lot more exciting since you came along,' he says. 'I got your package, some kid brought it round last night. I have to say, it's enough to put a lot of people away for a very long time.'

'I'm afraid the main players won't be making that, but I hope there is enough there to put a lot of the middle men out of business,' I say. 'Are you by a TV?'

'I can be, why?'

'Check out BBC News 24.'

'Ok, give me a sec,' he says, and I can hear his wheels softly whirring across carpet. I know what he will see when he gets it on – the hole in the side of Manchester Airport, and a story told by a couple of eyewitnesses who say an SUV slammed through the fence and smashed into the building, burying itself inside. It's the fourth story in this morning's pecking order, and is on loop every thirty minutes. I've watched it twice already. The story is just starting, and I've timed calling Salix just right.

'What am I looking at?' Salix asks.

'What recently went down at Manchester Airport. You need to get down here. Felix and Michael Davison are both dead in that hole you can see, and there is a woman in there who needs a lot of help. Listen to her – I think you'll find she has a lot to say.'

The line is quiet for a second, before Salix whispers, 'Jesus Christ.'

'I said I would sort it.' I want to approach this next part carefully. 'If you can keep my involvement quiet, I'm sure there is a lot more good we can do.'

That silence again, and I hope he is seriously considering it, because as long as my insurance policy is in place, I've got some time. I can make a difference where I can. I have to try.

I want redemption for what I did in the army. To show I'm not the traitorous scum they painted me as. To the memory of Jack and Zoe, not to mention my old dearly departed army brother, Stephen, whose death started my decline. Those people who didn't deserve what happened to them. Those people I could have saved, but didn't.

I think of the last line of my tattoo, the lyric inking my forearm:

'*tell them not to fear no more…*'

Once again, its meaning has changed.

'Ok,' says Salix. 'I will lie to nobody if asked, but I can keep my head down. Keep me in the loop. What are you going to do now?'

'I'm not sure, but… Hypothetically, if I was in an airport minded to take a little trip somewhere, perhaps where someone needed sorting out, where would I go?'

Jeremiah takes just a second this time. 'The Costa Del Sol. I think a man like you could have a lot of fun down there. If you call me when you get there, I can suggest some… activities.'

The departures board is lit up next to the bank of TVs over the bar.

202

I scroll down quickly with my eyes until I see it. Malaga, leaving in two hours.

'I'll be in touch a bit later then. Thank you, Jeremiah.'

'Thank you, whoever the hell you are.'

'Damn right.' I hang up.

Acknowledgements

I have always felt like a very lucky guy indeed. The following people are why.

Thank you to Carol Killman Rosenberg and Ted Gilley for their eagle-eyed editorial work. Thank you to everyone at Lume Books for this wonderful opportunity.

I feel so blessed and grateful to be represented by my agent Linda Langton. Her unwavering encouragement, dedication, guidance and support has kept this project moving forward. I extend my utmost gratitude to her and everyone at Langtons International Agency.

To my wife Becky, and my daughters Ava and Sylvia, I send all my thanks and love. You are my be all and end all. Thank you for helping me follow this dream.

To Mum and Dad – none of this would have happened without you. I hope you know how grateful I am. Your faith in me has me humbled. All my love.

To my whole family and my friends, right across, your support has kept me going from the beginning. All my love and thanks to you all.

Lastly, thank you so much to every reader who read my work in the early days, and every reader who picks up any book of mine going forward. You are the best.

CPSIA information can be obtained
at www.ICGtesting.com
Printed in the USA
BVHW030857180821
614616BV00007B/562